CAELIUM

THE CERULEAN AIRSHIP - BOOK THREE

RUXANDRA TARCA

1

London, May 1896

Of course, had it not been for the urgency of the situation, I would have never dared ask for such a favour. But I am certain you understand our position. The Paris Engineering School has a reputation to uphold, and I dare hope our longstanding friendship is an adequate justification for me to solicit the help we so desperately need from you. I believe Miss Ivy Blackwell is the most appropriate choice for bringing the last of our project's parts from Paris to London. Not only because she was a student at our school, but also for her excellent skills. Her recent airship journey to the Australian colonies did not pass unnoticed, and everyone here would be delighted to congratulate her in person for such an extraordinary achievement. Not only her, but Miss Hammond as well, if she is kind enough to join Miss Blackwell as an official member of the Engineers Order on behalf of the Gathering's committee.

Edmund Asher put the letter back on his desk. Without a word, he stood up and gazed for a few long moments at the continuous water stream of the mechanical waterfall in front of the Inspectorates before he finally turned to Theophilus Hollingsworth.

"I found their request rather odd," the temporary Senior Lord of the Engineers Order said, with his usual patience and good-natured demeanour. "In fact, the letter itself is rather odd, which is why I brought it to the Classified Affairs' attention."

Edmund took another look at the letter that had arrived at the Engineers Order's headquarters earlier that morning. "They could use plenty of other means to bring their project for the Gathering to the Crystal Palace without asking us to send Miss Blackwell to France. Better yet, their team could have brought all the parts themselves when they arrived." He returned to the window overlooking the square, his hands clasped behind his back. "As much as I loathe to speculate, I am quite certain we are dealing with a trap. One that doesn't concern Miss Blackwell but Annabella Hammond. She is not involved in the Gathering, yet they requested her presence in France."

Theophilus Hollingsworth started wiping his spectacles with a monotonous circular movement, his whole attention on the tedious task, as he always did when something bothered him.

"Edmund, I know you well enough to understand how you think," he said, putting his glasses back on and looking at the Chief Inspector of the Classified Affairs Office. "You are willing to let yourself fall into this trap because it is the fastest way to uncover it. However, I doubt it is a good idea, as it might put Miss Blackwell and Annabella in danger."

"If anyone wanted to murder Miss Blackwell or Annabella, they would have done so already," Edmund replied, his face an expressionless mask and his blue eyes distant. "The French requested their presence for other reasons, which we will find out soon enough."

"Then, at least send Jasper with them."

"No," Edmund replied curtly, his glacial tone an indication that there was no room for negotiation, regardless of his respect towards the negotiator. "If I send Jasper and this is indeed a trap, then the ones behind it will know we are aware of it, so they will step back and cover their traces. I trust those two to take care of themselves. Tell the French that Miss Blackwell and Annabella will fly to Paris."

THE CRUDE SPRING sun was piercing through the myriad of glass panes in thin, slanted beams of light, converging into the magnificent fountain that attracted the labourers who sought to escape the indoor heat in their brief moments of respite between mounting pavilions, stalls, and exhibits. Above the fountain, the grand brass clock that almost touched the arched roof of the transept was a silent reminder of the little time left until the Engineers World Gathering.

Overseers and labourers were scurrying about the exhibition grounds under the curious stares of the officials and onlookers who watched the general ruckus from under the protective shade of the elm trees. Pavilions in more or less advanced stages of completion delimitated the space, each marked with a flag and a large sign with the name of the country they hosted.

Among prototypes of steam-powered vehicles, mechanical installations, and household implements that awaited display to the public, the Crystal Palace buzzed in a cacophony of sounds and scents.

"And I thought the London airharbour was the most amazing thing in this city," Avery Hamilton said, taking in each detail of the crowded place. "I've never seen anything like this."

"Wait until the exhibition opens," Jasper said with an amused smile, his hands in his pockets and his wild black locks partly hidden under a canvas cap. "I'd wager you'll congratulate yourself for leaving Australia and coming here. Taking part in the Gathering is the dream of any engineer or aviator."

"My parents used to say it's *the most* prestigious engineering event in the world," Ivy added, emphasising the words, her voice loud with excitement. She kept checking the pocket watch attached to her aeronaut outfit's corset once in five minutes, and Jasper couldn't help wondering whether her presence had less to do with the exhibition preparations and everything to do with her Australian assistant, given that she was already late to pick up her assignment sheet from the Inspectorates. "Every country sends their best prototype, and this time England's chosen project is *The Cerulean Lady*. What I don't understand, though, is why everyone is working on mounting the exhibits so early. We still have a month left until the opening."

"Preparing such an exhibition requires time and expertise," Jasper explained as they continued their walk through the middle corridor of the immense structure made of glass and iron. "Each country needs to transport their project and assemble and test it here. As the host, England must assist with each participant's every need, which also means we are responsible for every little thing you see around."

When they reached the West End wing of the Palace, Jasper stopped in front of the metal stairs that led to the first floor, frowning at the sign hanging over the closest pavilion.

France.

"How strange," he said, starting towards the French stalls. "Their allotted space should be outside, not here."

"A correct assumption if our plans hadn't changed." The reply came in a slightly hoarse voice laced with a heavy French accent.

They turned around. Said voice belonged to a man in his

thirties and came attached to a round face, ginger locks in quite an advanced state of dishevelment, and a lanky figure Jasper recognised as Gilbert Fontaine, the French team's chief engineer and overseer.

"I expect a significant change for you to switch to an indoor pavilion," Jasper said. "Though I fail to see how an airship could fit into this space."

"We won't display *L'Étoile*." His words carried a hint of regret that Jasper didn't miss. "Maurice Gervaise decided our airship was not good or innovative enough to represent our flag, so he replaced her with another exhibit."

"Maurice Gervaise should understand that changing the project a month before the exhibition is barely within the rules," Jasper said, not bothering to hide his irritation. "I wonder what incredible exhibit made the dean of the Paris Engineering School replace *L'Étoile*."

The other man ran a hand through his hair and cleared his throat, looking in turn at Jasper, Ivy, and Hamilton as if assessing whether it was safe to answer. "It's a prototype Gervaise's laboratory started last November, but he wasn't certain whether they would complete it in time. If I am to believe Gervaise, we will display a new model of automaton that will shake the engineering world."

THE ROUND BRASS clock on top of the mechanical waterfall struck noon when Ivy Blackwell hurried into the Inspectorates' marble hallway. She was one hour late, and that was not done. Especially not on a Monday, the day when all aviators of the Order had to check the board for the week's official assignments.

She found her name on the third row, with nothing but a note next to it.

Jeremiah Barnaby's office.

"Rats and caterpillars!" Ivy swore, oblivious to the other aeronauts who were inspecting the rectangular brass board. "Last time the old fart summoned me to his office, he sent me to Sydney, devil take him!"

One hour late when called to the office of the Aviators Order's Senior Lord only added an extra layer to her misery. Taking two steps at a time, she conquered the grand staircase to the first floor and stopped before the Aviators Order's office to compose herself. Swearing under her breath, she wondered yet again whether Jeremiah Barnaby's innocence in his nephew's recent case had, in fact, been her doom.

Inhaling deeply and exhaling loudly, she entered, awaiting the imminent apocalypse – and possibly a journey to the Americas.

In an unexpected twist of her usually unfortunate luck, Barnaby had another guest. At the comforting sight of Rowena's father, Ivy let out a breath she didn't know she was holding.

"Here you are," Barnaby said, his frown so prominent that his two bushy eyebrows formed one thick line. "I shall overlook your belated arrival – which I would like to assume was not the result of your neglecting your duties – for I have more important matters to discuss. *The Skycradle* received an assignment on behalf of the Aviators Order."

Ivy clenched her fists, her nails digging into her palms. She didn't like where that conversation was going.

"Worry not, child." Theophilus Hollingsworth's soothing voice brought an ounce of reassurance. "No one sends you to the other side of the world this time. I daresay you will be most delighted to accept this assignment. Provided that you want to see Paris again and visit your old school, of course."

The glint in her eyes betrayed her surprise. "Am I to understand that I must fly to the Engineering School in Paris?"

"Indeed," Barnaby confirmed. "The school requested your

airship to send some parts and pieces of their project to London for the Engineers World Gathering."

A smile bloomed on Ivy's face. "Most wonderful!" She clapped. "Who will join me from the French team?"

The two Senior Lords exchanged a glance that tempered her enthusiasm. "I'm afraid no one from the French team will come," Master Hollingsworth replied. "This is why they commissioned your airship through the Engineers and Aviators Orders. They needed an official authority in which to place their absolute trust."

Ivy remained silent for a few moments, her gaze focused on the tip of her leather boots. As much as she wished to fly to Paris, she knew what such an assignment involved.

"You will not go alone," Barnaby said, as if reading her thoughts. "Miss Annabella Hammond will fly with you as the engineer in charge of this delegation on behalf of the Engineers World Gathering committee. And you can take your assistant with you if you wish so."

I bloody wish so. If Jasper is not an option, Avery should do.

"When are we leaving?"

The Senior Lord of the Aviators Order handed her the official, signed paper. "You will fly to France tomorrow and return in three days."

JASPER alighted from his hansom cab in front of the stone steps of the Inspectorates' entrance just as Edmund was coming out through the massive wooden doors. It was still early, certainly too early for his brother, who usually left his office late in the evening.

"You must already have plans for the night, but I hope you have a few minutes to spare," Jasper said. "I have some recent developments we need to talk about."

"My plans involve going home," Edmund replied matter-of-factly, walking towards the mechanical waterfall. "As it happens, I also have some developments to share."

Jasper followed him, a pang of worry constricting his chest. Edmund took his spymaster work way too seriously to just go home at such an hour unless he was utterly exhausted. In the past months, he had been chasing Benedict Quimby all over England and France, only to bump into dead ends. His face bore signs of fatigue and lack of sleep, of concern and frustration.

"I suppose you know the French changed their project," Jasper said. "However, the nature of this change bothers me."

Edmund stopped, squinting at his younger brother with tired eyes. "No, I was not aware of any change. Perhaps the committee did not consider it important enough to inform the Classified Affairs. Is it still an airship or something else?"

"Something else, and I doubt you will like this something else. They have a new automaton prototype that, according to Fontaine, will shake the engineering world. I wonder how they developed such a prototype in just a few months."

His older brother remained silent for a while, his gaze focused on the perpetual tumble of water plunging down the copper wheel of the waterfall.

"With the right help from the right person," he finally replied, facing Jasper again. "Last time Quimby was spotted on English soil, he was embarking on a ferry for France. I do not exclude the possibility that Quimby, if he indeed escaped to France, collaborated with them, perhaps even long before I arrested him."

Jasper took off his cap to run a hand through his tousled hair, delaying his answer. While most of the times Edmund's logic was infallible, this time he had his doubts – especially since his brother never relied on presuppositions instead of evidence.

"Automatons are indeed Quimby's obsession, which means

your assumption might be correct," he said, putting the cap back on his head. "However, a prestigious establishment such as the Paris Engineering School would never risk its reputation by hiding a wanted man and using his services."

"The same prestigious establishment requested *The Skycradle* to fetch some parts for their project from Paris," Edmund announced, to Jasper's surprise. "We could not refuse, as they are entitled to ask for anything the Gathering committee can provide. I believe it might be a trap, and this new piece of information only deepens my suspicion."

"Ivy was a student at that school, so it was only natural to ask for someone they know and trust. I fail to understand why this is a trap or how it involves Quimby."

"It is not about Miss Blackwell," Edmund said, unperturbed by Jasper's doubt. "It is about Annabella Hammond. They want her to join the delegation as a representative of the event committee. Why would they ask for the engineer who is exceptionally skilled in biomechanics, works on a secret automaton only a selected few know about, and has no official involvement in the Gathering?"

Jasper had to admit that his brother's reasoning was as sharp as ever. "The French couldn't have known about Annabella's biomechanics research unless Quimby informed them – which makes this trip even more dangerous. Allow me to go with them."

"That is out of the question." Edmund's voice could cut through steel. "I need you to supervise all activity at the Crystal Palace and report to me if you find anything amiss. I do not trust the committee – or rather I do not trust their judgement. Besides, your presence would only draw suspicion upon *The Skycradle*'s crew, which I can ill afford. If I miss this chance to catch Quimby –" Edmund stopped, unable to finish his sentence.

"Worry not." As much as he wanted to ease his brother's

worries, Jasper could hardly find the right words. "Nothing will happen at the Gathering."

His words sounded hollow, devoid of any substance. He looked up at the Westminster clocktower, watching how thick grey clouds were slowly covering the last patch of blue sky.

HAZEL WATERCRESS WRAPPED HER LONG, black cloak tighter about her as she hastened towards the hansom cab she had halted on the Strand, careful to hide her face under her hood. That night she was herself. No disguise, no secret information to extract. Her Madame had been kind enough to grant her a free evening, no question asked. She silently thanked Carmina Harcourt for her discretion, one of the many traits that had gained her Hazel's respect and loyalty.

"Aldgate," Hazel instructed the driver, who was staring blankly at her from the height of his box. Then she climbed inside with no other word.

The darkness seemed to stretch endlessly as the Cinnamon Dove and Covent Garden remained behind. She watched the changing landscape in silence, counting the broken streetlamps they were passing by. Inhaling deeply, she blew a patch of warm fog over the dirty window, which she wiped with the sleeve of her dress to have a better view of her surroundings.

Almost there.

Whitechapel never changed, no matter how many innovations the Reform brought to the rest of the city. Children still played in murky alleys. Facades still reeked of soot, barely visible under the thick black veneer. Air still stung. People still struggled in the dirt of the slums.

With a heavy heart, she pushed open the door of an old building, praying that her mother was all right. She wished to take her away from that place, but the stubborn woman never agreed. Her cloak on her arm, she entered the small room that used to be her home all those years ago, only to stop with her hand on the broken doorknob.

"Edwin –" she mumbled, staring at the man standing before her. "I thought – I thought you weren't in London. What are you doing here? When are you leaving?"

The young man threw her an amused look, flexing the fingers of his only arm. In the dim light of the lamp, his face looked sickly pale. "Lizzie, I see your sisterly love is as strong as I remember. As your older brother, I'm hurt. I even looked for you at that place – what was the name again? The Cinnamon Dove.

"I didn't find you," he went on, crossing the room to close the door. "But I saw something interesting. The Earl of Wyverstone entering that whorehouse. Who would have thought?" He laughed, his voice filling the space with a sinister echo. "Gentlemen such as him keep mistresses and never visit such places. I'm curious to know which girl has caught his eye."

Hazel's face turned white. The earl never visited their establishment when he could be seen, never interacted with anyone at the Dove, and always used the hidden backdoor that led to Madame's private quarters. Edwin couldn't have known about His Lordship's visits unless he had tailed him.

"I've never seen the earl at the Dove," she said, trying to not sound as uneasy as she felt. "Is this about the incident you had with his brother four years ago?"

"No, I was just curious," Edwin replied curtly. "Jade Asher caused my infirmity, but the earl saved my life, even against my will. How can I ever forget that?"

His icy voice sent a chill down Hazel's spine. She was almost certain that her brother had targeted the Earl of Wyverstone, which meant that Madame – the person who had saved her from misery and destitution – could also be in danger.

You won't touch them. She clenched her fists, small droplets of sweat forming on her palms. *I swear to God, I won't let you touch them.*

2

Annabella Hammond wiped the last brass part with a clean cloth before carefully placing it in the trunk on top of the others. She closed the lid and secured it with the padlock, then locked the pile of wires in her personal cabinet, where she kept the schematics for the circuits and mechanical limbs. Her eyes were watery from the artificial light of the laboratory and the long hours she wore her magnifying goggles. She unclasped their leather strap and put them on the workbench, blinking a few times to readjust her vision.

"Almost done," she said, turning towards the Earl of Ledburry. "But I fear I must leave now. I shall return in three days."

"Of course, of course," the Senior Lord of the Doctors Order replied, looking in turn at the trunk, the cabinet, and her. "You deserve some rest after a full month of uninterrupted work. A lady should not look *this* tired."

Annabella squinted at him, finding his sudden burst of exuberance rather bewildering. "I do what I must do. I have no time to rest. But I am close to perfecting the Humautomaton circuits, so perhaps you should discuss the matter with your hospital to provide us with test subjects. Soon, we shall need to test the Doctors Order's method of attaching the brass limbs to a human body through my circuits."

The Earl of Ledburry took off his work gloves and apron, starting towards the laboratory's sink. "We need to be careful before disclosing any information about Humautomaton." He washed his hands with circular, even movements, his eyes focused on his task. "This is the most important project of two Orders, and we cannot afford to draw unwanted attention upon us." He turned back to her. "Some people will consider it unethical, and others will want to steal it. Which is precisely the reason I cannot agree with your idea to present it at the Engineers World Gathering. Unless, of course, you complete and test it before that date."

Annabella inhaled sharply, struggling to keep her temper. The Senior Lord of the Doctors Order was not the easiest man to work with, and only the height of the clocktower in Westminster equalled his ego.

She was still fuming when she went out of the Inspectorates and into the square, where Avery was waiting for her. The lanky figure of her dearest friend brought a smile to her face, melting some of her anger.

"Hallo, Queen," he said in his usually cheerful voice, peppered with a pinch of sarcasm, before walking with her to the mews where she kept her newly acquired steammotor. "I almost thought you were dead and rotten in this damp place."

Annabella put on her driving goggles and started the engine. "Three full days with me, and you will wish I disappeared again."

"Perhaps. But for now, I'm glad you're coming with us. You have neglected your poor apprentice for far too long."

"That is because my project keeps me in the laboratory most of the time. Besides, your apprenticeship should be safe with Miss Blackwell and Jasper." She drove among the other vehicles, secretly wishing for the quiet streets of Sydney instead of the crowded ones in London. "Do you ever miss Australia?" she asked, a trace of wistfulness in her voice.

"Sometimes," he admitted. "But not enough to make me return. I have some things interesting enough to keep me in London, so I'll stay for a while."

Annabella turned to him with an impish smirk, poking him with her elbow. "Now tell me, Avery. Do those interesting *things* of yours include a *person* as well?"

Avery burst into heartfelt laughter.

JASPER ROLLED HIS EYES, barely controlling his exasperation. Half an hour had passed since their argument started, with no sign of yielding on her part. Leaning against the starboard wall of *The Skycradle*'s viewing deck, her arms crossed at the chest and her fiery green eyes throwing daggers, she didn't budge.

Count on Ivy Blackwell to drive someone out of their wits.

"How many times must I tell you until you understand? I can fly alone. There is no need to bother Miss Hammond. To me, going to Paris is like going home."

"How very noble," Jasper countered. "Only that it is not you who decides. You must follow Barnaby and Master Hollingsworth's instructions, and that's the end of it."

"Jasper is right." Annabella entered the gondola with Avery in tow, clad in her aeronaut attire and ready for travel. "As a member of the Engineers Order, I cannot turn down an official assignment." She took off her gloves and driving canvas coat and placed them on a wooden bench close to the viewing deck's railing. "But that is not the only reason I am here. You helped me with my hybriship when I most needed it, and now it is my turn to return the favour. Besides, I miss flying, and airships, and the airharbour. I spent too many days locked in that laboratory."

"I wouldn't have flown to Paris alone with you," Avery said, attracting Ivy's deadly look upon himself. "Under no circumstances."

"What?" Ivy clenched her fists, her voice trembling with anger. "Let me remind you, I flew this airship from as far as Sydney. You think I can't fly her to Paris?"

"What I think is very far from what your mysterious mind is concocting right now." Avery bent over to meet her eyes with a mischievous grin. "You have a special talent to twist my words and give them entirely new meanings, which I find fascinating."

"I think Hamilton's reaction has less to do with your skill and everything to do with him not seeing you as a colleague," Jasper said. "Perhaps you are not an aviator to him."

Ivy locked her astonished eyes on Avery. "Is this true?"

"Might," Avery replied in an amused tone.

"Listen here, you conceited oaf," Ivy said after a few long moments, her voice carrying a blend of anger and disappointment in equal proportions. "I *can* tolerate your hardly tolerable arrogance, but not your lack of respect. How can I work with a presumptuous dolt who doesn't even acknowledge me?"

Jasper exchanged a dumbfounded look with Annabella and Avery before all three of them started laughing.

Ivy looked at them with bewildered eyes.

"You are denser than London fog," Avery said, a warm smile on his face. "I assure you, I *do* acknowledge you. It was never about that."

"Then about what?" Ivy asked, squinting at him.

But Avery didn't continue. He started towards the piloting board. "It's time to do the pre-flight checks. Are you coming?"

"I don't like this commission at all," Jasper said in a low voice after Ivy and Avery disappeared into the piloting area. "The French changed their official exhibit to an automaton. This makes their request for your presence even more suspicious."

Annabella tucked a strand of black hair behind her ear. "The

French are renowned for their airships, not automata. I wonder whether *someone more skilled* helped them complete a project innovative enough to replace an airship that I am most certain would have rivalled *The Cerulean Lady*, laevium or not."

Jasper nodded in agreement. "My thoughts precisely. Be careful. I believe it is you whom they truly want."

THE OUTLINE of *The Skycradle*'s red envelope receded in the distance, slowly becoming a small point beyond the confines of London's airharbour. Jasper lingered for a while near the empty berth of Ivy's airship, wondering whether he should just take the next Paris-bound passenger airship.

As much as he loathed to admit it, he was keenly aware that his presence in France wouldn't be of much help to his friends.

Whereas his absence from London would be an inconvenience *The Cerulean Lady* could not afford. Not to mention that ignoring a direct order from the Chief Inspector of the Classified Affairs Office was a breach of protocol his brother would not overlook.

He had to stay.

The drizzle falling from the cloud-blanketed sky hastened his step towards the *Lady*'s hangar. He stopped for a few moments at the entrance, taking in the view of the colossal airship supported on her iron scaffolding, a corner of his lips curled in a satisfied grin.

She was as beautiful as he had imagined her when he and Ivy had drawn their first sketches over the Blackwells' schematics. The double-tiered gondola with the gilded wrought-iron railing of the observation deck, the four engine pods jutting out from the gondola's wall, the oval envelope painted in blue with golden leaf-like patterns, like the sun and the sky at the brightest time of the day.

Ivy's colours, he thought with a smile.

Elegant and magnificent, the *Lady* was almost ready to soar to the skies.

Almost.

For they still had work to do. Jasper strode towards the ship and climbed the ladder up to the gondola's upper level, nodding in silent agreement at the lavish furniture and curtains adorning the space, fit for the royal family. He went down to the navigation cabin, where Robert Elmstone, the engineer on duty, was checking the piloting board, a drawing in his hand.

"Asher." The man turned towards Jasper, interrupting his inspection. "I found no faults with the piloting board. Do you have a schedule for the tests?"

Jasper squatted to double check the range of levers, buttons and dials that made the pilot's board before facing Elmstone again.

"As soon as the factory sends us the engines, we'll schedule the first ground test," he replied. "Though I have no idea yet when that will be."

The engineer frowned, clearly not pleased with the vague answer. "I assume you have no idea about the test flight either."

"The Classified Affairs oversee all tests for the *Lady*," Jasper said apologetically. "Since Her Majesty is the owner of this airship, it is only natural for them to do so, especially after what happened to *The Golden Griffin* and Quimby's betrayal. I have no say in this."

"I understand," the other man said. "Still, the crew deserves to take part in the tests. Be careful, Asher. Your lack of trust might turn your most loyal men into your worst enemies."

THE LONG AND crowded corridor on the ground floor of the Inspectorates reminded Edmund why he loathed the rare moments when he had any business with the Constabulary. An acrid stench of sweat and filth filled the air, overpowering even the loud noises that translated into expletives and profanities unfit for a civilised place.

Edmund made his way towards the superintendent's office, avoiding – not without a considerable effort – the motley assortment of pickpockets, hookers, and hoodlums the constables were escorting. Inside the small, windowless room, the air was no less stifling, and the superintendent seemed as bored as the constables outside.

"I need to see Alistair Francis Montgomery," Edmund said.

"Not possible," the man replied, not bothering to lift his head from the ledger he perused. "He cannot receive guests."

Edmund slid his badge under the superintendent's nose. "Perhaps I was not very clear, so I shall repeat. I need to see Alistair Francis Montgomery."

At the sight of the small round piece of brass bearing the unmistakable emblem of Her Majesty's Office of Classified Affairs, the man finally noticed who the unexpected guest was. He jumped to his feet, sending the inkwell flying off his desk in the process.

"Your Lordship! Please, accept my apologies. Surely, you understand that with all these thugs filling the Constabulary each day of the week, it never occurred to me that someone of your station could visit my humble office. Of course, I'll see to your request immediately."

Minutes later, Edmund found himself face to face with the nephew of the Aviators Order's Senior Lord. The scant light coming through the barred window of the damp cell only accentuated the prisoner's sickly appearance. He had lost weight, and his pale countenance betrayed the worsened state of his health.

"What do you want?" Montgomery asked, squinting at Edmund without moving an inch. "My only answers are those I have already given when you questioned me in your bloody interrogation chamber. I have nothing else to say."

"They did not find you guilty of murdering Windstoneham." Edmund stopped for a few moments, as if to assess his next words. "*Yet*. I fear I must hasten the proceedings if you refuse to cooperate."

Instead of an answer, Montgomery burst into a coughing fit, choking under its power, which left him almost breathless. Edmund handed him his handkerchief, noticing the few drops of blood smearing the piece of cloth, no matter how hard Montgomery tried to hide them.

"Then hasten them," the young man said in a hoarse voice, still recovering after the unwanted outburst. "Guilty or not, it's the same for me."

"Are you saying this because you believe it or because you know you are dying?"

Montgomery's startled face told Edmund that his words had hit the mark. The moment he had prepared for had come, and he had only one card to play. The Engineers World Gathering was close. Quimby was still out of his reach, and he needed to catch him before the event turned into an unpredictable disaster. A bargain with Montgomery could change the odds.

"Your symptoms are signs of poisoning rather than of natural sickness," he said, his blue eyes expressionless. "Tuberculosis doesn't develop in such a short time." He strode towards Montgomery, standing in front of his cot, towering over him. "If I leave you here, you will die. Someone in the Constabulary finds you too dangerous to let live. However, if I move you to the Classified Affairs prison's medical ward, you will receive a doctor and – if you are fortunate enough – perhaps even an antidote."

"And why should I believe you?"

It only took Edmund a few steps to reach the cell's door.

"Then don't. Perhaps you will be more convinced in a few days –
though it might be too late. I do not make the same offer twice."

"I assume your offer comes with a price," Montgomery said
when Edmund's hand pressed the rusted door handle, his voice
laced with disgust. "What about Windstoneham and the
accusations?"

Edmund turned towards him again, his hand still on the
door handle, undaunted by the other man's hostility. "The
evidence is inconclusive, so it will be most likely a cold case." A
pause. "*If* you choose to cooperate."

THE LAST TRACES of daylight had disappeared beyond London's
smoky horizon when Edmund opened the small door hidden
into the Maiden Lane side of the Cinnamon Dove, careful to
remain out of sight, grateful for the broken streetlamp close to
the building. Once inside, he climbed the narrow flight of stairs
to Carmina's private quarters and opened the door to her study
just as Hazel was leaving the room.

"Your Lordship," the young woman mumbled in an almost
inaudible voice. She lowered her head and passed him in a
hurry before disappearing behind the door to the corridor
leading to the Dove's main wing.

"Is anything the matter?" Edmund entered Carmina's study,
glancing back with a lifted eyebrow.

Carmina rose to welcome him. "Her mother is unwell, so she
is rather distressed as of late." She took his hands in hers,
locking her green eyes with his. "Tell me about Montgomery.
Has your plan succeeded?"

"Like clockwork. You did excellent work as a constabulary
servant. The poison you slipped into his food scared him
enough to accept my offer."

Carmina moved her gaze from his eyes to their joined hands.

"You could have used a less ruthless method to make him talk. A few days longer and he would have died."

Edmund squeezed her hands, prompting her to look at him again. "No, he would have not. And nothing is too ruthless when it comes to the safety of the Engineers World Gathering, the royal family, and the people attending. I must find Quimby, and I need that man's help."

"Quimby is not that stupid as to reveal his exact location," Carmina said, a trace of weariness in her voice. "I doubt Montgomery possesses the information you seek."

"I am aware of that." Edmund bent over to touch his forehead to hers. "But I am quite certain he knows if he is indeed in France and how he escaped from prison. That information alone can be of great help."

"You will find him soon. It is not a matter of if but of when. Edmund, you are England's spymaster. So far, you proved yourself splendidly. I trust you. We all trust you." She wrapped her arms around his neck, gently pulling him closer. "You have the face of a man who has not slept in days." Her voice was almost a whisper against his lips. "Stay for the night. Stay with me."

"I am not going anywhere." Edmund kissed her, breathing in her delicate scent of violets and cinnamon. "Perhaps you are right. I might be indeed in need of rest."

If he was truly honest with himself, he was in dire need of rest. Or at least of a few hours of uninterrupted sleep without waking up in the middle of the night worrying amidst thousands of possibilities that might come to pass should he not be able to find Benedict Quimby.

And the only place where he could hope for some rest was with the woman he held in his arms.

He crushed her in his embrace and rested his head on her shoulder, aware of how heavy he ought to be against her small frame, yet unable to stand any longer under the unbearable weight of fatigue.

"Thank you," he breathed against the bare skin of her collarbone. "I do not deserve your kindness. Or your forgiveness. Not after what I have done. I was a fool, and yet you accepted me back."

He felt her hands through his hair in the softest of caresses. "I thought I explained it months ago," she said, cupping his face in her palms and locking her eyes with his again. "My reasons for having you back have nothing to do with kindness or forgiveness and everything to do with my desire to be happy. Have you forgotten?"

"No." He smiled. "I have not."

Edmund closed his eyes, remembering the day that had brought them together again after that dreadful night in London's sewers. He was in Jasper's chamber above the workshop, barely keeping his eyes open, on his knees beside the bed where Carmina had been sleeping for days without any sign that she would ever wake up again.

He had let himself rest for a bit, his head on the mattress next to her, the wet cloth he used to wipe her forehead still in his hand. Only to wake up to the soft sensation of her lips on his brow and eyelids, of her fingers caressing his cheek, of her voice whispering his name.

"You are awake, at last," he said, relief surging through his entire being. "I cannot recall the last time I was so scared. You should have never gone in there alone, and I should have come earlier, protocol be damned. I thought –" The words came out strangled and stuttering, his eyes drinking in the sight of her. "I regret everything I have done, every hour I spent away from you. I love you. I love you –"

Her lips on his interrupted the erratic whirl of his words. "I know," she said, her voice still weak. "You are here, and this is all that matters to me now. I am claiming you as mine again because I am selfish and cannot help it."

Edmund brushed his fingers over her damp forehead and bruised cheek. "I'm afraid I do not understand."

"If I were to follow the polite society's rules, I should send you away to preserve my dignity. But I am not part of the polite society, and I missed you with every inch of my being, every day of the last three years. Sending you away would only inflict more suffering upon my person, which I am too selfish to do. I want to be happy, and I cannot be happy without you. I love you, Edmund. I am not relinquishing you again for the sake of morality."

He shifted from his awkward position and moved his tall frame onto the bed, wrapping her in his arms. Outside, the dusk was turning into darkness, but he left the lamp unlit, revelling in the soothing obscurity of the room. His hand fished for the small silver locket he had been carrying in his pocket since the night Jasper had brought it to him. Surprise glowed in Carmina's green eyes when he clasped it around her neck again.

"I have yet to forgive myself," he had whispered, kissing her temple. "My choice only made us miserable."

She had held him that night just like she was holding him now, his island of reassurance amidst the troubling waves of uncertainty and doubt.

3

Jasper only needed a few seconds to spot the blue bonnet and the black curls, followed by a clearer view of a beaming face and a pair of hazel eyes as Rowena Hollingsworth came closer to the spot where he was standing, near the fountain in the centre of the Crystal Palace.

A welcome distraction from the overseer activities assigned to him for that first half of the day.

"Soon, you will know this place even better than I do," he said, greeting her and the Killen children with a wide smile. "I do hope you will find it interesting enough to visit after the opening as well."

"Certainly." Rowena rested a gloved hand on little Blake's shoulder. "This place is full of marvels. No wonder the children insist on coming almost every day. We were on our way to explore the first floor."

"Let me know if you need anything." Jasper waved, watching them disappear among the throngs of labourers who were preparing the stalls, before he went outside to check England's pavilion.

It shouldn't take more than two weeks to complete. Soon,

they would moor *The Cerulean Lady* to the berth, ready for everyone to see. And admire.

He couldn't help a grin, picturing the magnificent airship on display among so many other inventions.

But he had no time for daydreaming. His presence there had another purpose.

He strode back inside the gigantic iron and glass structure, crossing the aisle towards the French sector, where Gilbert Fontaine was instructing his men on how to mount the supporting scaffold for their exhibit.

"Oh, Asher, I'm afraid I have not much to show you. Our piece must wait for your colleagues' return from Paris. I'm told they are to bring the most important parts of our automaton."

The most important parts? Jasper didn't particularly like that bit of information.

"I fail to understand why the school didn't send the fully assembled automaton," he said, throwing a suspicious look at the French team's overseer. "Why let such a precious cargo in our hands?"

The French engineer snorted, as if Jasper's question was the most outlandish thing he'd heard that day. "We could not risk damaging the automaton during transportation," he explained in a pedantic tone Jasper found rather irritating. "What if something happened to the airship? Say, because of bad weather or engine failure? Besides, we had to wait until these last parts and pieces were completed, and now they are. Of course, the school could only use a most trustworthy carrier to send them."

"I see," Jasper said, not entirely convinced by Fontaine's explanatory diatribe. "Perhaps I would understand better if I knew the novelty your automaton brings."

"Unlike other automata programmed for only one specific task, ours can be programmed for several tasks, for both industrial, and household use," Fontaine replied.

"An automaton with multiple uses?" Jasper asked, suddenly

interested. "What mechanic principle do you apply to switch between the automaton's functions?"

"It's a secret patent, and I told you too much already," Fontaine said. He took one step closer, lowering his voice. "But, from one engineer to another, I can tell you that the switch is possible because of some extraordinary circuits similar in their design to the vessels and nerves in the human body."

Jasper caught his breath, struggling to hide his surprise at the unexpected revelation.

To his knowledge, the only person to have developed such circuits was Annabella Philippa Hammond. And they had requested her presence in Paris.

THE BRASS TIMEPIECE hanging from Annabella's leather corset showed half past noon when Ivy and Avery entered the impressive three-storey building on Rue des Écoles, a stone's throw from the Sorbonne. Before going in herself, she looked up to read again the letters painted in gold above the massive wooden door carved with symbols fit for the institution it hosted.

L'École d'Ingénieurs de Paris.

The Paris Engineering School.

One of the most prestigious science universities on the Continent, and the dream of any engineer. She wondered whether they would have accepted her biomechanics research the University of London had rejected with contempt and mockery.

But that was too old a memory to linger upon. They had work to do.

And some time to spare, apparently, as the school's dean was not available to welcome them.

"Maurice Gervaise has quite the nerve," Annabella hissed,

glaring in the general direction of the students scurrying down the hallways. "Requesting our presence here, only to make us wait in a bloody corridor."

"Who says we have to wait for that old dolt here?" Ivy threw them an impish grin, fiddling with an auburn tendril that had rebelled out of her loose chignon. "Allowing me to show you around the school would be a much better option."

Annabella and Avery didn't wait to be invited twice. They followed their aeronaut friend towards the stairway that led below ground, glancing inside the halls and amphitheatres they were lucky enough to find open. She couldn't help but marvel at the sight of so many installations and mechanisms mounted there for the students' benefit.

The corridors beneath the ground floor were quieter, with fewer open halls, lacking the natural light coming in abundance through the large windows on the floor above. The wall sconces and fixtures fitted with bulbs in various sizes and intensities were the only sources of light in the cavernous stone passage.

"Should I be afraid for my life?" Avery asked, bending over until he was the same height as Ivy, mischief glowing in his eyes. "Where are you taking us?"

"To sacrifice you to the almighty god of wisdom and science," Ivy replied, returning the stare with one eyebrow raised. "Though I doubt he would be pleased with such an insufferable arrogant."

"Most doors have metal reinforcement," Annabella said, ignoring their banter. "Are they laboratories?"

"No, they are experiment rooms. They design all new projects in the laboratories, then assemble them and bring them down here for testing. This way, if something goes bonkers during the tests, the laboratories remain intact."

Annabella nodded in understanding as they continued their walk down the long corridor, passing a few students and assistants on their way. Just as she was about to ask Miss Blackwell another question, her eyes fell on a portly bespectacled man dressed in a white laboratory scrub, who was opening a door at the very end of the hallway.

Holy saints! What is Benedict Quimby doing here?

The man disappeared inside too fast for her to confirm his identity. Forgetting about Avery and Ivy and paying no heed to the students eyeing her with curious looks, she ran after him. She had to find out whether that man was indeed Benedict Quimby. Was the school harbouring a criminal? Was his presence related to *her* presence?

The door she sought opened just as she reached for the handle, and she found herself in front of a tall and sturdy man in his late fifties, wearing round spectacles and sporting an impressive beard the same silvery colour as his shoulder-length, thick hair.

"*Mademoiselle*, what are you doing here?" the man asked in French. "Are you new to this school and are not familiar with the rules, perhaps? This area is off-limits if you do not have an access pass. Who is your coordinator?"

"*Monsieur* Gervaise, it's been quite a while," Ivy said, her French flawless. Her flushed face indicated she had followed Annabella in haste. "I'm happy to see you in good health. As I still have my access pass, I showed my friends around while waiting for you. We had no intention to intrude."

"Ivy, my dear child!" The man, who Annabella identified now as Maurice Gervaise, the dean of the Paris Engineering School, squeezed Ivy in a hug. "How wonderful to see you." He turned to Annabella again, switching to heavily accented English. "Then you must be Miss Hammond. I apologise for mistaking you for one of our students."

"I need to check that room," Annabella said, nodding towards the door that might hide the former Senior Lord of the

Engineers Order. "I am quite certain I saw an acquaintance of mine entering there. Perhaps I should inform you he is a wanted man in England. Your school might be in danger if you harbour a criminal."

"I assure you, only my students are in this room, working on a practice project I have just assigned to them. Now come with me, and I'll show you the laboratories." He ushered the group towards a set of stairs in the opposite direction, ignoring Annabella's frustrated grunt. "Miss Hammond, I want to show you something and hear your expert opinion about it."

Maurice Gervaise's good-natured smile and his willingness to show them the most important part of the school didn't appease Annabella's doubts. If anything, her suspicions only grew stronger with each quick step they took further away from the underground level of the building and closer to the laboratory area on the second floor, where the school master's assistant joined their little group.

"Claude, be kind and help our dear Miss Blackwell and her friend with the cargo. The papers are prepared and signed on my desk. A part of the load goes into the airship today, and the rest tomorrow before our guests' departure."

He turned from his assistant to Annabella. "In the meantime, I'll show Miss Hammond our newest prototype. The laboratory is two doors away."

Alarm bells rang in Annabella's brain. Why would he want to separate her from her friends? Why was she even invited there?

"As the person in charge of this commission, I'm afraid I cannot leave Miss Blackwell and Mr Hamilton to see to the cargo and papers by themselves. I shall join them."

"Seeing a new prototype must be a thousand times more

interesting than loading boxes in *The Skycradle*," Ivy said. "Avery and I are capable enough to take care of everything, so you have nothing to be afraid of."

I have quite a lot to be afraid of, starting with this charade to split our group.

"Very well," Annabella agreed at last. "I shall see the prototype while you see to the cargo."

She followed Gervaise into what he presented as the school's most advanced laboratory. Cabinets filled with tools, instruments, and measuring devices lined the walls, along with tall bookshelves and a gas evaluation machine. A strange installation of copper pipes and glass containers whose function Annabella could not fathom occupied half of the space, while long metal workbenches covered the other half.

On one of them lay what appeared to be an open automaton in human shape.

"Is that the prototype?" she asked, nodding towards the mass of brass on the table. "Shouldn't prototypes be a secret until their completion? Are you not afraid to show it to me?"

"It is indeed," Gervaise replied, beckoning her to come closer to the workbench. "You are a famous engineer and a member of the prestigious Engineers Order of England, so your opinion would be very valuable to us."

"But I am an airship engineer, not an automaton engineer," Annabella insisted, foreboding creeping down her spine. "I cannot offer an opinion on a matter I know nothing about."

"When we created this prototype, we thought of something different," Gervaise said, ignoring her words. "A purpose that would deviate from ordinary automata. We believe we can adapt this prototype to the human body. More specifically, merge it with the human body. Miss Hammond, do you think it would be possible?"

Annabella needed all the self-control she could muster to hide her shock. "I am neither a technician nor a doctor, so I cannot give a qualified answer," she said in a neutral tone, crossing the laboratory towards the workbench. "But I confess I do want to see this prototype of yours. Any engineer would be curious."

She bent over the automaton to inspect its inner workings, careful to not look too interested, only to find herself staring at her past four years' work. The same brass parts and fittings, the same circuits still unfinished, the same materials. The automaton prototype was not similar, but identical to her own.

Annabella turned her gaze back at Maurice Gervaise, her face ashen. A sneer was pasted on his face, any trace of a smile gone, and then she knew.

Someone had stolen her schematics, and she had just received a warning. She and her work were no longer safe.

Ivy and Avery would not return from the airharbour for another hour – enough time for Annabella to go to their hotel and request to make a speakerbox call. If her Humautomaton schematics had indeed fallen into unwanted hands, the only route she could think of was the Doctors Order's laboratory in London. As unlikely as it seemed, one of Ledburry's assistants had betrayed them.

She typed the code with trembling fingers, her head spinning, still processing the image of the automaton, stuck in the back of her mind.

"Miss Hammond, if I had not trusted my assistants, I would have never opened the laboratory," the earl said on the other end of the line. Judging from his unconcerned tone, Annabella's question hadn't bothered him at all. "I personally chose all three of them – or are you implying I am not capable of selecting my own team?"

Annabella's palm sweated over the receiver. "The French

automaton is hardly different from my Humautomaton plans. They must have my schematics, but how? I only shared them with our laboratory."

"My dear, it is not unheard of for two engineers to have the same idea," the Senior Lord of the Doctors Order said, his voice more understanding. "All the more reason for you to complete those connecting circuits and finish Humautomaton. If you succeed, we shall reveal it at the Engineers World Gathering. The sooner it becomes public knowledge, the smaller the risk to see it done in a foreign laboratory."

"I fear my plans are no longer safe in my cabinet," she tried, aware that there was no way to convince Ledburry.

"Your plans are perfectly safe in your cabinet. I suggest you enjoy Paris and forget about work, at least for a day. Now, I'm afraid I really must return to the worktable."

His last words before she returned the receiver to the hook carried to her, perhaps because he'd failed to secure his own receiver, and the connection lingered.

"Was that Miss Hammond? Is anything the matter?"

"Women hysterics. Nothing more."

THICK, grey clouds looking as if they were going to burst any moment loomed over Whitechapel with the menace of impending rain. The late afternoon's dull shadows crept up the dirty pavements and broken windows of wretched courts and narrow alleys riddled with the foul stench of squalor.

Hazel stopped at the entrance to Angel Alley, looking past the lodging houses and the gin bar that lined it, to the dead end where bare-knuckle fights used to be a regular occurrence. Had it not been for that night when her brother had challenged Jade Asher – Blackhand, the invincible fighter known in all

Whitechapel – Edwin would have been a whole man, and none of that bad blood would exist.

Alas, it was too late for what-ifs.

She hurried to the old red brick building where her mother lived, but the sight of her brother coming out of it made her jump behind a wheelbarrow, grateful for the shadow that covered her – and for the unexpected chance to find out what Edwin was scheming.

As soon as he disappeared inside a hansom cab in Aldgate, Hazel followed him in another conveyance until they reached Fleet Street and Edwin alighted in front of *The Londoners' Journal*'s headquarters. He emerged one hour later – too long if he only wanted to place an announcement, and just about the right amount of time if he intended to consult the archives. Hazel walked up the street behind him, keeping a safe distance, watching him enter a restaurant that a Whitechapel lad would never afford.

Who is paying for his dinner? This is a place for toffs, not for troublemakers raised in the slums.

She peered through the window, careful to remain hidden, waiting for his companion to arrive. But he ate alone and left a short while after, leaving her with more questions than answers.

The brougham waiting for Edwin at the street corner added to Hazel's suspicions.

Whoever sent that conveyance must be an affluent person, an aristocrat perhaps.

To her dismay, the thick curtains of the carriage and the darkness that had already descended prevented her from seeing who else was inside. She took a hansom cab and continued her pursuit, wiping the dirty window to have a better view of her surroundings in the dim light of the freshly lit streetlamps. Soon, she recognised the familiar buildings around Covent Garden, where her vehicle came to a stop.

"Lost 'im, Miss," the driver said apologetically. "'e must be around 'ere."

Hazel threw him a coin and nodded, hurrying into the maze of narrow streets where her brother had disappeared. She turned around a corner, aware that she was almost behind the Cinnamon Dove, only to find herself face to face with Edwin.

"I hope you enjoyed tailing me this afternoon, dear sister," he said, his mouth curled in a malicious grin. "I surely enjoyed making you believe I wasn't aware of your presence."

Hazel took one step towards him, schooling her features to hide her surprise at the sudden appearance.

Even the way he speaks is different from what it used to be. Who is he working for?

"Who is your sponsor, and for what?" she asked abruptly, her voice carrying no trace of the fear that gripped her. "If you can afford to eat in such places and ride such conveyances, they must be paying you handsomely. I wonder what they require of you for such an amount of money."

"My very generous employer is a discreet man who loathes attention," Edwin replied, his mocking grin still plastered on his pale face. "However, the Earl of Wyverstone's interest in the Dove intrigues him. If you behave like a good sister and help me decipher the mystery behind his presence in your establishment, we will have much to gain."

Cold dread crept down Hazel's spine. "Your employer should mind his own life and business and not pry on others' affairs. The matters at the Dove are discreet by their nature."

Edwin's laughter filled the space between them with a sinister edge. "Don't worry, my sister. I already have some answers."

"What do you mean?" Hazel's heart threatened to burst out of her chest. "Edwin, why did you return after all this time? What are you after?"

His face turned serious again. "Lizzie, I noticed your

remarkable tailing skills and wondered how often you use them and for what purpose. If I were anyone else, you would have done an excellent job." He bent over, his words a whisper in her ear. "But you failed to consider that I am as skilled as you in this art, so I will never be easy prey. You will only know what I decide to tell you."

4

A mild wind and unusually clear skies welcomed *The Skycradle*'s return to London that morning – a pleasant change from the drab clouds and soot hovering over the airharbour most of the days. The engines' roar stopped as soon as the airship's anchorage grapples secured her on the berth and Ivy finished all the post-flight checks. She peered through the glass pane above the piloting board to look for the French team. No one was waiting for them – neither at the base of the berth nor on the landing.

"I see no steammotor, no carriage or other vehicle bearing the official emblem of the French pavilion," she said when she joined Annabella and Avery, who were leaning over the observation deck's railing. "They should have been here to wait for their cargo."

"I'll go to the Assignments Office to ask Hayes," Annabella offered. "He should know whether they are coming anytime soon."

"No need, Miss Hammond, no need." All eyes turned to Hayes, whom none of them saw entering the gondola, with a man dressed in work clothes in tow. "I am here for the cargo you brought from Paris."

"Why are *you* here for a cargo that is no concern of yours?" Annabella's sharp tone and piercing look made the airharbour clerk take a step back. "Where is Fontaine? He should have arrived ages ago."

"Monsieur Fontaine won't come," the other man replied in broken English. "He sent me to bring our load to the Crystal Palace."

"Do we look like a bunch of fools to you?" Avery's thundering voice, combined with his height, could be quite intimidating. "If this cargo was important enough for the French to request the Engineers Order's help to bring it, then it should be important enough for their overseer to come to the airharbour."

"Young man, you are forgetting your place." Hayes bristling at Avery who was towering over him made a rather absurd image. Ivy could hardly contain her laughter. "Nobody asked for your opinion."

"I am the official coordinator of this assignment." Annabella interfered before Avery could reply – or worse, land a fist at Hayes' jaw. "I refuse to hand our cargo to anyone else but the French team's chief engineer. The boxes are not going anywhere until Gilbert Fontaine comes to fetch them himself."

The other man handed her a paper. "Is Monsieur Fontaine's signature enough?"

"No, it is not," Annabella replied sharply. "The cargo remains inside *The Skycradle*'s hold."

"This paper is an official document," Ivy said after checking it herself. "We have no choice but to give him the boxes." She turned from Annabella to the Frenchman. "But you can't handle the containers by yourself."

"Our airharbour workers will help him load those trunks into the steam cart, and his team will unload everything at the Crystal Palace," Hayes said, his face red with irritation, visibly displeased to be in a place he did not fancy, in the company of people he did not like. "Now, Miss Blackwell, stop being such a nuisance and give us access to the cargo hold. I don't have the entire day."

Ivy gritted her teeth, conjuring all the patience and composure she was capable of. The last thing she needed was for her foul mouth to land her in trouble again.

She nodded and disappeared inside the piloting area. A welcome change, as the air was becoming suffocating in the gondola's main room. Taking a deep breath to steady herself and calm her nerves, she pressed the lever that opened the cargo hold's hatch. Another push and the ramp went down, allowing for the wooden boxes to glide to the far end of the berth's base, where four sturdy men were waiting.

THE GENERAL OPINION had long since established the Engineers World Gathering as one of the greatest gifts the Reform had given to the country – and a proof that involving the High Orders of Sciences and Crafts in the state affairs had been an auspicious, though radical, change. Allowing scientists to decide the future development of England – under the strict eye of the Crown – had proved a winning wager, though many of the oldest families had strongly opposed the shift that altered everyone's lives profoundly.

Once in two years, London became the world capital of technology, the distinguished event's exhibits attracting visitors not only from England, but the Continent as well. And quite a few from lands as far as America.

From the height of his spot, perched on a ladder just outside the Crystal Palace, Jasper saw the airharbour's transportation steam cart approaching, carrying three boxes and just one passenger. He squinted at the vehicle, his leather-gloved hand shielding his brow. He recognised the steam cart's driver as one of Fontaine's men.

This must be the cargo Ivy has brought from Paris. But Fontaine should have fetched it from the airharbour himself. Why the devil is that man alone with the trunks?

Jasper climbed down in a hurry. Wiping his hands on his work trousers, thus adding to the vast collection of grease and oil stains on the fabric, he entered the Palace, striding purposefully towards the French pavilion.

"Right on time, Asher, right on time." Gilbert Fontaine rubbed his hands, watching his men unload the cargo from the steam cart, with an excited glint in his eyes. "I was just about to open the boxes we received from France, so you'll have the chance to see this marvel of automaton I told you about. I trust an engineer such as yourself will understand the novelty it brings."

"Except that I am more interested in understanding why you didn't go to the airharbour to receive, check, and register the cargo yourself. As the procedure requires. And I must add, we are rather strict when it comes to procedures."

"Why would I waste my time with an activity suited for a labourer? I am a busy man." He gave a derisive snort. "Leave the workers by themselves and you'll find them drinking instead of working. Why do you think the Engineering School asked your Order to send a reliable airship?"

Jasper clenched his fists, one eyebrow raised. The man had no respect for anything or anyone. "I have a few ideas."

"It was precisely because we had no time for your bloody procedures." Fontaine's disdainful gaze moved from his boxes to Jasper, and then again to the boxes, a corner of his mouth moving in a nervous twitch. "I can very well check the cargo here, and this is exactly what I'll do now."

The first two boxes contained a few brass parts looking new and polished, carefully placed on a soft bed of sawdust. Jasper bent over the open trunks to take a better look, but he found nothing of much interest – and certainly nothing to justify the request for *The Skycradle*, which he considered increasingly outlandish and suspicious.

"I wonder whether it really was necessary for your school to ask for an English delegation," he said, his stern voice matching the irritation he felt. "Those parts look rather ordinary to me."

"Oh, but you are mistaken." The other man threw Jasper a smile that spoke about superiority and entitlement, trying his patience in an exceptional manner. "The reason we commissioned that airship is in the last trunk. Let me show you the circuits and central engine, and you'll understand – hopefully."

Without waiting for Jasper's answer, Fontaine broke the seal of the last container and unlocked the three heavy padlocks, pushing the lid up.

His hand remained glued to the trunk's lid, his mouth agape, his eyes as wide as saucers.

"What's the matter?" Jasper hurried beside him, an apprehensive itch creeping down his spine. "What's in that box?"

"Precisely nothing!" Fontaine stood up from where he was crouched beside the box and turned to Jasper, pointing an accusatory finger at him. "Instead of the circuits and engine expected to turn our automaton into a functional prototype, this damned trunk carried garden soil! *Garden soil!* Care to explain the meaning of this?"

He was shaking with anger. Rage thickened the French accent that laced his bellowing voice. The labourers in their vicinity had halted to stare openly, with curious and amused eyes.

"Calm down." Jasper checked the empty box – or almost empty if one considered the fresh soil that filled half of it – with a sudden surge of exasperation. His patience was running thin.

Yet he couldn't shake the persistent feeling that the scene unfolding before his eyes was a carefully orchestrated ploy.

"This container had the Paris Engineering School's seal," he said, summoning an amount of self-control he was not entirely sure he possessed. "There is no doubt regarding its provenance. Perhaps they loaded the wrong trunk by mistake."

"An institution such as ours would never make such a foolish mistake." The Frenchman slammed the heavy lid of the box with a loud thump. "You understand, I hope, that *anyone* could have replaced the box and forged a fake seal. Your crew had just one duty, and that was to protect it." He strode towards the closest door, with Jasper in tow. "I'll place a speakerbox call with the school immediately." He turned towards Jasper, his eyes almost red with fury. "If Gervaise confirms they don't have the circuits and have indeed loaded them into that bloody English airship, then Miss Hammond and Miss Blackwell will have to take responsibility for their carelessness."

THE DISTANT WHOOSHING sound of the mechanical waterfall outside was the only intrusion in the heavy silence that had settled in the office of the Engineers Orders' Senior Lord following the account of the disastrous events at the Crystal Palace. Jasper, Ivy, Avery, Annabella, and Gilbert Fontaine – who were waiting for Theophilus Hollingsworth's answer – made the room seem more crowded than usual, their attention entirely on the elderly royal mechanic.

"From what you have just told me, I am to infer that two members of our delegation with an impeccable professional reputation bear the blame for losing the most important items of the French cargo." Master Hollingsworth took a few steps from his desk towards the centre of his office where the peculiar group stood, his hands clasped at his slightly bent back.

"Precisely so," the Frenchman replied, his voice carrying a mixture of anger and haughtiness. "Of course, we demand an explanation and the due compensation for this incident."

"I do hope you understand the gravity of your accusations and the terrible consequences they might bring," Theophilus Hollingsworth said, cutting off whatever angry retort Annabella and Jasper were about to spew in the French engineer's face. "I believe you should think carefully and make sure this is not a mistake."

"My superiors at the Engineering School assured me they loaded all the correct containers in Miss Blackwell's airship. Moreover, all of them were opened and checked before the English crew's eyes. However much you would like to think otherwise, this was no mistake. It was crass negligence."

The temporary Senior Lord of the Engineers Order locked his gaze on Annabella and Ivy. "Have they checked the cargo in front of you *after* loading it into *The Skycradle*? Is this true?"

"It is," Annabella replied, taking a deep breath to calm her fury. "Which does not mean we lost the contents of that bloody trunk on the way. How on earth would that be possible? I have no idea how that odd replacement happened, but I tell you for certain that none of us touched those containers after the French put the School's seal on them."

"There are only two possible explanations," Jasper said. "They loaded a part of the cargo one day before our delegation's return to England. Which means that the trunk's content could have been replaced in Paris, the night before *The Skycradle* left the airharbour. However, this is highly unlikely. It would have been too difficult to break into Ivy's airship and replace such a big container without being seen." He started pacing around the room, his eyebrows creased in a concentrated frown, his arms crossed at his chest. "This leaves us with the other possibility. I'd wager that the trunk or what was inside it was replaced in London after the containers were unloaded from the airship."

"Your theory is most insulting!" Fontaine bellowed, his small eyes smouldering with rage. "Why would we sabotage our own project?"

"And why would *we* sabotage *your* project?" Jasper retorted. "Your theory is as insulting as mine." He turned towards Ivy "What time have you unloaded the cargo off *The Skycradle*?"

"Nine in the morning," Ivy replied promptly. "I checked my timepiece because I needed to write the exact delivery time in *The Skycradle*'s activity ledger."

"The airharbour's steam cart arrived on the Crystal Palace's grounds at noon," Jasper announced. "You only need one hour at most. Not three. The steam cart must have stopped somewhere else along the way – possibly to replace what was inside that trunk."

"Lies!" Fontaine's face turned dark crimson. "According to our registry, the cargo was unloaded from that airship at half past ten! Not nine."

"Miss Blackwell is telling the truth," Annabella said, without as much as a glance in the Frenchman's direction, her voice harsh and commanding. "We placed the cargo in the French delegate's care at nine in the morning. You can confirm with Hadrian Hayes from the Airharbour Assignments Office, as he was there as well. Though I do not trust that man's mouth to ever utter an honest word."

Another moment of silence. Theophilus Hollingsworth crossed the office with small steps, staring thoughtfully at the clocktower dominating that part of Westminster Square. "As we are the Engineers World Gathering's host country, it is our duty to take all theories into consideration," he finally said. "The Inspectorates will open an investigation."

Fontaine's red face contorted in a burst of mocking laughter. "How can we trust such an investigation if Miss Blackwell and Miss Hammond won't take any responsibility while we wait?"

"A board of the Engineers, Aviators, and Doctors Orders'

representatives will meet in an hour to decide what happens to Miss Blackwell and Miss Hammond during the investigation," Master Hollingsworth said, his eyes heavy with apprehension. "I will inform you of our decision later this afternoon."

EDMUND ASHER HAD ALWAYS FOUND hospitals and medical wards repugnant, the mixed odour of laudanum, carbolic acid, sweat, and illness never failing to assault his nostrils and make his stomach roil. His adversity towards such places had become almost unbearable since an incident four years before, when circumstances had forced him to approve the amputation of a man's arm to save his already wretched life, condemning him to live as a cripple. He had never really forgotten about Edwin Sheridan or the fact that his own late brother, Jade Kendall Asher, had been the cause of his decision – and that man's misfortune.

He forced the unwanted memories out of his mind. His presence in the Classified Affairs' medical ward had a different purpose than reminiscing about the fateful night that had started a downward spiral ending up with his brother's death and that man's mutilation.

Alistair Montgomery was sitting on a narrow hospital bed, his back leaning against the cold wall. Though still pale, his cheeks had started to recover their normal colour, and his eyes were more focused and alert. He had discarded his fake glasses since his arrest, as he had no need for them anymore.

The earl took the chair beside the cot, beckoning the nurse to leave them. "I see your health has improved."

"A little," the other man snarled, throwing a spiteful glare at his unwanted visitor. "They did not allow my uncle here and informed me I was to receive no visitors. As I understand, I have certain rights, even as a convict."

"My specific instructions override any rights you think you might have," Edmund said, unperturbed. "Speaking of visitors, to my knowledge, the Constabulary had received the same instructions. Yet you had a fair share of guests in the past months, a matter that I am very interested in discussing with you."

"I have nothing to discuss," Montgomery retorted, his voice never losing its venomous tone. "My only visitors at the Constabulary were my uncle and a few friends unrelated to my activities."

Edmund took out a small notebook from his coat's pocket. "And the names of these friends are?"

He scribbled the names Montgomery spit out, before returning the notebook inside his coat. "Perhaps you need to be reminded of our deal. If my memory serves right, you agreed to share whatever information you possess about Benedict Quimby in exchange for protection and treatment. I am here to collect that information."

Though he spoke in a low voice, his tone was as commanding as ever, laced with a hint of menace. His words were barely audible in the ample space of the ward, but clear enough for Montgomery to understand he had no choice but to comply.

Montgomery's eyes rested on the small particles of dust dancing in the slant of daylight coming through the small window mounted high into the wall before turning to Edmund. "And perhaps you need to be reminded that my innocence in Windstoneham's murder case was part of the package I agreed upon."

"That part stands only if I am satisfied with the information that you will pass on to me," Edmund replied matter-of-factly. "Which is not the case at the moment."

"Damn you!" Montgomery shouted, hatred and rage

contorting his plain features. "This is not what we discussed at the Constabulary."

"As I have the upper hand, I can change the terms of our deal whenever and however I see fit." Edmund's cold voice showed no remorse. "You might have forgotten that someone is after your life, so you need the Classified Affairs' protection. Which leaves you with a rather limited range of choices."

Montgomery spat in disgust. "And how can I be certain you will keep your word if you have already changed the terms of our deal to your advantage?"

"You cannot," Edmund replied. "It is entirely your choice. However, I should say that a wager to trust me could prove more helpful to you, as I might actually keep my part of the deal if you cooperate. Whilst your silence would only ensure you will either be found guilty of Windstoneham's death or murdered. Shall I also add the tiny detail that I saved your life?"

"But you told me there is no clear evidence against me. That it will be a cold case."

"Only if you choose to cooperate," Edmund said in the same chilling voice. "I can always find evidence when necessary."

A visible shiver shook Montgomery's thin frame. "All right, curse you! I'll tell you what I know."

He brought his knees to his mouth and started talking, his eyes focused on some distant, invisible point in the whitewashed room. "I was aware of Quimby's plan to escape. He had secured the help of someone inside the Inspectorates. That person killed the guard, then made sure the four loose slabs in the pavement close to Quimby's door were still loose and could be moved, as no one had used them in a very long time. Of course, no one except Quimby knew about them. They opened into a tunnel that led to London's sewage network."

A light cough interrupted his story. Edmund waited for him to continue.

"I knew Annabella would come, as I had sent her a note to make sure she visited Quimby that night. I came through the tunnel one hour before Annabella would arrive, changed into the clothes of the dead guard, hid in the alcove, and waited for her. Then I drugged her with paralysis serum and carried her through the tunnel. The plan worked like clockwork, as no one was there except for Quimby and his guard." He gave a sarcastic laugh. "Perhaps it was what the Classified Affairs deserved for being all high and mighty and believing that your fortress is unbreachable."

Edmund's carefully schooled features showed nothing of the anger boiling inside him. Not at what Montgomery had said, but at the stark truth of his words. Trusting the security of the Classified Affairs premises had been his worst mistake.

"That guard was murdered in the exact manner as Windstoneham," he said, crossing his arms at his chest. "Which only leads me to believe that you were the one who did it."

"I never said I killed Windstoneham." Perhaps what he saw in Edmund's icy gaze determined Montgomery not to press the issue further. Instead, he continued his recount. "I did not kill that guard, but I did give the paralysis serum to Quimby's trusted messenger the night before it happened. Unfortunately, I cannot tell who he was, as he never actually revealed his identity. That time, I met him in a church in Whitechapel. He always wore a mask, so I never saw his face. But I can tell he was tall and short of an arm."

Tall and short of an arm.

A familiar sense of foreboding sent a creep down Edmund's spine. Edwin Sheridan, the crippled man whose arm had been amputated by Edmund's physician, at Edmund's request, after Jade had almost killed him, had disappeared three years before, leaving only a note on the doctor's table.

A note scribbled with the shaky scrawl of a man who barely knew how to write.

Wyverstone, ye'll pay tenfold for this arm. I swear on me dad's grave, when we meet again ye'll wish ye was dead.

"Are you listening?" Montgomery asked, and Edmund realised that for a moment he had lost himself again in a memory he wished he had the right to forget.

"Tell me who in the Inspectorates helped Quimby escape."

"I am not privy to such information," Montgomery said. "I only know that the guard had been bribed to keep silent about the messages Quimby exchanged with his acolytes."

So, the only lead to the traitor was dead, Edmund thought bitterly.

"Do you have any knowledge of Quimby's whereabouts?" He already knew the answer, but asked anyway.

"Will they hang me for murdering Windstoneham?"

Edmund kept silent for a moment, quickly pondering his options. He didn't have too many of them. "I give you my word that I shall protect you from any charges if you honestly help in any way you can with this investigation."

"I am not aware of his exact location, as our ways separated when we came out of those bloody sewers," Montgomery said. "Quimby left without giving any details about where he was going. However, I heard him saying that one of his strongest allies is in Paris. Given his fugitive status in England, I'd wager he fled to France."

Edmund stood up. He knew that was the most he could extract from Montgomery. "I shall make sure your help will be rewarded accordingly." He stopped in the doorway. "I suppose you do not know who Quimby's man in Paris is."

"No, I do not," Montgomery replied flatly. "Quimby shared little with me outside my own role in his experiment. But from what I can infer, I assume he must be an engineer."

Back to his office on the Inspectorates' second floor, Edmund unlocked a cabinet and took out Carmina's list of persons who had visited Montgomery at the Constabulary. He sat in his leather upholstered armchair and stretched his legs, crossing them at the ankles, before placing Carmina's paper and his notebook side by side on his desk.

The names on both lists were identical, and none of them even remotely related to anything that might provide a clue.

Edmund clenched his fists and closed his eyes, allowing himself a moment to gather his thoughts. Then he strode towards the tall window, staring at the mechanical waterfall with distant eyes, as if it were thousands of miles away.

Should I be happy that I now have two new clues? That I now know about the traitor inside the Inspectorates and about Quimby's engineer in Paris? Or should I despair because I have absolutely no idea how to find them?

THE EARLY EVENING light enveloped the Orders' conference hall in a mild, serene glow, in stark contradiction with the ominous air in the room. Seated at the long table that occupied the centre of the space, the Senior Lords of the Engineers, Aviators, and Doctors Orders, along with Gilbert Fontaine, waited for Ivy, Annabella, and Jasper to enter and close the heavy door behind them.

Jasper stared at Theophilus Hollingsworth, Jeremiah Barnaby, and the Earl of Ledburry, trying in vain to guess the Board's conclusion.

"The difficult decision we had to make was the result of a long – and intense, if I may add – debate," Master Hollingsworth said, adjusting his pince-nez, clearly uncomfortable with the entire story. "In the end, our priority was to prove our goodwill towards the French team and show that the English would not take advantage of their dire circumstances." He cleared his voice. "Furthermore, as the host country, England has a particular responsibility towards all participants."

The foreboding preamble didn't sit well with Jasper. He glanced at Annabella, the only other person in the room who knew Master Hollingsworth as well as he did, hoping she could still read the royal mechanic's tired face and unsteady gestures. She nodded, silently confirming her fears matched his.

She also expected the worst.

"The Constabulary will start investigating tomorrow," Theophilus Hollingworth went on. "However, following our Board's decision, Miss Blackwell's flying permit and Miss Hammond's research activities will be revoked for the entire duration of the investigation."

Annabella jumped from her seat, her gloved hands clenched in the fabric of her black skirts. "You cannot do this!" Her voice shook with a burst of anger she made no effort to disguise. "If the French team is – as we believe – behind this pitiful charade, your unjust decision will only help the enemy and sabotage your own team."

"Miss Hammond, if you are so kind as to allow me to finish," Master Hollingsworth said, beckoning her to take her seat. "Moreover, as a token of trust, our Board also decided to suspend the construction of *The Cerulean Lady*'s berth until the investigation is finished."

This time it was Jasper who sprang up from his chair. "This must be a sour joke," he said, a corner of his mouth curled up in a sarcastic sneer. "We all know that the Constabulary do not have the brightest of men in their employ. What happens if they don't finish the investigation in due time? Perhaps I should remind the Board that time is not quite on our side."

The Earl of Ledburry, Senior Lord of the Doctors Order, was the one to answer. "In that unfortunate circumstance, I fear we will have no choice but to open the Engineers World Gathering without England's project."

"I do hope they don't expect me to just sit and wait," Annabella said after the meeting was over and she was alone with Jasper on the mobile promenade surrounding the mechanical waterfall. Ivy had left first, too furious to stay at the Inspectorates one moment longer. "I do not trust the Constabulary, and I must complete those bloody circuits before the Gathering. Waiting is out of the question."

"Annabella, please do what they say and try not to make matters worse," Jasper said. "I understand why you do not trust the Constabulary. They are just a miserable assemblage of ill-prepared lads. I do not trust them either, for the same reasons. However, I do trust my brother."

5

As soon as Annabella's hansom cab left the square, Jasper returned to the Inspectorates to report to Edmund.

"Now I have no doubt we were framed," he concluded after finishing his account, trying to read his brother's expression. "Fontaine's accusations and the Board's decision are equally absurd for me to think otherwise."

"I agree," Edmund replied, to Jasper's surprise. It was not an everyday occurrence for Edmund to support an opinion without asking for further evidence. "I shall add these recent developments to Quimby's case file without waiting for proof to relate his disappearance to what happened today at the Crystal Palace."

"This is –" Jasper paused for a moment to search for the right word. "Unexpected."

"This is necessary." Edmund crossed his arms at his chest, leaning against the windowsill, his back to the mechanical waterfall. "I believe you are right, and I have no time to wait for some miraculous piece of evidence. It is quite clear that someone intends to sabotage not only England's participation at the Engineers World Gathering, but Annabella's Humautomaton as well. And the only person who knows about both projects and is capable of such a deed is Benedict Quimby. That man is a menace to the event. Perhaps even to the Crown."

The late evening light shrouded the room in a warm glow, leaving Edmund's tired face half in shadow. Jasper felt a pang of guilt for adding to his brother's burden, but he had no choice.

"*The Cerulean Lady* is not yet completed," he said. "Neither is Annabella's project. And we only have a few weeks left until the opening. As things are now, quitting seems a rather attractive idea."

"An idea which I hope will remain just that." Edmund ran his long fingers through his hair, his blue eyes more concerned than he probably wished to show. "Instead, you should revise the Board's decision more carefully. You might be surprised."

Jasper squinted at him, not following.

Edmund explained. "I am quite certain that Theophilus Hollingsworth was behind the final decision. You are missing some important details. Whilst they did suspend Miss Blackwell's flying permit, *The Skycradle* has no such restrictions, so she can ask her Australian friend to pilot her when needed. Although the construction of our airship's berth was paused at the Crystal Palace, the *Lady* has no restrictions, so you can complete her." He stopped, creasing his brow in a frown. "However, what worries me the most is Annabella. She is the only one whose work is completely stalled, and her project is of utmost importance. This little detail makes me believe Quimby is indeed behind this charade."

He poured himself a glass of water, but Jasper guessed he would have traded that for something stronger had he been in his study at home. Edmund drank it all in one gulp and turned to Jasper again.

"If the new information I extracted from Montgomery today is true, Quimby is in France," he announced. "Someone from the Inspectorates helped him out of the Classified Affairs' prison."

"A traitor," Jasper spat. "How will you find him?"

"I shall work with Herdforthbridge for that. But there is more. I found out who Quimby's messenger was all that time. According to Montgomery's description, a tall, black-haired young man." A pause. "Who had one arm amputated."

A chill ran down Jasper's spine. His mind travelled back to the night he had found out that his twin brother Jade – an officer in Her Majesty's Safety Corps – had made a name as the most fearsome bare-knuckle fighter in Whitechapel, leading a double life among the destitute. That night from four years ago, Jade's last opponent was Edwin Sheridan, whom he almost killed. Jasper let Jade take his place aboard *The Golden Griffin* to redeem himself and receive a promotion, and Edmund left Sheridan in his physician's custody. Sheridan had lost his arm. Jade had lost his life.

Jasper clenched his fists. "Sheridan," he finally said, his voice bitter and broken.

Edmund nodded. He unlocked a drawer of his cabinet and extracted a thin leather-bound file. "This is all I have on him. Find out his whereabouts and everything else there is to know."

HAZEL ADJUSTED her bonnet and gloves and plastered an innocent expression on her face, satisfied with her prim and proper look, before entering *The Londoners' Journal's* headquarters just as they were about to close for the public. A few distressed tears and a trembling hand convinced the clerk to let her search for an important family incident in the newspaper's archives regardless of the late hour, so the good man handed her the registration ledger right away.

"Miss, make sure you fill out your name, request, and purpose. Here." He pointed at a blank space under the last name on the page.

"Thank you, sir," Hazel said, gratitude and relief in her voice. "You can't imagine what a great service you have done to a family whose good fortune depends on what I'll find."

Wiping an imaginary tear and tucking a black lock of hair under her bonnet, she took the ledger to the nearest table, searching for her brother's name after the clerk returned to his reading and paid no more attention to her. She found it on the previous page, along with the date and number of the magazines he had perused.

"Newspapers from ten years ago seem in high demand these days," the archivist muttered when he brought her a pile of the *Journal*'s older issues, squinting at her over the rim of his spectacles. She was the only person in the reading room, and the man clearly had no wish for a late visitor he had to accommodate instead of going home.

Ignoring the librarian's frown, Hazel took out her gloves and started reading the newspapers, trying to find anything, any piece of information, even remotely related to the Earl of Wyverstone.

She found none. Most of the articles in the magazines her brother had requested documented the tragic untimely death of some aristocratic debutante with no relation to the earl. Almost an hour later, after making sure she left no line unread, Hazel let out a long breath of relief. Nothing in those papers could compromise the earl.

The best course of action, Hazel decided on her way back to the Dove, was to drop the matter and not worry Madame uselessly. Carmina Harcourt and the Earl of Wyverstone had suffered enough and deserved some happiness.

~

"I SHOULD LEAVE for France at once," Carmina concluded when Edmund shared with her the details of the day in the privacy of his study at the Wyverstone house. She was standing close to his desk, under a wall sconce whose electric bulb engulfed her in a mild yellow glow that cast slants of light on the silk of her blue dress and in the violet curls of her hair.

Her green eyes sparkled with the excitement of a new potentially lethal assignment. Strong, yet delicate, mysterious, dangerous, and strikingly beautiful. After all those years, the depth of his love for her still shook him to the core and scared him witless.

"No," he replied, keeping those thoughts to himself. "It's too early. We have no knowledge where in France he is hiding, so I need to make further inquiries."

Carmina nodded and poured tea for both of them. He followed the elegant movement of her wrist as she returned the teapot back onto the tray.

"So natural," he mused aloud, his eyes drowning in the sight of her. It was one of those rare moments when he felt at peace. "You fit so well."

She gave him a surprised glance. "I'm afraid I do not follow."

Edmund rose, his tea forgotten, and joined her on the other side of his desk. "Here, in this house." His long fingers cradled her cheek. "You always come here as yourself. No disguises. Which makes me happy because it allows me to imagine you are the lady of this house."

"You are treading on dangerous waters." Carmina's voice was but a whisper against his touch. "This is the most we can have of each other, a fact both you and I know too well. For a thousand reasons. For the need to hide my past. For my desire to keep my freedom. For our work in the service of the Crown."

A slight frown shadowed his handsome face and darkened his blue eyes. She rested her hand on his against her cheek.

"But know this," she continued, her intense green gaze on him. "Although we met in the wrong circumstances, although we both accepted this life when we became lovers, although we must hide our feelings, you are the only one for me. I knew that from the moment we first met at that ball in Paris, when your father brought us together to work on the Humautomaton case. I love you, Edmund Asher. Never forget how much I love you."

As if her words were the reassurance he had been waiting for, he closed the narrow distance between them and crushed his lips on hers, pulling her to him in a desperate embrace. His fingers tangled in her tresses, her hairpins falling on the soft carpet, soon followed by her bodice and his waistcoat.

She was his world, and he was losing himself in it, everything else nothing but a distant echo in the back of his mind.

A GENTLE, almost transparent darkness enveloped the small makeshift bedchamber attached to the study, as the thick blackness dissipated into the early dawn's milder shades. The outline of the mahogany desk, the tall windows with drawn velvet curtains, and a trail of clothes discarded on the floor were barely visible through the open door in the soft dimness of a night that was about to end.

Edmund breathed in the scent of the woman he held in his arms and closed his eyes, his thoughts travelling back to the day they had first met as agents of the Crown, an encounter decided by his father, the late Earl of Wyverstone. He had briefed him in the same study he was using now, explaining all the details of the mission. Benedict Quimby was under suspicion of conducting illegal experiments, and the Office of Classified Affairs had to find evidence to arrest him. They were about to start a chase that would last for months, torn between London and Paris.

"You assign me such a dangerous and difficult case, yet you ask me to work with a woman?" Edmund lifted an eyebrow in an incredulous frown. He was younger then and had yet to master the talent of hiding his emotions. "Father, this must be a mistake."

"She is no ordinary woman," his father replied, a corner of his lips curled in an amused smile. "I have yet to find an agent with better disguise and infiltration abilities. Edmund, I trust Carmina as much as I trust you. And so should you."

Edmund nodded, aware that trying to further challenge his father's decision would be a useless undertaking. "I only have her name and an invitation to the private ball in Paris where I am to meet her. How shall I recognise this woman?"

The earl's smile turned into laughter. "Oh, believe me, son. You shall."

And, by gods, he had. She had entered the ballroom bringing with her the fresh scent of early summer, of roses and cinnamon, the most beautiful woman he had ever laid his gaze upon. All eyes were on her, on the low neckline of her daring green silk gown, on the black locks of her hair, carefully arranged over her bare nape, on her mysterious smile, on her elegant bearing when she danced, on the sensual movements of her arm. Everything about her was a cold calculation towards one purpose – to attract attention.

His attention.

From that very first moment, Edmund knew. Not only that she was the woman his father had partnered him with, but also that he wanted her as much more than just a partner. He left the ballroom and slipped outside onto a secluded balcony. Carmina followed, light and shadow dancing on her lithe figure.

She was a stranger to him, yet there was something familiar about her. He could not escape the feeling that, in some hidden corner of a distant past, he had already met her.

"His lordship informed me we are to live as husband and wife," she said without any introduction. Carmina's confidence in her ability to spot her partner without mistake equally amused and awed him. "As I understand, we have rooms close to Hotel de Ville. I shall come tomorrow morning."

"The flat is rather small, with just a parlour and a bedchamber," Edmund explained. "For that, I apologise. My father insisted we keep all appearances of a happily married couple. As I am certain you already know, in our line of work, keeping up appearances is capital."

"Of course, I was prepared for that," she said, no emotion and all practicality. "I shall be there at eight."

She started towards the French doors, but he was not yet ready to let her go.

"Miss Harcourt," he said, his voice more intense than he had wanted, prompting her to stop and turn the fiery gaze of her green eyes at him. "Have we, by any chance, met before?"

"No, my lord, I'm afraid not," she replied before disappearing among the throngs of dancers.

When he returned inside the ballroom, she was gone.

The next day she appeared at the door of their rented rooms at eight sharp, with a single travel trunk as her only luggage, wearing a plain carriage dress, her hair styled demurely in a chignon at her back, and as beautiful as she had been in green silk the night before.

Living together for months in that small flat, slowly opening towards one another, peeling thin layers of each other's soul, had been their undoing. By the end of their mission, he was utterly, completely, irrevocably in love with her. And he was terrified.

"Where are we going from here?" she asked one day, shortly before their final departure for London, breaking the pleasant silence that enveloped their small parlour in Paris. They had grown so used to each other's presence that those moments of silence never felt awkward. "I understand that your station comes with certain responsibilities, but I would rather we left no thoughts unspoken."

She was standing before the tall window overlooking Rue du Temple, watching the dusk fading into night, her palms leaning against the windowsill. Edmund looked up from the report he was writing, aware that her question had nothing to do with their mission.

He joined her at the window. Outside, the dying light of the day blended with the murky glow of the streetlamps, which turned people and carriages into patches of shadow. "I'm afraid you need to elaborate, otherwise I might misunderstand the meaning of your words."

"I believe you *perfectly* understand the meaning of my words." Carmina locked her eyes on him, bold, and brave, and true to herself. "I am referring, of course, to our mutual attraction, which, so far, both of us have struggled to ignore. Alas, I cannot ignore it any longer. His lordship gave no specific instructions about this when he sent me here as your partner, so I cannot know for certain how many rules I have broken. But, against all protocol, I'm afraid I have fallen in love with you."

Her words lifted a weight he had not realised he had upon his soul.

"I am fully aware of the duties my station and my future role in the Office entail," he whispered, his thumb caressing a corner of her mouth. "But I am also fully aware of what I feel. Of what I desire." He pulled her closer, his brow touching hers. "I love you. For your brilliant mind, for your spirit, for everything you are. Carmina Harcourt, if you'll have me, we shall find a way."

Her kiss, the passion of her embrace, the way she felt in his arms that first night of their love were the only answer he needed.

Months later, when he became the next Earl of Wyverstone and the new Chief Inspector of Her Majesty's Office of Classified Affairs after his father's death, he received full access to Carmina's file, which revealed her real identity as the Marquess of Windstoneham's eldest daughter. And then he understood.

His father had chosen her not only as his partner but also as his future wife. For that reason, he had provided no specific instructions about their relationship.

Only that the late earl could not have foreseen his son's mistake – one that had separated him for three years from the woman he loved and thrown him into a loathsome marriage to a traitor.

Edmund opened his eyes, unwilling to dwell on that particular part of his recent past. The regular beats of Carmina's heart against his chest and the soft, almost inaudible sound of her breathing indicated that she was still asleep.

Something inside him had shifted profoundly after the night he had taken her out of Quimby's underground den, more dead than alive. Their stolen nights and hidden moments were no longer enough for him.

"Rebecca Beatrix Asher," he whispered in the mild darkness of the room, caressing her bare back, his voice heavy with longing. "Countess of Wyverstone."

Only the early morning's bitter chill announced the approaching dawn, as the darkness was still thick enough to shelter London's nocturne endeavours, such as someone determined to break into another person's home.

Jasper pulled his cap over his eyes, although chances for anyone to recognise him in the deserted street were slim. Soon, the city would come to life again, the shrill of the day's first gondotram heralding the start of a new day. But four in the morning was too early for intense activity.

Throwing a quick glance around to make sure he was alone, Jasper crouched to peek through the windows into the kitchen of the house Gilbert Fontaine had rented in Knightsbridge, close to the Crystal Palace. His vision had grown used to the murky glow of the streetlamps, or at least enough to ascertain that the room downstairs was empty. Fontaine's servants slept either in the attic or in their own homes. Either way, they would be down there soon, so he had to make haste.

If Fontaine was part of the charade the French had prepared for them, he would find out.

It only took him a few moments to extract the lockpick from his pocket and work the service door to gain entrance into the house, the amplifier in his ear. Careful not to make any noise, he climbed the carpeted stairs to the first floor, two steps at a time, stopping in the shadows next to the study's closed door to listen. No sound came.

Jasper searched the French engineer's shelves and cabinets at the light of the small pocket lamp he carried with him, but they had no secrets to reveal. He flipped through the sketches and prototypes spread in disarray on the desk, finding nothing incriminating about them. Some quills and pens completed the image of industrious disorder, along with an inkwell placed on a small, slim piece of paper that Jasper identified as a cable. He pulled it and read the message written in French.

The last pieces will arrive tomorrow. No need for you at the airharbour. Expect them at the Palace.

He read the cable again, trying to understand. Was it possible that Fontaine played no part in that sordid affair? Was he just following an order? His doubt and anger with the English were actually genuine?

He had one way to find out.

Jasper arrived at the Crystal Palace just as the first dull light of dawn cracked through the clouded sky. The place was still deserted, except for the guards and a few labourers who had started the day working on a scaffold outside the exhibition building. Among them, Jasper recognised one of the junior engineers assigned as helpers to the French team, who had been around the pavilion the day when *The Skycradle*'s cargo arrived from the airharbour.

"May I have a word?" Jasper said, prompting the man to turn and climb down. "Do you remember any particular detail about yesterday? About how the French brought their cargo from the airharbour?"

The man frowned, as if trying to fathom what Jasper was talking about, then rubbed his chin, recollecting the events. "Yesterday? No. But I do recall some incident from two days ago. Their engineer informed us that the following day he would go to the airharbour, so we had to work unsupervised until his return. Then one of his men required his urgent attention. They talked in French, so I didn't understand, but I can tell it was an angry conversation. Fontaine returned to let us know his assistant would go alone, and he would wait for the cargo at the Palace with the rest of the team."

The problem is not Fontaine but his superiors at the school. But why? What do they stand to gain from this affair?

"Thank you. That was helpful."

"Wait!" The man stopped him just as he was about to leave. "When Fontaine and his assistant had that conversation, they were not alone. I remember a lady who was close enough to hear them. Usually, ladies speak French, ain't it so?"

"They do," Jasper confirmed, suddenly interested. "Tell me about this lady."

"She was a beautiful woman. Not too tall, but not too short either. She had black curls and a blue bonnet, and wore a pale blue dress. The children who were with her called her Lady Rowena."

6

"There, done!" Annabella clapped her hands, staring in delight at the small clockwork frog gleaming in coppery shades on her workbench. The late morning sun invaded the room turned into workshop on the uppermost floor of the Windstoneham house, throwing a glossy sheen over the brass parts, gauges, wires, and contraptions spread all over the place.

She wound up the key on the toy's back. The frog made a few tentative jumps before leaping in a wide arch from the workbench's tabletop straight onto the face of Oscar Bashford, the Duke of Herdforthbridge, who had made a stealth appearance to surprise her.

"Bloody fiendish contraption!" He took a step back, catching the toy with one hand. "Are you by any chance designing a weapon?"

Annabella turned to her soon-to-be husband, a wide, startled grin brightening her face. "Oscar!"

She threw her goggles on the workbench and welcomed him with a kiss, glancing at the open door behind him as if she expected her mother or Ethel to appear that instant in the doorframe.

"Oh, how I missed you." She ran her fingers through his

blond, shoulder-length hair. "When did you return from Herdforth Hall? I wasn't expecting you back in London for at least another week."

"Last night I found out about the incident at the Inspectorates and left for London at dawn. You should have told me."

"But you had so much work to do at the estate, and I did not want to worry you."

"No work is more important than you." He squeezed her bare hand, oblivious to the grease transferring to his pristine glove. "Tell me what happened."

She recounted the events of the previous day, anger burning in her eyes. "This sordid story's only purpose must be to hinder Humautomaton so that the French can flaunt their work at the Gathering."

A frown creased the duke's handsome face. "I fail to comprehend how your work has anything to do with the French. As I recall, Humautomaton is still a heavily guarded secret, so how on earth would they know of its existence?"

"Not so heavily, it seems." Annabella hugged herself against the chilling memory. "Do you know what I saw in the Engineering School's laboratory in Paris? My very own automaton design. Not a similar, but an *identical* one. Of course, I wondered how that was possible. But after the pitiful sham with *The Skycradle*'s cargo, I am quite certain that the man I saw in Paris that day was indeed Benedict Quimby, and he had a hand in this."

"What?" Herdforthbridge's clear blue eyes turned one shade darker. "This would mean that the Paris Engineering School is protecting a criminal, which is a serious offence."

"I have no means to confirm what I've seen," Annabella said, a bitter smile echoing her helplessness. "I ran after him, but they dragged me out of there, and now I have no access to that bloody laboratory. Perhaps I should have returned when no one was aware and tried to –"

The duke kissed her forehead, his hands still holding hers. "No. You did well. We should talk to Edmund. Before it's too late."

~

THE MORNING DREARINESS had disappeared into the midday's pleasant sunlight and unusually clear sky, peppered with scattered clouds and a few small cruise airships flying above the gondotram's iron tracks spread high over Holborn. The cheerful noise of the streets mingled with the busy tumult of the neighbouring skystation, like a huge artery pulsing with life inside the giant that was London.

"A fine day for a walk around your school," Jasper argued, offering his arm to a still undecided Rowena Hollingsworth, who didn't enjoy the prospect of abandoning her work even for a short while. She finally conceded, putting her gloved hand on the crook of his arm.

"The children seem to love their visits to the Crystal Palace," Jasper said matter-of-factly. "You bring them there almost every day."

Rowena laughed. "For such inquisitive minds, the Gathering is a treasure trove. They always find some novelty to marvel at, a new contraption being mounted right before their eyes. Though you should know they are eager to see the *Lady*."

"I'm afraid there might be no *Lady* to see at all at the Gathering." Jasper's smile faded. "Not after what happened yesterday. Our airship seems the target of some vile sabotage attempt."

Rowena held his concerned gaze. "Father told me about that unpleasant incident. I do hope the constabulary will sort out this misunderstanding soon."

"I do not trust them to sort it out, so I shall investigate myself."

She looked at him with startled eyes. "But you are no constable. Jasper, you should trust the authorities more and let them help you. Stop worrying so much."

"You did not have the same opinion when your school turned into a pile of rubble." Jasper regretted his words the second he uttered them.

"That was a different matter," she said. To his relief, she betrayed no distress at the previous summer's painful memory.

No, it was not, he thought, but didn't press the issue further.

"Rowe, I need your help." Time to explain the reason for his unexpected visit to her school. "I understand that Fontaine and one of his assistants had quite a heated exchange two days ago, and you were around when it happened. What can you tell me about that? I think the French planned this entire story with the cargo, and I need any information I could use."

"It is not much," Rowena said after the few moments of silence it took her to recall the episode. "This man, Fontaine, who I believe was their main engineer, wanted to go to the airharbour to receive the cargo they were expecting. But his colleague reminded him that their superior in Paris had instructed him otherwise, and he was under strict orders. As I understand, Fontaine was not allowed to leave the exhibition site the day the cargo arrived from France. He had to arrange for transportation with the airharbour instead."

"Thank you." Jasper took her hand in his out of impulse, forgetting for a moment that they were in the middle of a crowded street. He had acquired the information he needed, but was well too aware he could not use it. Such a conversation could not count as evidence, and he did not want to involve Rowena. But at least he had a lead in his search for the truth.

"Lady Rowena!" Little Blake Killen's loud voice made him

release her hand. "Ye need to come to the school. Yer new assistant is 'ere!"

"ARE YOU CERTAIN IT WAS QUIMBY?" Edmund asked, his icy gaze matching his inflexible tone. "Think carefully, Annabella. However much I want to arrest that man, I cannot risk a diplomatic incident, accusing one of the most prestigious science institutions on the Continent of harbouring a wanted criminal."

"Not entirely, but almost," she replied, returning his cold stare. Chief Inspector of the Classified Affairs or not, Edmund Asher would not intimidate her. "After yesterday's events, I am even more inclined towards the affirmative."

The tense atmosphere in the dowager Marchioness of Windstoneham's drawing room had become almost unbreathable as Annabella, Edmund, and the duke kept talking in low voices, fearing a servant could hear them. The tea had gone cold, but Annabella made no move to ask for a fresh teapot.

"By the time I reached that door at the end of the corridor, he had already disappeared inside the workroom," she said, looking in turn at Edmund and Oscar. "I tried to explain to the dean that I might have spotted a dangerous man who was wanted in England. But he denied it so vehemently and assured me in such definitive terms that no one except his students was there, that I came to really believe it myself. However, seeing my prototype in their laboratory and yesterday's events rekindled my doubts."

"Damnation!" Edmund cursed in a rare burst of frustration. "Annabella, I'm afraid you made a monumental mistake. But I cannot blame you, as you are no agent of mine and have no proper training to understand how to behave in such circumstances."

Annabella threw him a dumbfounded look. "Care to explain what you mean?"

"Let me explain what Edmund meant, but you must understand that nothing of this is your fault." Herdforthbridge took her hand in his, his blue eyes as reassuring and comforting as ever. "Seeing Quimby and making a clear statement that you recognised him might be problematic. Now he and those who are hiding him are on high alert, and they will be more careful. Those people must have guessed you would relay the information regarding Quimby's presence at the school, so they will take precautions. In other words, we might have missed an important opportunity to find him."

"*We?*"

"We, England," Herdforthbridge explained hastily, under Edmund's deadly glare.

Annabella rose, her skirts swishing with the sudden movement. She pressed her fingers against her forehead, trying to ignore the headache that squeezed her temples. "Good Lord, you are right. I should have thought of the consequences of my actions. I have made an unpardonable mistake."

"Anyone else would have done the same in your stead," Edmund said, his composure back in place. "Worry not, we still have a good chance." He started pacing around the drawing room, his arms crossed at his chest, his attention focused on the invisible stream of his thoughts. "If Quimby is working to sabotage England's participation at the Gathering or has some other wicked plan afoot, then he has no time to go into hiding again. Moreover, he will consider your setback as an advantage, because he will probably believe you will direct your efforts towards returning to your workbench, and not towards solving the mystery of the man you identified as Quimby."

"But how will you find him?" Annabella asked. "We cannot

know for sure whether he remained in Paris or returned to London."

"I have a few ideas." Edmund stopped beside the tall window, staring at the clear sky outside. "The information you provided is extremely valuable, but I still need your help. Do you happen to have any sort of smaller contraption similar to Humautomaton?"

"I do," Annabella said. "I designed and built some small toy automatons for practice."

"It would be most excellent if I could use the schematics of such a toy. I need those plans to infiltrate one of my agents into the school."

REBECCA BEATRIX ASHER, *Countess of Wyverstone.*

Hours later, Edmund's low, beautiful voice still echoed in Carmina's mind. She sipped her tea, glancing at the sunset's shades of intense, dark red from the privacy of her study at the Cinnamon Dove. His words, whispered in the welcoming darkness of the chamber where they lay in each other's arms, had shattered her heart, filling her with devastating pain.

But she couldn't have let him know she was awake. It was better like that for both of them. No matter how she longed for a life with him, that was the most they could have of each other.

"Fool." Her voice, barely audible in the pleasant silence of the room, carried an equal measure of yearning and sadness. "Edmund, you fool."

She was grateful for the soft knock at the door interrupting the unwanted train of her thoughts. Hazel entered her study, the latest issue of *The Londoners' Journal* in her hand.

She left it on the small round table beside her Madame's armchair. "The evening newspaper." Then started back towards the door.

"Wait." Carmina stopped her just as she was about to leave the room. "Is anything the matter? You seem rather distracted as of late, and I want you to know you can always ask for my help should you need it."

"I'm all right, Madame, just need some sleep," Hazel replied, then opened the door with a smile. "Thank you for your concern."

Alone again, Carmina lit the lamp on her desk and opened the newspaper, searching for some useful information she could add to her files for later research, but found nothing of interest.

She reached the last page, where an announcement in big black letters framed in a thick border was glaring at the unaware reader.

EXPLOSIVE INVESTIGATION!

If our esteemed audience had any doubts about the rot plaguing the upper echelons of English society, our next investigation will shatter them to the wind. The Reform should have brought trust and stability, yet our most sacred institutions are riddled with fraud and dishonesty. Be prepared, dear reader, for we shall reveal truths that will shake the entire establishment. We are now assembling the last pieces that make the big and grisly picture, which we will deliver to you in one of our future issues.

"Bloody scandal sheet," Carmina muttered in disgust, throwing the newspaper on her desk. "I wonder who the target of this nefarious inquiry is."

The chime of her speakerbox diverted her attention from *The Londoners' Journal.*

"You are leaving for France," Edmund announced from the other end of the line. "I shall expect you at the Inspectorates tomorrow."

∼

Angel Alley was the last place where Jasper wanted to be that evening.

The lane hadn't changed much in the past four years since the night he'd found Jade embroiled in a bare-knuckle fight with Edwin Sheridan on the patch of dirt at its end, surrounded by a grisly assortment of dock workers, hookers, and street urchins who were cheering for his brother – for Blackhand. That night, in this wretched place, Jasper had discovered, unwillingly, Jade's other life, one he hadn't been aware of. The recollection of that night, the image of his twin brother in the clutches of near madness while punching the other man's face, still burnt his memories.

But he could not afford to run back to the safety of his workshop, as he was inclined to do as soon as he stepped into the narrow alley lined by lodging houses covered in a black layer of soot. Grateful for the heavy stench of ash and urine that invaded his senses and distracted his bleak thoughts, he entered the only pub in that murky corner of Whitechapel.

"Jolly ol' place," he said in an accented voice after he found an empty chair, squinting around in the general direction. "Reckon it ain't that changed since I came 'ere last."

He put his pint of ale on the table, waiting for a reaction, aware that no one recognised him.

"And when was that, lad?" one of the burly men at the nearby table asked, his bulky, dirty fingers clasping a tankard whose contents had partially spilt out in a frothy trail. "Can tell ye're not from 'ere."

"Came four years ago to see a fight," Jasper replied. "What a night that was, mind ye. Blackhand crushed that poor sod to a bloody pulp. Sheridan was 'is name, I fink."

"Blackhand, what a magnificent fighter that lad," the other man said in a wistful voice, wiping his brow with the back of his greasy hand. "'E disappeared after that bout with Sheridan. Weeks later, there 'e was, in the newspaper. Tis how we found out the lad was a toff by the name of Jade Asher. Brother to the Earl of Wyverstone, no less!"

"'E died soon after that." Another man joined them at Jasper's table. "Twas a pity to lose 'im. Such a young and strong lad, and never put on airs. We all respected 'im 'ere."

"Reckon it was a pity," Jasper replied, fighting the knot that constricted his throat. "And Sheridan? I didn't see 'im in other fights."

"No one did," the burly man said. "Last we 'eard, the day Sheridan challenged Blackhand, he'd lost 'is job at the Sleepy Mutton near Aldgate. Ol' Jack Sheffield, the owner, found out he was embroiled in some mischief and sacked 'im."

His friend finished the story. "Sheridan thought a victory against Blackhand ought to bring 'im some ready. But 'e barely escaped with 'is life that night."

Jasper nodded, as if captivated by their sordid account, swallowing his drink in large gulps. As soon as he finished, he thanked the men and hurried out to find Jack Sheffield, Sheridan's former employer.

Tucked in a back alley, the Sleepy Mutton didn't stand out too much. Though old and rather shabby, with a pair of gas lamps mounted on each side of the entrance, the small establishment was clean and well-kept on the inside. Jasper took a stool at the counter and ordered a mug of ale from the old man who owned the place.

Jack Sheffield directed a suspicious gaze at the unfamiliar guest. "New around here, lad?"

"I'm after a man who was in your employ," Jasper said, wiping his mouth with the back of his hand. "Edwin Sheridan. What can you tell me?"

A shadow darkened the barkeep's wrinkled face. "Drink your ale and leave." He turned his back to Jasper. "I've nothing to tell you."

"He's after my family," Jasper pressed, his voice laced with the right amount of desperation to make the man face him again. "Can't protect my girl and my mum if I have nothing on him."

The barkeep kept silent for a few long moments, as if assessing whether to recount what he knew. "I helped that man when he first moved to London with his mum and sister," he finally said, resting his gnarly fingers on the wooden countertop. "Twas 5 or 6 years ago, but I ain't too sure. I employed him and paid for the rooms they kept at a lodging house three streets away from here."

Sheffield stopped to drink a few gulps of water, then locked his gaze on the blackened beams of the ceiling, lost in the sour memory. "But he had no good bone in him, that lad. One year – or it might be a year and a half – after he started here at the Mutton, I found out he used a band of ragamuffins to pick pockets for him. One night, I caught him beating a poor street urchin in a back alley. Ain't one to tolerate such cruelty, so I sacked him. The next morning, when he left, he stole my knife, the one I used to prepare poison traps for vermin. Lord knows what he wanted to do with that rusty, vicious thing."

He tried to stab Jade with that knife, and Jade stabbed him with it instead, Jasper thought, but said nothing, waiting for the man to continue.

"Heard he lost an arm, but he disappeared, and I knew nothing of him anymore. Saw him again only a few days ago. Came here to show me how well he was faring, just to spite me. He almost looked like a gentleman."

"Didn't you find it odd for someone like Sheridan to do this well?" Jasper asked, his ale forgotten.

"Sheridan's ilk could never do well on their own merit." The old barkeep almost spat the words. "He must do the dirty work of some toff who pays him well, and now the scoundrel wants his own business. I have a cellar he wants to turn into a prize fighting room. Promised to bring the best fighters in London and the likes. But I'm good with the Mutton as it is, so I told him to leave. He did, but I reckon he still thinks I'll change my mind. Told me where to find him.

"He keeps rooms on Stangate Street in Lambeth, close to the Inspectorates," the barkeep added, answering Jasper's silent plea. "But be careful, lad. That man is vile. And as cunning and slippery as a serpent."

7

"What's yer business 'ere?" The doorkeeper squinted at Jasper with a bored look, stretching his legs under the table in the cold, semi-darkened hallway.

"I've a message for Edwin Sheridan, and my master would appreciate a swift delivery," Jasper said, sliding two coins on the wooden top under the man's nose. "Jack Sheffield from the Sleepy Mutton expects 'im tonight to finish their little talk from two days ago."

The coins disappeared into the doorkeeper's pocket. Jasper waited for him to climb the first flight of stairs before following him, keeping himself close to the wall, careful not to make any sounds. On the third floor, he crouched inside a narrow alcove that hid the door to the service stairs and waited.

Message delivered, the doorkeeper passed Jasper's hiding spot without a glance. Minutes later, Edwin Sheridan followed, his steps echoing down the stairs until fading into complete silence.

Jasper hurried down the dimly lit corridor and picked the lock to Sheridan's rooms in haste, aware that he had no more than an hour until the man found out he'd been tricked and returned from Whitechapel.

The small parlour had no secrets to reveal. Just a few pieces of furniture and a set of thick curtains covering the tall windows entirely. No papers, no books, no letters, and no objects that could relate Sheridan to Quimby.

Holding back a frustrated grunt, Jasper continued his search in Sheridan's bedchamber, which was as sparsely furnished and decorated as the parlour – with the solitary exception of a thick package wrapped in brown paper and tied with rope, left on a chair close to the wardrobe.

Daniel Marlowe – only a name with no address was written on the package, in a handwriting Jasper had a hard time deciphering.

For Maurice Gervaise, The Paris Engineering School, Rue des Écoles, Paris, France.

Jasper opened one side of the package, careful not to tear the paper, and let the contents slip out in his hand. Two old books with cracked spines and damaged covers with gilded titles, which he had already seen a few months before, on a table in Herdforthbridge's cottage at Herdforth Hall.

An In-Depth Treatise on Biomechanics

Compendium of Biomechanics and How It Can Be Applied to the Living World

Jasper stared at the worn-out tomes in astonishment. Those biomechanics books were the last thing he had expected to find in Sheridan's lair. He flipped through the pages, their edges filled with drawings and notes, the owner's name marked in small letters, in a familiar handwriting, under the books' titles.

A. P. Hammond

He returned the books inside the paper wrap and secured the rope, aware he had to leave no trace of his visit.

Annabella's books, he thought as he found his way out on the service stairs. *Someone has stolen Annabella's books so that Sheridan could send them to the French under a false name.*

For the first time in months, some sort of peace had settled on Edmund's handsome features that morning, his eyes focused and his voice clear and resolute while explaining the details of their mission. After days of doubt and dead ends, he finally had a strong lead.

"I have secured you a ticket for tomorrow's airship bound for Paris. You are a young lady from a wealthy bourgeois family in the countryside who loves tinkering and reading science books, but they are no longer enough, so you wish to attend the lectures at the Paris Engineering School."

"And my name is Berthe Hamel," Carmina said. "My main purpose is to find out how Quimby is related to the school and where he is hiding. But are you that certain he is there?"

"Annabella saw him enter one of their underground laboratories. She helped us with her schematics of a miniature automaton." Edmund handed Carmina a thin file containing drawings and notes. "This will be the project you will show them. Can you copy it? I would not risk someone recognising Annabella's handwriting."

"I can. With the engineering guidance I have received from Jasper in the past few weeks for this mission, I gather I shall be able to even understand those notes and explain them – or at least pretend to explain them. But something about this case keeps bothering me.

"I wonder whether Quimby was aware of how important the medical part was for Humautomaton's success," she continued, under Edmund's questioning gaze. "I wonder whether he knew when he started the experiment that he could never complete it without the Doctors Order's participation."

"Annabella must have the answer to that, but your point is valid." Edmund rubbed his chin, his brow creased in a frown.

"Quimby ought to have known from the very beginning that he needed another Order's help." He stopped for a moment, staring at her with a look she could not fathom, a strange mixture of rage and fear darkening his blue eyes. "If Quimby used the Doctors Order's help to create the mechanical hound that almost killed you in the sewers, then we might have a traitor within the Inspectorates, outside the Engineers Order. I must admit this possibility never occurred to me until now. I shall instruct Herdforthbridge to ask Annabella about this."

Jasper opening the door cut short Carmina's reply. He looked deprived of sleep, dishevelled and tired, as if after a full night of work – or drink at the Copper Kettle.

"What happened to you?" she asked as he wiped his brow, tucking a few strands of black hair behind his ears, fully revealing his troubled eyes. "Where have you been?"

Edmund nodded towards the upholstered armchair beside the tall cabinet, which Jasper took before starting his recount.

Tailing Edwin Sheridan, the man so tightly connected to Jade's death, tracing his whereabouts from Whitechapel to Lambeth, breaking into his house, and discovering Annabella's stolen books ready to be sent to Paris – all within a single night – were enough reasons for Jasper's roguish appearance.

"I doubt Daniel Marlowe actually exists," Jasper said, finishing his story. "Most certainly, it is Sheridan's assumed name. I could not take the package with me, but I don't think Annabella will be pleased to discover her biomechanics books, filled to the edge with her notes, are missing."

"Worry not," Carmina said. "I shall find out who will peruse those books, and how. Then I shall bring them back."

❧

THE MORNING'S clear sky and gentle sunlight had disappeared under an overcast blanket of clouds huddled over Belgravia, puffed with the promise of rain. A light wind swept the streets and the carefully scrubbed entrance steps of the townhouses in Grosvenor Crescent, carrying the smoky odour of the city with it. Late spring's brittle air made summer feel rather like a faraway dream.

Annabella emerged from the Windstoneham house, clad in a black silk dress, her reticule in one hand. Herdforthbridge hastened his step, reaching her mechanical horse-drawn carriage just as she climbed inside and settled herself on the upholstered bench. He followed, taking the bench across from her and earning a delightfully surprised look on her face.

"Where are we going?" he asked when the mechanical horses started their monotonous clop. "Should I infer you have forgotten I was to call on you today?"

"Of course not. But I had planned to return before you came."

"Return from where?"

She sighed, her dark eyes' gaze moving from him to the vehicle's window. "The Inspectorates. I need to retrieve my things from the laboratory and maybe see Ledburry and understand what the devil is going on."

"A rather terrible idea." The duke's low voice signalled his disapproval of her rushed decision. "You cannot show your face at the Inspectorates while they are investigating. Please, Annabella, do not get yourself into more trouble."

Annabella clenched her fists, her eyes fiery with rage when she turned to face him again. "Oscar, I thought you loved me for what I am, and I am a woman of action, not one who cowers in fear. I thought you of all people understood what damage their unfair judgment brought upon my work. But perhaps I should remind you I am still a member of the Doctors Order and I deserve some explanations. Waiting while the Constabulary decides the fate of my career is out of the question."

Herdforthbridge took her hands in his, squeezing them gently before pressing his lips on her gloved fingers. "Forgive me. I should have not said that."

"Oscar, I was not expecting you until afternoon." She leaned towards him and caressed his cheek, squinting at him with a worried look. "Is anything the matter? Why are you here so early?"

"I was wondering whether Quimby was aware from the beginning that Humautomaton would not be possible without a doctor's help."

Her hand stilled on his face as she understood the implications of his question. For a few moments, only the even trot of the mechanical horses and the clatter in the streets outside crept through the open carriage window, distant and unwanted sounds. "Yes," she finally said. "While I have studied human anatomy extensively, as I needed to create brass parts and circuits that perfectly emulated the human body and limb, I am an engineer, not a physician. I can only attach my brass parts to a living human body with a surgeon's assistance. Quimby has always been aware of this fact."

"Which means the Doctors Order might have worked with Quimby."

"I have no evidence of that. However, they were not the only ones Quimby needed. If we were to attach a mechanical limb to a body, only the Chemists Order could create an anaesthetic powerful enough to put a man to sleep for the entire duration of the procedure."

If three Orders are involved in Quimby's plans, this affair is much more dangerous than any of us could have predicted, the duke thought, the cold pang of fear slicing his chest. *I must keep her away from them no matter what it takes.*

"Francis was the only one who did not understand the need to involve other scientists. He was certain the entire work was my responsibility."

So Montgomery was nothing more than Annabella's guard. That man is in a quite vulnerable position, and only Edmund can protect him.

~

"ARE YOU NOT COMING?" Annabella asked when Herdforthbridge did not make any move to alight from the carriage when they reached Westminster and the conveyance halted before the Inspectorates' steps. His unexpected presence had helped her think more clearly and regain her composure. Anger would not have been a reliable ally.

"I prefer to avoid this place whenever possible," he said, leaning against a corner of the carriage and stretching his legs as best as he could in the small space. "Besides, it would be rather improper if the lot here saw you emerging from a carriage with me and without a chaperone. Not many people know of our engagement, and you are supposed to be in mourning."

"I gather it will not take long." She left him waiting and disappeared inside the Inspectorates, up to the third floor, to the research laboratory where she had been working until the Orders' decision.

"Miss Hammond! What are you doing here?" One of Ledburry's assistants – and her colleague until a few days before – stared at her in astonishment, as if she were a ghoul. "You are not allowed in the laboratory!"

Ignoring the brazen nerve of the young man who could have been her apprentice and whom she did not deem worthy of an answer, no matter how tempted she was to crush his audacity, Annabella strode to her cabinet, only to stare blankly at the glass windows – and the empty shelves.

She unlocked it, certain that no one except her had the key. All her things had miraculously vanished in the last few days, except for a biomechanics book, a pair of broken magnifying goggles, and a stack of blank tracing paper sheets.

"Who opened this cabinet in my absence?" she asked, but none of the three assistants looked at her. "Very well, I shall find out myself."

Taking a deep breath, he crossed the laboratory to the Earl of Ledburry's private office and opened the door without knocking, slamming it shut behind her. "Care to tell me where the devil are my things? Who has my Humautomaton schematics? And the brass circuits and my other books?"

The Doctors Order's Senior Lord lifted his head from the thick ledger he was perusing, a frown creasing his wide forehead.

"Is this how a young lady of your station enters a gentleman's office? Miss Hammond, this is London, not Sydney – a place where, sadly, you seem to have forgotten your manners. Your rogue behaviour is unacceptable in civilised society."

"I have neither the time nor the inclination to listen to such boring diatribes. Where are my Humautomaton schematics and my books? This laboratory's door is as secure as a fortress, so I doubt anyone else except you and your assistants had access here. One of you opened my cabinet and took my things, and I would very much like to know who."

The earl pushed his spectacles up his nose, his right eye twitching with irritation. "Miss Hammond, I was wrong about you." He stood up and closed the ledger, throwing her a repulsed look. "Such manifestation of your hysterical nature, which I could have never anticipated, given your respectable upbringing, is not only bothersome but also vulgar."

He took a step towards her. "However, I shall be lenient enough to overlook this delirious episode and assure you I have no idea what you are talking about, for no one opened your cabinet while you were away. The past day's events might have troubled your mind considerably, which is understandable. Now please leave, and I shall see you again when the investigation is over."

"Someone not only opened my cabinet but also took what was inside it," she said, without budging an inch, aware that everyone in the adjacent laboratory heard them. "My Humautomaton schematics are missing, yet you are not bothered at all. What am I to believe?"

"I am not bothered because our project is almost completed, so your schematics are rather useless at this point, should someone else get their hands on them. But as proof of my magnanimity, I shall personally look into this matter and see whether someone had indeed stolen your things. However, until your stunt with the Engineers Order is over, I must ask you to keep away from my laboratory, as the Doctors Order has a reputation to uphold. Until your name is cleared, I am not willing to associate myself with your person."

Annabella took a deep breath, in a failed attempt to calm the blind rage boiling inside her. "My person would happily leave this instant. But not without my books and schematics."

"Miss Hammond, I have nothing else to say to you. Now please leave. Otherwise, I shall be forced to call the guards to drag you out." He strode to the door and opened it. "Certainly, you would not want to be humiliated in such a manner."

"Pre-flight checks done. Now we wait for Miss Hollingsworth," Avery announced, joining Ivy on the viewing deck. A light rain rapped on the gondola's glass panes, blurring the sight of the overcast sky looming over the airharbour. "You'll scare the children with that murderous look." He poked her side, a playful smile on his lips.

"Rats and caterpillars, I can scare all of London for all I care." She kicked the wooden panelling of the railing with the tip of her leather boot. "I can't pilot *The Skycradle* myself because of a stupid misunderstanding. No one wanted to listen to us. How is this fair? You tell me."

"It could've been worse." Avery leaned his tall, slender frame against the deck's railing, his arms crossed at his chest, and his deep dark eyes on her. "You can at least use your airship with my help, and I'll pilot her for you whenever you need me. But think of Annabella. Her work was put on hold altogether."

"Should we add the Crystal Palace on our route today?" Avery was right, Ivy decided, changing the subject to the more pressing matters of their commission. "The children will surely love to see it from above."

"An excellent idea." To Ivy and Avery's surprise, the voice was not Rowena's. It belonged to a man they'd never seen before, who had entered the gondola with the children in tow. "Oh, my apologies. I am Daniel Marlowe, the new tutor at Miss Hollingsworth's school. I'll take her place today as she had some other urgent matters to attend to."

Avery nodded and disappeared into the piloting area to start the engines. A few minutes later, they were flying over London, the children huddled near the railing, trying to get a glimpse of the scenery below through the thin rain. Ivy stood close to Avery, watching him with the inquisitive eyes of a hawk. A little hand tugging at her canvas skirts made her turn to see Blake Killen.

"What's the matter, Blake?" She squatted to be at the same height as him. "Why are you not with the others? The piloting board is not a place for children."

"I'm sorry, Miss Aeronaut. If I stay with the others, Lady Rowena will be sad, and I don't want to 'pset 'er."

"Why would you upset Rowena?" Ivy asked, trying to hide her amusement.

"She told us to be'ave like nothing's wrong with the new tutor, like 'is problem doesn't exist, fer 'e is no different from us. But I can't do what she said. I know it's wrong of me, but I can't 'elp staring at 'im. Miss Aeronaut, thing is I've ne'er seen a man wiv just one arm."

8

Annabella smoothed her black skirts with a mechanical movement of her hands, a repetitive gesture that helped her calm her anger. In the small confines of the carriage she shared with Herdforthbridge on their way back to Belgravia, she collected her thoughts enough to provide a coherent account of her exchange with the Earl of Ledburry, keeping her voice low and composed not without considerable effort. Patches of shadow danced on her face and in her hair as they rode past St James' Park in the dull light of the early afternoon.

"I cannot trust Ledburry to really look for my papers and books and return them to me. Oscar, this is beyond unfair. No one has the right to just take my work and use it as they please."

"Are you telling me you have no other copies of those papers?"

"I do have my own copy of the schematics at home, which I fear I cannot use without the technical support only the Engineers and Doctors Orders can offer. However, my books included a lot of my notes. If I don't find them, those notes are forever lost to me."

Her words sounded strangled and desperate, and the duke

88

squeezed her hands, the touch bringing her the comfort she so much needed. "Oh, Oscar, the very thought that my work is in someone else's hands makes me ill. Long ago, I had given up on you, on my family, on my happiness, just to keep that project safe. And now –" She bit her lip, the raw pain preventing her from breaking.

Herdforthbridge pulled her to his bench and into his arms, holding her close to his chest, his long fingers caressing her back in a soothing embrace.

"I shall acquire a special license so that we can marry before your mourning year ends," he said after a while, cupping her cheek, his blue eyes staring into the depths of her dark gaze. "This affair might be more dangerous than you believe. What if you have become a liability to those who want to use your work? What if they will try to dispose of you now that they have your schematics?"

"We cannot know for sure that my schematics fell in Quimby's hands," Annabella said, in a shaky attempt to dismiss his fears, which mirrored her own. A mischievous grin bloomed on her face. "I want to marry you as soon as possible, but my reasons are vastly different from yours and rather unrelated to my safety."

"Much as I would have otherwise loved your brazenness, I'm afraid this is not an appropriate moment for that. Not when your life is threatened. And think of your mother. If you become a target, she might be in danger as well. Let's wed soon, so that I can properly protect both of you."

Annabella's smile vanished, worry shadowing her eyes. "We will do as you say. But let me give you a fair warning. If we marry while I'm in mourning, we will be the centrepiece of yet another scandal. Are you certain you want to do this?"

This time, it was his turn to offer her an impish grin. "I have never cared about gossipmongers. Besides, this particular scandal will have a happy ending."

Annabella laughed and kissed his mouth hard, her worries gone – at least for the remainder of their ride.

~

Robert Elmstone, the engineer supervising *The Cerulean Lady*, threw Jasper a questioning look, as if unable to understand his request.

"I need you to be careful and allow no one but our labourers in the hangar," Jasper repeated, his patience running thin. Ivy and Avery were flying *The Skycradle*, but he would talk to them later. For now, he had to make sure no one tried to sabotage their work. "This airship here belongs to the Crown, so we need to take all the necessary precautions, no matter how strange they might seem."

"Is it true that the *Lady* won't fly for the Gathering?" the other engineer asked.

"No, it is not," Jasper replied, more hastily than he wished. "And pray do tell the lads that all of you will have a free day the day after tomorrow."

"How can we afford a free day in the middle of the week, when there is so little time left until the Gathering?" Elmstone squinted at Jasper as if about to ask whether he was in his right mind.

"I need to do some checks for the Inspectorates as part of the investigation they are conducting," he lied. "One free day won't do much damage. One failed investigation will."

The other engineer nodded and returned to his work without other questions. Jasper left the hangar and crossed the eastern area of the airharbour towards the skystation. On the platform for the Blackfriars-bound gondotram, he found Ivy and Avery waiting for the next aerial train.

"Do you have any commissions the day after tomorrow?" he asked without any introduction. "The manufactory will deliver the *Lady*'s main engines, and I need both of you at the hangar. All the others will have a free day."

"You dismissed the entire team for a day?" Ivy shouted. "Have you gone bonkers?"

"I only need trustworthy people to work with me on those engines. The three of us and Annabella would be enough."

"But why the secrecy?" Avery asked, as confused as Ivy. "I doubt the lads at the hangar would damage the *Lady*. They seem quite invested in her."

"I cannot take risks. Mounting the engines is one of the most vulnerable moments when building an airship. Anyone with enough ill intent and knowledge can rig them. Four years ago, I made a mistake that cost innocent people's lives. A mistake I do not intend to repeat."

WHILST IT LACKED the historical prestige of the older, more established gentlemen's clubs, the Epystemus Club had risen to stellar fame among the aristocrats invested in the new scientific and technological developments. Founded by the Duke of Litchborough in the early days of the Reform and soon after Her Majesty signed the decree that had turned the High Orders of Sciences and Crafts from a bold idea into a startling reality, the club's success was almost instant. Now, membership was de rigueur for any respectable nobleman, and a mark of open-mindedness and passion for knowledge.

For Herdforthbridge, membership was a convenient way to keep an eye on the upper echelon of the Orders, an activity simplified considerably by his professed hatred against the radical change in favour of science, a sentiment that protected him from the other members' unwanted attention. Many regarded his presence as an oddity that only the club's popularity among the fashionable male society could explain.

If he wanted to catch a hint of what was going on within the Orders, the Epystemus was the place to start.

The duke alighted from his carriage in front of the club's steps on Pall Mall, certain he would find there all the men who could give him an answer or two. A few games in the card room, a couple of bland conversations in the library, a promise to offer a financial contribution to an excellent project of the Architects Order in the smoking room, and his search finally brought him to the dining room where Baron Hydenhollow, Senior Lord of the Chemists Order, was filling his plate with shrimp canapes while talking to the Earl of Ledburry, Senior Lord of the Doctors Order.

"Herdforthbridge, what a surprise to see you here." The baron greeted him, a wide smile plastered on his red, prominent cheeks. "It's been a while since you last crossed our doorstep. Since before your airship adventure in Australia, if I am not mistaken."

"No, you are not," the duke replied, his face displaying the most affable expression he could conjure. "I must admit that the journey in question rather opened my appetite for the wonders of technology, so it was only natural to seek the company of like-minded people."

"Then you should not miss Lady Ledburry's ball on Sunday," Hydenhollow continued, and the duke wondered whether his excessively cheerful mood was the result of too much brandy. "All of Society and all the Senior Lords will be in attendance."

"I see you are full of surprises as of late." Ledburry threw Herdforthbridge a look that the duke could place anywhere between doubt, caution, and annoyance. "I could have never imagined that a conservative such as you would embark on an airship to the other side of the world, neglecting your social and political duties." The earl sipped from the brandy glass he was holding. "Speaking of social duties, my wife's ball is actually an event I wish I could avoid. Women cannot understand that some men prefer scientific pursuits in their laboratory instead of a crowded, stuffy ballroom."

"I beg to differ," Herdforthbridge countered. "I know a few women who are better fitted in a laboratory than certain men."

The earl nodded. "No doubt, no doubt. However, I must say I am utterly dismayed by the latest developments involving a certain female scientist of our mutual acquaintance. These developments are unexpected and disturbing for the research my laboratory is conducting, which the lady in question risks jeopardising."

"I fear I have no idea what you are talking about, so I am not in a position to give my opinion."

"Mark my words, Herdforthbridge," Ledburry continued, his voice carrying the superior tone of someone who believed his opinions to be above all the others'. "If you have certain intentions towards Miss Hammond – as some of Society's gossip is currently suggesting – you should abandon them while you can. If you care about your name, your station, and your sanity, that is. That reckless, impulsive woman had already dragged you into a scandal once, and she will happily do it again if it suits her purposes."

Herdforthbridge clenched his fist and opened it again, mustering all the restraint he was capable of not to plant it on the arrogant face of the Doctors Order's Senior Lord. "Perhaps I should remind you that Miss Hammond is a member of your Order upon your request. Why bring such a reckless, impulsive woman into your fold?"

Ledburry laughed. "That is an entirely different matter. She is a brilliant scientist and a great asset for the Order, which unfortunately makes her no less difficult to deal with."

The duke offered a cold, tight smile that looked more like a grimace. "I shall consider your advice. Now, gentlemen, if you'll excuse me, I shall take my leave." He stopped two steps later, turning to face the two men again. "Oh, send the countess my regards. Her ball is on top of my list of events to attend."

And an excellent opportunity for a discreet search of the earl's townhouse.

~

DEFINITELY NOT A GOOD evening for tinkering in the workshop, Jasper decided, throwing his magnifying goggles over a pile of wires and cogs on his workbench. He had tried to play with contraptions to keep his mind and hands occupied, but his thoughts turned back relentlessly to the investigation that most certainly led nowhere and did nothing but delay them.

He grabbed his coat and went out. Hands in his pockets, he walked to the Blackfriars skystation and took the exterior lift to Platform 3 to wait for the Whitechapel-bound gondotram. The lights of the platform's lamps glared against the dark sky. Only a few people were inside the station, the late hour visible on their tired faces and sunken eyes.

Much as he loathed Whitechapel, the place would keep him busy enough to forget for a while about the Board's decision. He had found out where Sheridan's mother lived, and he intended to make good use of that information.

Turning left past the Sleepy Mutton, careful to remain out of Jack Sheffield's sight, Jasper found himself in a court tucked behind a dark alley choked with the acrid smell of soot and human waste, a sorrowful reminder of London's slums from before the Reform. In such forgotten patches of misery, change had yet to come.

The building he was looking for stood at the far end of the court, its original red colour long washed out. Two women whose age was hard to guess in the murky light of the only lamp were chatting while pulling a set of ragged clothes off a line and into a large wicker basket. Jasper's presence attracted their suspicious squint upon himself.

"What be yer business 'ere, lad?" one of them asked, a sturdy woman with watery eyes and silvery hair.

"I'm looking for someone who lives here. Or used to. A tall man with dark hair by the name of Edwin Sheridan."

The woman wiped her plump hands on her apron, a disgusted look on her face. "He ain't 'ere, that devil. Lost an arm four years ago, and that made 'im more vicious. Became obsessed with his infirmity and terrified all the good people around 'ere. Thank Lord he left soon after that. To recover his lost limb, he said."

Recover his lost limb? Jasper thought. *Had Quimby offered him a brass arm in return for his help with the horrors of his twisted version of Humautomaton?*

"Looks like disappearance is a common occurrence in that family," the other woman said. "Lizzie, 'is sister, had disappeared 'erself 'bout a year before 'is accident. But the lass was beyond salvation, picking pockets or selling herself at street corners. She most likely ended dead in a gutter."

"Lizzie ain't dead," the sturdy woman countered. "She just left, and her mother's circumstances vastly improved soon after that. At first, we thought she'd found 'erself a sweetheart to provide for her, being pretty and all that. But she is still a harlot. My son saw the lass at an establishment near Covent Garden, all clean and proper. Same Lizzie Sheridan, but now goes by the name of Hazel Watercress."

Jasper froze. Carmina's most trusted helper was the sister of Edmund's sworn enemy.

"Perhaps I should find her to ask about her brother's whereabouts," he said. "She must know something."

"Oh, don't fink so, lad. Those two hated each other."

Jasper let out a slow, long breath he didn't know he was holding.

Shortly past midnight, when Herdforthbridge left the Epystemus Club to return to an eerily deserted Grosvenor Crescent, the Wyverstone house stood dark and quiet, its only light coming from the pair of lamps mounted on each side of the front door. But the duke knew Edmund was still awake, working in his private study overlooking the garden, and the matters he had to bring to his attention could not wait until morning.

"If Quimby's treason involves not one, but three Orders, then this affair is more rotten than I have imagined." Edmund refilled the two glasses and strode to the tall windows encased in wrought-iron frames, his gaze locked on a distant point in the darkness outside. He drank his brandy and rubbed his chin, thinking for a few long moments at what the duke had just reported. "Conducting this investigation only within the Engineers Order was a terrible mistake on my part."

"Since Annabella informed me that Quimby was aware of the help he needed from both the Doctors, and the Chemists Orders, I keep thinking about that war airship he was building underground," Herdforthbridge said. "And about the mechanical hound Carmina encountered in the sewers, and the Chemists Order's eagerness to close the Laevium Works and do another thorough inspection, just to find something against Jasper's project. There must be something more about them."

The Earl of Wyverstone turned to his friend again, the mild light of the wall sconce revealing his tired face and the troubled look in his blue eyes. "Humautomaton might be just a means for a larger plot, involving several Orders. Which means the treason within their ranks might be wider and deeper than I have thought. I shall try to extract more information from Montgomery."

"Montgomery is only an insignificant cog," the duke said. "He is not aware of the other Orders' involvement and believes

Annabella can complete the project on her own. Now that his role has ended, and he is in your custody, he is ripe for a mysterious demise. You should be careful."

Edmund returned to his leather armchair behind the desk. "He is still an important witness. I shall protect him."

"One more thing." Herdforthbridge put his empty glass on the small table beside his chair. The clock on the mantel showed long past midnight, and he was ready to take his leave. "Annabella's schematics and her biomechanics books disappeared from Ledburry's laboratory. But I shall find them before someone more dangerous can use them."

"Jasper has already found those books." Edmund rested his elbows on the desk's polished tabletop, his chin on his clasped hands. "However, they might help us in our search, so he could not retrieve them. The package containing Annabella's books is bound for the Paris Engineering School. Carmina will steal them back when the opportunity presents itself. In the meantime, I need you to keep an eye on Ledburry and his whereabouts. His wife's ball on Sunday is an excellent occasion to take a look here and there around his house." He curled his lips in a sarcastic smile. "Since my divorce, my invitations to social functions have decreased considerably, so I cannot be of any help."

"Worry not." The duke rested his hand on the door handle for a few moments. "If there is anything to find in Ledburry's house, I shall find it."

9

"I was expecting you half an hour ago," Edmund said when Jasper entered his office at the Inspectorates the following morning. "I received the final approved route for *The Cerulean Lady*'s maiden flight at the Gathering."

Looking in the general direction of the windows to avoid his brother's disapproving stare, Jasper settled himself in an armchair across from the desk, gritting his teeth to suppress a yawn. After spending several sleepless hours dissecting the information he had received about Hazel, he had decided against passing said information to Edmund. For now, he would focus on the matter at hand, namely the royal airship's itinerary, and think about the Sheridan siblings later.

"She will depart from the Crystal Palace and stop for a quarter of an hour near the clocktower in Westminster, where Her Majesty will appear on the observation deck to greet the crowd in the square." Edmund's gaze rested a moment too long on Jasper, but if he noticed something was amiss, he did not say. "This precise moment requires the tightest security we can provide. Master Hollingsworth has mounted the trap I requested for the clocktower. That contraption will lock any intruder inside and alert the Inspectorates."

"A good plan – if that airship will fly," Jasper said. "The berth's construction at the Crystal Palace is stalled, and the only thing that can clear our names is finding the French's circuits and proving that hiding them was their own doing. But I'm afraid that will be difficult."

"You did not actually believe I would leave this matter in the Constabulary's hands, did you?" Edmund said. "I have a parallel investigation underway."

"And how do you intend to find the missing cargo?" Jasper countered. No matter how good his brother's network, how well-prepared his spies, such a search was a fool's errand. "It can be anywhere in London. Or Paris."

Edmund poured tea into two cups, his composed expression in complete opposition to Jasper's torment. "Using our cognitive abilities would be a good start. I am already working with Herdforthbridge to estimate all possible locations, and I need you to help him. While he searches Ledburry's house during the countess' ball, you will infiltrate his laboratory and Hydenhollow's office at the Inspectorates. They will be at the ball, along with most of their assistants, so no one of importance will be at the Inspectorates that night."

Outside, after the briefing was over, Jasper stopped near the mechanical waterfall, staring at the massive red brick building of the Inspectorates, his soul heavy under the weight of crushing doubt. What if he was wrong? What if he should have informed Edmund about Sheridan and Hazel?

Regardless of the countless questions plaguing his mind, he did not waver. As soon as Carmina left for Paris that afternoon, he would talk to Hazel Watercress.

No, he would talk to Lizzie Sheridan.

Carmina closed the lid of her unassuming travel trunk and secured the two leather straps that kept it in place before emerging from her dressing room. The warm light of the afternoon sun filled her bedchamber at the Dove through the tall windows, casting a golden shroud over the bed, washstand, two armchairs, and walnut escritoire – the only pieces of furniture she needed in her most private space, where Edmund was waiting for her to finish preparing her new persona.

He gave her a long stare, his intense blue eyes hiding their secrets with the easiness of long-time practice. Yet, they were too much alike for him to be able to hide his thoughts from her. She knew where his mind travelled that instant. She knew he remembered a lonely young woman with black curls and thick spectacles he had met at a ball over ten years before. A woman who had materialised again in front of him.

"I had to change the colour of my hair," she explained, adjusting her hat, a simple piece in the same dark blue as her travelling dress. "A wig would not have been enough. And yes, these are the same spectacles I wore the night of my demise. They were of great help to me back then and I trust them to help me again this time as well."

"You look too much like the woman who died ten years ago, and I am not certain I like the idea," Edmund said in a low, slightly hoarse voice. He made no move towards her, standing tall and commanding like an ancient Greek god on his spot near the velvet curtain, the most beautiful and sophisticated man she had ever encountered. "What if someone recognises you?"

"Rebecca Beatrix Hammond was too dull for any respectable member of society to remember her." Carmina closed the distance between them and cupped his face in her gloved hands, pressing her lips on his, her green eyes seeing straight into his soul. "Edmund, I shall not die. Berthe Hamel is just a disguise like all the others."

"The landlady has your letter of approval from the

Engineering School," he said, once again the calculating, composed Chief Inspector of Her Majesty's Office of Classified Affairs. "Annabella's toy automaton had the effect we expected. Maurice Gervaise and the school's board are interested in the contraption and agreed to let you attend the lectures."

He took her travel trunk and started towards the door, but Carmina stopped him. "We cannot leave the Dove together in broad daylight. I shall go alone."

"Be careful." Edmund's hands gently squeezed hers. "There will be no speakerbox calls. You will only send me a short, encrypted cable when you have the information I need, and I shall know what to do. However, until then, I strictly forbid any form of communication between us."

Carmina nodded and picked up her suitcase, but Edmund pulled her to him, holding her close for a few long moments. "This time you will follow the protocol. No matter the stakes, your life and safety come first."

She opened the bedchamber's door and left without replying, without looking back, keeping to herself the overwhelming thought that clenched her heart.

I love you.

REGARDLESS OF THE time of the day, Covent Garden's noises and odours never disappeared, only changing in nature and intensity. Costermongers' curses and flower sellers' shouts filled the air thick with an odd mixture of the fragrance of primroses and violets and the foul stench of rotten vegetables and fish kept on stalls for far too long. Street urchins with deft hands helped themselves from piles of fruit, under the nose of unassuming merchants. Young girls carrying flower baskets walked around the busy market shouting their wares.

Making his way among wheelbarrows, donkeys, carts, and a

motley assortment of people of all stations, Jasper found Hazel chattering with a group of flower sellers at the end of a long line of stalls in the market's piazza. He had searched for her at the Dove, only to find out she was out with business in Covent Garden – another name for her information gathering errands. If one wanted to find out the latest gossip about everything, from the latest sordid murder in a Whitechapel alley all the way up to the newest mistress of a duke, Covent Garden had it all.

He watched her for a few moments, the woman he'd known for over four years, with whom he had a special camaraderie, whose bed he used to share when he'd sought comfort other than in a bottle of gin after Jade's passing. She wore her disguise flawlessly, an excellent apprentice of Carmina's. Clad in a simple grey wool dress covered with a stained apron that used to be white in times now long forgotten, her black curls gathered in a loose chignon at her nape, she blended among the other flower sellers as if she truly were one of them.

Doubt crept into his thoughts again. Would Hazel truly choose her Madame over her brother? What if those women were wrong, and she'd protect her family no matter the cost?

In the end, he had little choice but to trust her. He strode towards her, making sure she saw him and came to meet him. He beckoned her to follow him to the Russell Street's edge of the market, far from the crowded area where he'd found her.

Hazel locked her caramel-brown eyes on him. "I suppose you ain't here to buy violets."

"No, I'm not." Jasper leaned against the wall in the most casual manner, his right knee slightly bent, and his arms crossed at the chest. "I'm here to ask about your brother's whereabouts."

Hazel turned pale. "Jasper, I don't fancy talking about my brother. I don't have much to tell you."

"Does Carmina know who you are? Or rather, does she know your brother is her lover's sworn enemy?"

"No." Her trembling voice carried a tight mixture of guilt and fear. "No one knows about Edwin. If you discovered he is my brother, it means you were tailing him, ain't it so? What did he do to attract the Classified Affairs' attention?"

"I'm not here in an official capacity, but to ask for your help. Sheridan might be Benedict Quimby's underdog. If you know anything about that, you should tell me. I understand he is your family, but there is more at stake than you could imagine. Please, Hazel. Tell me what you know."

Hazel's face contorted in a grimace of disgust. "That lunatic is not my family. The only family I have is my mum, Madame, and the people at the Dove. I want to help you, but I don't know where Edwin was or what he did while he was away. I know nothing except his mad obsession with how His Lordship maimed him. He complained to everyone and swore revenge, but no one paid attention to him back then. Who would believe the feared Earl of Wyverstone had anything to do with a poor mongrel from Whitechapel? His return surprised me as much as it worried me, so I tried to follow him, but I found nothing suspicious. I only saw him twice, and I don't even know where he lodges."

To Jasper's dismay, his hope to find a real clue was slowly vanishing. "What did he say? Can you remember any particular detail that we might use?"

"Somehow, he found out about His Lordship's visits to the Dove, so I thought he sought revenge, and I was afraid for Madame. But then he just stopped. Our doorman confirmed that no man with only one arm came to the Dove after the day I followed Edwin and told him to leave me and the Dove alone. So I considered the matter closed."

Jasper kept silent for a while, lost in thought. He pulled his brown canvas cap over his forehead, lightly tapping its brim. "You could give me a hand. I'll give you his address, and you'll make some discreet inquiries to find out about his habits and visitors."

Hazel nodded, and they started back towards the market's piazza.

"That day when you followed him, did he do something unusual?" Jasper asked before turning to leave. "Visited any odd place?"

"Nothing except having dinner at an expensive coffee shop – which made me believe his employer pays him handsomely – and a one-hour visit at *The Londoners' Journal*."

"*The Londoners' Journal*?" Jasper's recent history with said newspaper made him cringe at the name. "What could he possibly have done there?"

"He requested some ten-year-old newspapers from their archives. I checked those journals to make sure, but they contained nothing of interest or related to His Lordship."

Ten years ago. What happened ten years ago worth checking the archives? "Do you remember the date of those newspapers?"

"I do. It was the 20th of April 1886."

As soon as he left Covent Garden, Jasper hurried to the clocktower in Westminster to meet Theophilus Hollingsworth for a practical demonstration of the mechanism he had recently completed. The tower had been closed almost a year before – after he and his master had done the last oiling and checking of the clock's mechanisms.

He climbed up to the clock faces' room and, with the help of an unassuming lever hidden behind a beam above the small wooden door, let himself be trapped and then released.

"Excellent, dear boy!" The royal mechanic's watery eyes sparkled with excitement behind his spectacles. "This mechanism will trap all unwanted visitors in here. Edmund will be pleased."

"An excellent contraption indeed," Jasper said, not entirely convinced of the utility of such a trap. "However, Her Majesty will be in clear view for a full quarter of an hour on the *Lady*'s observation deck. If someone is truly intent on harming her, they will do it with or without your trap, for I doubt they care what happens to them."

"Worry not." Master Hollingsworth patted him on the shoulder, a reassuring smile on his wrinkled face. "Your brother will detach a special detail to secure the area without anyone noticing. He requested my trap only as a further precaution, but I don't believe we shall need it."

"Yet Edmund has not taken the same measures for the other buildings in the square. What about the Inspectorates and the mechanical waterfall? Why aren't we mounting such contraptions there?"

"The *Lady* will stop near the clocktower for Her Majesty's speech, so securing it will be enough," Theophilus Hollingsworth said. "The other buildings are too far to be targets."

Jasper stared into the distance, taking in the airharbour's line basking in the warm light of the sunset, his mind far away on Paris and Carmina. If she found Quimby soon enough, all those traps and contraptions would become unnecessary.

He turned back to Master Hollingsworth. "Can you recall whether anything of importance happened on the 20th of April 1886? Something that might involve Edmund?"

"That might involve Edmund –" the royal mechanic repeated in a low voice, his head bent as if searching through forgotten memories. "No," he finally replied. "Back then, the earl was only a young officer of the Classified Affairs under your father's command. And the same discreet man. He could not have been involved in anything."

Carmina alighted from the steam carriage that had brought her from the airharbour to the three-storey building on Rue de la Sorbonne, where Edmund had rented rooms for her, and halted for a few moments to take in the familiar surroundings. The entrance to the old university with its ornate columns, just across from her lodging. The ochre buildings whose cafes and restaurants catered to every taste and pocket, from students engaged in literary debates, up to gentlemen of the fashionable society discussing the latest political decisions. The elegant, polished steam carriages. In the early evening's mild sun, the motley assortment of colours, shapes, and textures appeared more vivid, tightly woven into the grand tapestry of the beloved city.

She smiled, inhaling the air filled with the scent of Paris and of her memories.

Inside, the windowless hallway carried the fragrance of lavender, spices, and wood, the musky scent of nostalgia and past. The mellow light of the wall sconces threw a golden shade over the small paintings lining the wall whose flowery-patterned, striped wallpaper had long since lost its original vivid green colour. Edmund had chosen a place cosy enough for her to feel comfortable, and rickety enough to avoid unwanted attention from outside.

After one glimpse in the tall mirror near the front door, she pushed her spectacles up her nose, fixed her blue bonnet, and knocked at a door painted in white, whose sign read *Mme Blanchet.*

"Oh, you must be Madame Hamel. Come, I'll show you to your rooms." The landlady, a small woman in her late fifties with a good-natured smile, climbed up two flights of stairs, with Carmina in tow. She stopped before a door tucked in the furthest corner of the corridor and opened it to reveal a small vestibule.

"Your husband paid me considerably more than the price I

asked, so I gave you the best room I have." Madame Blanchet invited her inside the flat consisting of a parlour, a dressing room, and a bedchamber. "I tried to provide everything that could be of use for a young woman, but if you need anything else, pray do tell me. The maid will clean the room once a day, in the morning."

As soon as she was alone, Carmina threw her bonnet and spectacles on the only armchair in the bedchamber. She lifted her trunk on the neatly made bed and opened the lid to unpack the few items she had brought with her from England. Two elegant dresses and matching bonnets in yellow and green, fit for a middle-class French lady visiting the capital, came out first. Only one disguise was far from enough, but she couldn't bring her entire arsenal without risking discovery by the landlady or the cleaning maid.

With her suitcase emptied and tucked under the bed, she could concentrate on the task at hand. The raucous noises and the red hues of the sunset filled the parlour through the tall windows overlooking the busy street, helping her clear her thoughts and adopt her new persona. Comfortably settled at the escritoire, she took a blank sheet of paper and her pen and started writing.

Monsieur Gervaise,

I am humbled and honoured to have received such a positive answer from your esteemed person and colleagues. The opportunity to attend the Paris Engineering School's lectures and further discuss my automaton proposal is more than I hoped for, and I am deeply grateful to be the recipient of your scientific trust and regard. I have arrived in Paris and will come to school for the lectures no later than tomorrow.

With the deepest consideration,

Berthe Hamel

Carmina folded the letter and inserted it into an envelope, staring at it for a while.

It has begun. The last act of the battle we started all those years ago.

She put on the spectacles again and came down to the landlady's office.

"Madame Blanchet, I fear I must already take advantage of your generous offer to help me. Would you be so kind as to have this delivered for me to the Engineering School this evening?"

10

Seven in the morning was a rather ungodly hour for a visit. Yet Jasper didn't give it too much thought when he lifted the brass knocker and struck it to the plate mounted on the front door of Gilbert Fontaine's rented townhouse in Knightsbridge. If all else failed, he had to appeal to his good sense – provided he had any – and make him see reason.

A butler with an inscrutable face led him to the study, where Fontaine was having breakfast at a desk crowded with papers, drawings, and writing tools.

"You must have a solid reason to appear at my door at such an hour." The French engineer forked a generous amount of bacon and eggs from his breakfast plate without inviting Jasper to sit. "Whilst I was sorely tempted to send you your way, I confess that curiosity got the better of me. What do you want?"

Jasper took a quick look around before answering. He recognised some of the books laying in disarray on the desk and chairs. The drawings spread on the desk's corner contained the unmistakable schematics of an airship.

"You are an airship engineer. This is why they sent you here in the first place."

"And how exactly is this related to anything?" Fontaine asked.

"Changing the project at the last moment must have been quite a blow for you, ain't it so?"

"I must admit I would have preferred an airship representing France at the Gathering. But I am nonetheless impressed with my country's new project, which I must still oversee regardless of its nature. However, because of the negligence of two women, our exhibit might not be displayed at all."

Jasper cleared his throat and took a deep breath, in an effort to contain a retort at the insulting remark. He had to refrain from provoking the man further, yet his words irked him too much to just ignore them. "The two women in question are highly skilled professionals who know how to do their work."

"Skill has nothing to do with indolence," Fontaine said, disdain lacing his high-pitched voice. "You still haven't told me why you are here. My time is not an unlimited resource."

"I'm here to ask for your help in my search for the truth."

"The *truth*?" Fontaine stared at him with an incredulous look. "*Merde*, the nerve you have! The only truth I know, which is as clear as day, is that our cargo has mysteriously disappeared. What other truth is there to find out?"

"England has no reason to sabotage the French team. We have nothing to gain from that. However, someone in the French team might have such intentions."

The French engineer's laugh could be placed anywhere in the wide range between mockery and astonishment. "This is outrageous! Who on earth would sabotage their own project?"

"We need to think of all possibilities." Jasper leaned against the tall cabinet, his hands crossed at the chest, facing Fontaine. "You should have gone to the airharbour to sign for your cargo, yet you changed your mind at the last moment. I need to know why. Did you follow someone's instructions?"

Fontaine froze, his eyes focused on the food already gone cold.

"Our team's only fault was to accept helping another team, and now we risk being unjustly punished for that. I am told you are a man of honour, so if you remember anything, pray do tell me."

A long stretch of silent seconds followed until Fontaine stood up and poured a glass of brandy, swallowing the strong drink in one gulp. "Yes, as the chief engineer of my team, I wanted to go to the airharbour myself. Anyone would have done the same in my stead."

He started pacing around the room, running his calloused fingers through his thick red hair. "But I received a cable from Gervaise, who ordered me to wait for the cargo at the Palace and never leave the exhibition grounds. At first, I intended to go anyway." He turned to face Jasper. "You see, I thought he just wanted to make sure our labourers didn't stop working while I was away. But I trusted the lads enough to leave them out of my sight for a few hours. Just as I was about to leave for the airharbour, I received another cable, with the same request. I could not disobey a direct order from the Engineering School, so my assistant left without me."

"And you want me to believe you didn't find that request odd?" Jasper asked.

"Of course, I did. Who wouldn't? This is precisely why I had a speakerbox call with a friend who works as Maurice Gervaise's assistant in the automaton laboratory."

Jasper wondered why he didn't call Gervaise directly, but kept the thought to himself. The only reason he could think of was that Fontaine did not fully trust his superior. Though he wasn't certain whether the French team's change of project played a part in that.

"My friend confirmed that Gervaise wanted me to stay on the exhibition grounds and not go to the airharbour, a decision which baffled him as well. Then he told me a most unusual thing."

"Which is?"

"That he had long since stopped questioning Gervaise's decisions, of which the least understandable one was to send an unfinished circuit to London."

Jasper gave the French engineer a long, hard stare, afraid to hope he truly was one step away from the piece of evidence he sought. *An unfinished circuit* meant they were not able to fully replicate Annabella's work. And, most importantly, it meant Quimby was indeed at the Engineering School in Paris. "Whatever do you mean by that?"

"My friend slipped the information believing I already had it, but Gervaise never warned me I was to receive an unfinished circuit. I assumed they would send someone to complete it. So, this incident is quite a troublesome interruption, for I am not certain we will finish that automaton on time if we don't resume working on it soon."

"Are you certain that none of the briefings you received from France included this detail?" Jasper asked.

"I assure you I could not have overlooked such information."

Jasper let out a deep, long breath he didn't know he was holding. "In which case, I can only infer that your school sent those wires and parts with the sole purpose to make them vanish and hold us accountable, an outcome that your presence at the airharbour would have prevented. I hope you agree with me that our team has nothing to do with the cargo's disappearance."

Another stretch of silence before Fontaine slowly nodded with a haunted look in his eyes, his shoulders slumped, like a defeated soldier on a ravaged battlefield.

Carmina Harcourt stood still for a while, assessing her Berthe Hamel persona in the tall mirror of her dressing room. She wore a dark blue dress with matching bonnet, thick spectacles, and a lace parasol – an attire elegant enough to make her pass as an upper-middle-class lady whose interest in technology was signalled solely by the latest issue of *Le Journal Hebdomadaire des Ingénieurs*, which she carried in her hand.

With a satisfied nod, she left her small rented flat and took the five-minute walk to the Engineering School on Rue des Écoles, without thinking too much of what awaited her, of what was the most difficult mission she had ever been assigned. Until then, all her missions were within her realm of knowledge and control. But Berthe Hamel was an engineer, albeit a self-made one, and Carmina's expertise in engineering only encompassed two weeks' worth of lessons from Jasper, which barely covered the basics. She was not Annabella. A few words out of place and she would reveal herself.

Though she loathed to admit it, fear gripped her heart. Not of death, for she had long ceased to fear death. Fear of failing and disappointing the trust Edmund had placed in her.

She arrived early enough to secure herself a seat in the front row of the amphitheatre where Monsieur Gervaise gave his lecture. He was a tall and sturdy man, good-natured and kind, answering all questions and offering further explanations when asked. For a moment, Carmina wondered whether such a considerate man was indeed in Quimby's league. But she was no fool. Her years in the Crown's service had taught her to never trust her quarry and follow the brief and her instincts.

Gervaise's highly technical lecture on mechanical engineering only deepened Carmina's apprehension, making her aware that she couldn't keep her pretence for too long. She had to find Quimby soon, before they uncovered her as the imposter she was.

"Monsieur Gervaise, may I have a moment?" Accosting him

in the corridor after the lecture was a necessary impertinence if she wanted him to acknowledge her. "I'm Berthe Hamel."

"Oh, the self-taught engineer from Soissons. I remember your letter and your toy automaton schematics." The school dean offered her a wide smile. "Whilst a toy, your project was nonetheless intriguing, and I should like to hear more about it."

"I want to develop it into something bigger," Carmina said. "Like a new kind of automaton. Alas, I don't have the expertise for that. I wish I could attend the Engineers World Gathering in London to see all those astonishing exhibits with my own eyes and learn new things, but my husband was firmly against it. To compensate, he agreed to let me attend your lectures and improve my automaton, and I intend to make good use of my time here."

"I see. And do you have a specific purpose in mind for this automaton you want to design?"

"As a matter of fact, I do. I intend to turn it into an assistant for the unfortunate people who cannot perform certain activities by themselves. Our poor coachman had a terrible accident two years ago and lost a leg. And I wondered. What if he had an artificial limb that would serve him the same way his original, anatomical one had? I first designed that toy, and now I want to build a full prototype to replicate some of the human body's functions."

Carmina didn't budge under Gervaise's long, inquisitive, and certainly doubtful stare. But she had taken care to sound genuinely interested and look appropriately unassuming. He could not have seen beyond her cover. At least not now, not so early.

"We could have a beneficial collaboration," he finally said, his amiable smile back in place, but not as impressed as she'd hoped with her passionate diatribe. "I hope to see you again at my lectures. Now I'm afraid I must hurry to my laboratory."

With her hopes to gain access to said laboratory shattered,

Carmina remained in the middle of the hallway, watching him disappear among the throngs of students. It was too soon for her to be admitted to an off-limits space.

But she would find a way. By the time Gervaise was out of sight, her mind was already concocting a new strategy.

THE MILD LIGHT of an unusually sunny day crept inside the hangar through the rectangular windows lining the upper half of the high walls, bathing the blue envelope and its golden leafy patterns in a glowing sheen. From her tall scaffold, *The Cerulean Lady* dominated the space in all her glory.

That day, only Jasper, Ivy, Avery, and Annabella were at the hangar, working with the doors locked, their presence unnoticed at the airharbour. The four new engines, which the manufactory had sent that morning, waited on wheeled platforms to be mounted on the ramp and pushed up to the engine pods in the lower half of the envelope.

"I'm sending up the first one!" Jasper shouted at Annabella, who was perched on the highest ladder leaning against the front right pod. He pulled the ramp's lever, setting the mobile slope in motion. The engine started to move slowly towards its capsule.

"Received!" Annabella shouted back after a few minutes, shifting her position with a deft move from the ladder's rungs to the square platform of the ramp. "I shall guide the engine into the pod, and then we'll pass on to the next one. Miss Blackwell, this one is yours!"

She pushed the engine inside. After one last check to make sure everything was in place and the ramp lift damaged none of its parts, she climbed down to where the others were waiting.

"I'll send the rest of the engines, and Annabella will secure them into their pods," Jasper explained once again, his attention on Ivy and Avery. "In the meantime, you two will connect each secured engine to the engine room inside the airship. You'll find in the pods all the cables, tubes, and other parts you need. When you finish, Annabella and I will do the final checks, and then we'll be ready for the first engine test."

Half a day later, with all the engines mounted and connected, the four of them congregated in the piloting cabin, on the gondola's lower deck. Jasper pulled the main lever of the piloting board and turned the three brass knobs next to it, starting the engines. They held their breaths for a moment, an oppressive silence filling the air around them.

And then, the hissing of the pressure gauges broke the stillness. A louder, humming noise followed. Lasted. Intensified. Announced that their airship was ready to take the skies.

"They work!" Ivy squeezed Jasper in a grateful embrace and kissed his cheeks with a joy she didn't bother to contain. "A year ago, this airship was just a pile of papers I was desperately trying to keep secret. Now, look at her!" Her eyes glittered with unshed tears. "She is so beautiful and ready to fly."

"Just a few more pieces of furniture to receive, and we can schedule the test flight." With a boyish grin, Jasper stopped the freshly mounted engines and took off his leather gloves, running his fingers through the unruly locks of his black hair. "Now we should take one more look at the pods to make sure all connections are still in place, and we're done for the day."

"I hope you prepared a convincing explanation for your workers," Annabella said. She had climbed on the ramp's platform again, facing the starboard wall of the gondola, a brush in her hand and a bucket of white paint beside her. "Otherwise, you risk losing their trust for what you did today behind their backs."

"Worry not," Jasper replied, without noticing what she was doing. "I have an official paper to prove I only followed the Classified Affairs' specific order, for security purposes. I doubt anyone would dare challenge my brother's decisions."

"Miss Hammond, are you painting the gondola?" Ivy's startled question resonating in the hangar's vast space prompted the others to come to Annabella's side of the airship. "What are you writing?"

"You will still need to paste golden foil over the paint." Annabella stood aside, revealing the letters she had drawn in beautiful calligraphy.

"*Ea Caelium Superabit,*" Avery read in a tortured spelling. "What is that?"

"Latin," Annabella replied. "The *Lady* uses a lifting gas called *laevium,* so I thought a Latin motto would be most appropriate."

"What does that mean?" Ivy asked, as confused as her assistant.

Jasper read the words again in perfect Latin spelling and translated them with a wide, happy grin.

"*Ea Caelium Superabit. She will conquer the skies.*"

"MAY I HAVE A WORD?" Jasper asked after Ivy and Avery left to prepare *The Skycradle* for the following day, and Annabella started towards the airharbour's mews to retrieve her steammotor. "I have some news you might want to hear."

Annabella nodded, and they made their way to the vehicle among steam carts and carriages. The airharbour throbbed with the early evening activity, as the flying season had just started. Airships moored and took off in a continuous flow, overseers were running among the numbered berths, and the light wind carried the pungent odour of tar and smoke.

"The French sent an unfinished circuit," Jasper said when they were at a safe distance from unwanted ears, in Annabella's steammotor. "I paid Fontaine a visit this morning and extracted this piece of information from him."

Annabella stilled, one hand clutched on the steering lever and the other holding her driving goggles, forgetting about starting the vehicle's engine. "An *unfinished circuit*? Are you certain?"

"I am. Fontaine was not even supposed to be in the possession of this detail. He chose to share it with me, so I doubt he is involved in whatever scheme his school is concocting."

"Now everything makes sense." She took a few more moments before finally starting the boiler. "They could not complete *my* circuit, so they sent it in such a state with the precise purpose to wreak havoc and turn us into their scapegoat."

"I fear there is more to this." Jasper settled in the passenger's chair, waiting for her to steer them out of the airharbour and on their way to his workshop on Tallis Street. "What if the real purpose is to keep England out of the Gathering?" She turned to look at her. "And to remove you from the laboratory so that they can steal your schematics and pass them to Quimby? They must have tried to complete that automaton faster than you. But couldn't, so they are running out of time and decided to use your work."

"Your theory has its merits, and I am inclined to believe it is correct," Annabella agreed over the steammotor's roar. "In which case, the only way for that bloody school to get their hands on my schematics would be from someone who works in our laboratory."

"Exactly. Perhaps Ledburry offered you all you needed to develop your own version of Humautomaton with this in mind. Perhaps he is in Quimby's league and wanted to help you conduct your research and use your work to their advantage when it's completed – or in an advanced stage of completion."

"That is quite a serious accusation," Annabella said, without taking her eyes off the street in front of them, driving the vehicle expertly in the flow of carriages, hansoms, and steammotors.

"But I started having my doubts as well after my altercation with Ledburry the other day when I found my cabinet empty. He must have stolen my books and notes because he realised they cannot complete their automaton without me." She turned her gaze to Jasper for one moment, a wide, mischievous smile on her face. "Rest assured. Even if he has my schematics, neither Quimby nor anyone else can use them without my help."

But Jasper didn't return her amused grin, as her words only confirmed his suspicions. Using her was the only reason they had kept her alive. As soon as they completed Humautomaton's circuits, with or without her help, they would dispose of her.

"Be careful," Jasper said before Annabella continued towards Grosvenor square, after dropping him in front of his workshop. "I am not sure how safe it is for you to roam about London alone."

"Oh, please!" She threw him an indignant stare. "Do not expect me to just lock myself in my house and wait for my books to return miraculously. Send Master Hollingsworth my regards."

With that, she pulled her goggles back over her eyes and drove on without waiting for a reply, leaving Jasper to stare after her with a concerned look. When she disappeared around the corner, he entered his workshop and climbed the short flight of stairs to his bedchamber. He only had an hour to wash and change his work clothes before leaving again.

"What is troubling you?" Rowena asked later, when he had arrived at Master Hollingsworth's house and they were all comfortably seated in the drawing room, waiting for dinner.

"Nothing," he lied. He had no intention of burdening her or her father with his worries about the English team and Annabella. "It was an exhausting day, this one. Forgive me for the sour company."

"Lately you seem to have forgotten how to rest." Theophilus Hollingsworth poured a glass of brandy for him, which Jasper drank in one gulp. "Perhaps you should employ an assistant, as Rowena has. Her new assistant has proven to be quite an asset, regardless of the physical infirmity that many, unlike my daughter, would not have ignored."

Jasper turned to look at Rowena, a smile brightening his tired face. "Employing someone who is in unfortunate or dire circumstances only proves what a kind and generous person you are. I expected nothing less of you."

"I would rather you stopped embarrassing me," Rowena said, avoiding Jasper's gaze, her cheeks flushed. "Moreover, I believe both of you misunderstood my intentions. Employing my assistant was not an act of mercy, for I would never disrespect someone as much as to pity their physical infirmity. I just happened to need an assistant and found the right person. That was all."

"My dear, forgive this old man for being so inconsiderate," her father said with an apologetic look. "I assure you, it never occurred to me you would do such a thing out of pity." He leaned towards Jasper again. "Tell me, dear boy, have you found that information you were searching for?"

Jasper stood still for a few moments. Had his master found out about Fontaine and the French team's scheming? No, he couldn't have. He'd left straight to the hangar, without even informing Edmund. "I'm not sure I understand what you mean."

"The 20th of April, 1886. Have you found out if anything happened that day?"

"Oh, that." He shook his head. "No. I assumed that if you didn't remember anything important from that day, probably nothing actually happened."

"Your assumption is erroneous," Rowena said, making the two men turn to face her with curious looks. "Something did happen that day. Or more exactly that night."

"And was this incident in any way related to Edmund?" Jasper asked, suddenly interested. "What was it about?"

"I doubt that tragic event had anything to do with the earl, but it kept the newspapers' headlines for several days."

Jasper frowned, trying to search through long-forgotten memories, but nothing came. "Tragic event? What tragic event?"

"I was still very young back then so I would not know the details," Rowena said. "However, I remember that the 20th of April 1886 was the night when Rebecca Beatrix Hammond, the Marquess of Windstoneham's eldest daughter, died in a carriage accident, the night of her debut ball."

11

B ent over the thin brass rim of the protective glass wall that sheltered the workbench, Carmina stared with what she hoped to be rapt attention and keen interest at her colleague who was handling a small contraption spread on the tabletop, carefully turning a screw with one hand, and holding it still with the other, his eyes two strange hazel-coloured bulges behind the amplifying goggles. The spring sun of the early afternoon cast a golden glitter over the metal objects on the laboratory's worktables.

Nothing looked amiss. Scale models, gauges, cogs, and other parts and instruments filled the tall shelves lining the walls. Wires and undefined metal pieces were stuffed inside locked cabinets with glass windows, next to engineering books and piles of papers covered with exquisitely drawn designs. No trace of Annabella's biomechanics books or schematics anywhere. Or of anything that could lead to Benedict Quimby. By the looks of it, that one was only an ordinary laboratory, which regular students used for their experiments. If she wanted hints and answers, she had to search for them elsewhere – preferably in the off-limits automaton laboratory of the school's dean.

"Monsieur Gervaise is full of surprises," the young man said, finally pulling off his goggles and lifting his head to meet her gaze, tucking a few damp curls behind his ear. "To give us your toy automaton as an assignment, that was quite unexpected. But I must admit that your schematics are quite good. I wonder how this automaton would work on a larger scale."

"I hope Monsieur Gervaise will help me with that soon enough," she replied. "But this doesn't seem an appropriate laboratory for developing automata. I gather it is not the only one in this school, is it?"

The young student laughed, throwing her a pitiful look clearly directed at her ignorance. "You come from Soissons, yes? I understand that, for a province woman, this laboratory might seem grand, but I assure you it is not. This is but a small experiment room usually occupied by first-year students. The real research is done in Gervaise's underground laboratories." He put his goggles on the workbench with a sigh, a trace of sadness in his brown eyes. "But only a chosen few are allowed there to work with the dean and other renowned professors on developing ground-breaking projects."

"Oh, I see," Carmina said, ignoring her colleague's diminishing remark. "I have only seen lecture halls, study rooms, the library, and this working space. I wonder where these remarkable laboratories are."

"In a separate wing of the school, quite far from here," the student promptly replied. "Gervaise's laboratories are in the western part of the building. But you can't go there without Gervaise's permission."

This must be where Annabella saw Quimby, Carmina thought, but Gervaise entered before she could ask another question.

He walked among the tables, taking his time to check each student's toy automaton, which they were building following Berthe Hamel's schematics – Annabella's schematics. A nod here, a few corrections there, before he reached Carmina's workbench.

"Madame Hamel, I do hope you agree with my decision to share your schematics with the other students," he said with a pleasant smile on his plump, reddish face. "I found it a most inspiring project, and an excellent assignment for these future engineers."

"Yes, yes, of course," Carmina replied, a humble blush blossoming on her cheeks. "This school is most fascinating, with so many talented students as colleagues. Thus far, I only worked alone, in the solitude of the workroom I improvised at home, so I could never have imagined the joy of being part of a team. Though I'm afraid I have yet to find a way to improve my automaton."

"Oh?" The dean lifted an eyebrow. "Do you need something more specific for your research?"

Carmina threw him a pleading stare. "As a matter of fact, I do. I was hoping to receive proper guidance from someone so skilled in automata such as you. This is the reason I am here."

Gervaise laughed, his baritone voice reverberating within the vast space. "As I am most curious about your plans with this automaton, I shall reward your diligence. I shall prepare a pass to grant you access to my laboratory no later than next week."

Next week is too vague. And too late.

THE SUPERINTENDENT of the building on Stangate Street in Lambeth where Edwin Sheridan had rented rooms, a thin, tall woman in her late fifties with a stern face and rigid demeanour, squinted at Hazel with an accusatory frown, pushing the thin rim of her round spectacles up her nose. Whilst she had never seen one, Hazel imagined this is how the headmistress of a boarding school for young ladies ought to look like.

Decidedly, a visit from a stranger was not the most pleasant thing to expect so early in the morning, when most of the building's occupants were not even awake, and the woman had to oversee breakfast preparation for the tenants. But she could not just close the door in the face of a respectable young lady of the middle class looking all prim and proper in her pale blue dress and matching bonnet, her reticule in her gloved hand, and a small basket of violets on the crook of her arm.

"Good morning, Mrs Honeywell," Hazel said, a sad smile plastered on her face. Her conversation with the doorkeeper the previous evening had offered her all the details she needed to know about the lady in charge of managing the lodging house. "You must excuse me for visiting at such an hour, but I'm afraid this is the only time I could extricate myself from the duties of my home, as I am leaving London soon. I'm Lizzie Sheridan. As I understand, my brother Edwin has been in your care, and for that I must extend my heartfelt gratitude. I am aware he is not precisely the easiest person to deal with, given the unfortunate accident that brought such a damaging infirmity upon him."

She offered the flower basket to the perplexed host, who took it and invited her in. They entered a small room – which most probably served as Mrs Honeywell's office – that only sported a table, two chairs, a brass cabinet, and a worn-out wooden cupboard.

"I can see some physical similarities between you and Mr Sheridan," the woman said with an analytical stare. She put the basket on the table and sat on a chair, beckoning Hazel to take the other one. "But he never mentioned a sister, and I confess I find it odd that you have never come here before."

"Oh, that was indeed terrible of me." Hazel's apologetic tone complemented the distraught expression on her face. "But I found out only recently where he lodged, for he never informed me or Mama that he had returned to London." She extracted a handkerchief from her reticule and dabbed the corner of her eyes. "How I wished he were more open towards me. But I hope he has a good life and someone to take care of him, for his infirmity has isolated him from the world."

The housekeeper's pitiful look indicated that Hazel's story had the intended result. "You, poor darling." She assembled a plate with cookies and sweets from the cupboard and poured hot tea for her guest. "I'm afraid I have no good news for you on that front. No one visited your brother while he lodged with us. No lady, no man, no one. He was indeed a solitary man. I didn't know much about his endeavours, as he was away for the most part of the day, and never had breakfast or dinner with the others in the common dining room."

The woman's words only confirmed what Hazel had already found out the night before from the doorkeeper. However, her use of past tense didn't go unnoticed.

"May I ask to be allowed into his rooms? I tried to reach him earlier, but I received no answer."

"My dear, I fear I can't help you. Your brother doesn't live here anymore."

"He left?" This time, Hazel's surprise was genuine. The doorkeeper had said nothing about that. "Pray, when did he leave? Are you telling me I've lost my brother again?"

"Last night. He left in quite a hurry, mind you. I asked if anything happened, but he only said he had personal affairs to attend to and must vacate his rooms. I'm afraid I'm not able to tell you where to find Mr Sheridan."

SPRAWLED on the wooden bench of the skystation's crowded platform, his arms folded, and his legs crossed at the ankles, Jasper stared blankly through the open wall in front of him at the ever-expanding fat grey clouds spewing out a thin drizzle over London. In the near distance, the airharbour's yellow lights impregnated the dull bleakness of the evening with a tinge of colour, breaking through the gloom along with the noises and shouts around the berths. Close to the entrance, half of the *Lady*'s hangar's front wall jutted from among two soot-covered warehouses, its massive metal doors locked for the night.

He checked the central round brass clock dominating the platform. Ten minutes until the Blackfriars-bound gondotram arrived. Still plenty of time to muse about that day's work.

She was almost ready to fly, their airship. Jasper lifted a corner of his mouth in a shadow of a smile, rubbing the sore muscles of his arms to ease the pain of a full day of carrying and mounting the last furniture pieces. According to his calculations, all the interior spaces would be completed in a few days. Then she would be ready for the final tests, which he had already scheduled for the following week.

And yet, it could be all for nothing. The *Lady* might be ready on time, but the berth and the mooring mast they had to build at the Crystal Palace wouldn't, and she might as well be denied her well-deserved participation in the event.

Unless we find those bloody circuits.

They had to. He owed that to the Blackwells and to Jade.

A frustrated grunt escaped his throat, the grim possibility of their exclusion turning more and more into a real probability. The Countess of Ledburry's ball remained their best chance to find a lead. Neither he nor Herdforthbridge could afford mistakes. Sunday night, while the duke searched the earl's house, he would break into Ledburry's laboratory.

A mass of silky black curls on his cheeks and a pair of slender arms around his chest interrupted his thoughts. He lifted his gaze to see Hazel standing behind him.

"A penny for your thoughts, guv'nor," she said, then bent her head even closer over him, her voice a whisper in his ear. "I reckon you might be interested in what I have for you."

He squeezed her hands to play her game, then stood and

pulled her close to him, leading her towards an iron pillar to the far edge of the platform, away from other people's curious eyes.

"Edwin vacated his rooms last night, and I have no idea where he went," she announced, looking at Jasper as if waiting for him to concoct an idea to find her brother. "I'm not even sure he's still in London."

The same bugging doubt crept into his soul again. Sheridan's disappearance was too sudden and unexpected to bode well. And the timing was too perfect to be mere coincidence.

"I swear I have nothing to do with it," Hazel said, holding his doubtful look. "Jasper, Madame saved me from the gutter, taught me how to read and speak properly, along with many other things that made me what I am now. I would never betray her. You need to understand this."

Jasper stared at her for a few moments, aware that his decision could put the people most dear to him in danger. But the resolute expression on her face and the determination in her eyes could not lie.

"I believe you. However, this doesn't solve our problem. In all probability, he's still in London. We need to trace him. Soon."

"If he's still in London, I'll find him. Let me help you. Please."

Jasper nodded. Sheridan could wait for now, as he'd found nothing to classify him as an immediate threat. Besides, Edmund was perfectly capable to take care of himself. Edwin Sheridan was not the first – and certainly would not be the last – man who tried to kill him.

For now, he would keep silent about Sheridan's disappearance. Edmund had enough on his mind as it was, working until late with the Queen's advisors on the full arrangements for the Royals' participation in the Gathering.

"All right," he finally said, his voice overlapping with the shrill of the gondotram arriving at the platform. "We'll search for your brother together. However, we'll leave Edmund and Carmina out of this."

∾

HERDFORTHBRIDGE CLIMBED the last flight of narrow stairs up to the Windstoneham house's attic and stood in the doorway to watch Annabella, who was too absorbed in her work to notice his presence. Wearing her plain, black cotton work dress and a canvas apron stained with a generous amount of grease and paint, with her goggles over her eyes and a few black strands coming out of her loose chignon, she directed her entire attention upon the gauge of a wooden box wired to something he could not see. The gauge's needle moved a few lines forward, then stopped with a thud and a thin plume of smoke coming out of its container.

"Blimey!" Annabella cursed and took off her goggles, throwing them on the floor with a frustrated grunt. "Just work already!"

Herdforthbridge entered the workshop and picked up her goggles "Should I call for tea? You look like you need a break."

Annabella turned towards him, her eyes wide and bright with joy at the unexpected sight. "Oscar! Shouldn't you be home preparing for the ball? It's almost evening."

He pulled her to him, oblivious of the stains transferring onto his impeccably tailored coat – or to the fact that Ethel, Annabella's former governess, or a maid could appear any moment. "What is there to prepare?"

"Of course, your evening attire, which will have to be quite exquisite to match your dashing looks." She lifted her head, locking her eyes with his. "How I wish I could go. It's been ages since we last danced together."

"We shall have plenty of opportunities for dancing." He smiled, wiping a smudge off her cheek with the back of his finger. "I received the special license. If you agree, we shall marry the following Saturday."

"The following Saturday? How on Earth can we plan a wedding in just one week?"

"As I recall, a wedding only needs the bride, the groom, and a priest, which does not involve much planning. The sooner you move into my home, the more protected and safer you will be. A week is longer than I wanted, but that was the best I could do. The countess and Ethel will stay with us until the Inspectorates clear this mess with Quimby and the Gathering."

Annabella wrapped her arms around him again. "I love you, Oscar. I love you so much."

The duke held her for a few moments, their embrace offering him a full view of her workbench over her shoulder. A few wires connected the wooden box to a metal part in the form of a human arm.

He frowned. "Will you tell me what exactly are you working on? That pile of brass looks oddly familiar. Wasn't it in those trunks you kept at Herdforth Hall?"

Annabella returned to her workbench and disconnected the wires from the box. "I couldn't afford to wait for the Constabulary to clear my name to resume my work. If I want Humautomaton completed before the Gathering, I need to work on those bloody circuits here. Only that I cannot figure out the right frequency to make them functional, no matter how hard I try."

Protect her. Jasper's words from the other day's speakerbox conversation resurfaced in his mind with a new, amplified intensity. *Those incomplete circuits are the key to the entire project. And the only reason Annabella is still alive. She is a liability to them. Her testimony could send Quimby straight to the noose.*

"If I ask you to stop working on those circuits, at least until our wedding, will you do it? Now that you lack the Inspectorates' protection, this is a most dangerous endeavour. Quimby has always been after your work. If you complete it, he will find out."

Annabella squinted at him. "So what if he finds out? I am not afraid of him."

"If he finds out, you'll die." His voice sounded cold and ghastly even to his own ears. "Which is the one thing I shall do everything in my power to prevent."

For Oscar Bashford, the Duke of Herdforthbridge, balls had long ceased to be a source of entertainment. He rather regarded them as a social necessity or, as it was the case that night, the perfect milieu to collect information or evidence.

The Countess of Ledburry's annual ball was an excellent occasion to have the most prominent members of the aristocracy in the same place. The duke had arrived fashionably late, aware that he and Annabella Hammond were again the centrepiece of the latest gossip. Skilfully navigating through the biting remarks of Society's disconsolate Mamas suddenly deprived of their most sought-after prize, he made his way to the refreshment room, searching for Ledburry, but finding the earl's wife there instead. His late mother's distant cousin, Herdforthbridge loved her intellect and sharp tongue. The idea of her becoming a collateral victim of her husband's ill-managed affairs made his stomach turn, but he had no choice. He could not warn her without betraying his mission and his position as an undercover agent of the Crown. Besides, however outlandish the prospect, he could never exclude the possibility of her involvement in the Earl of Ledburry's business – in which case, blowing his cover would prove utterly disastrous.

"My dear Herdforthbridge, I'm afraid you positioned yourself dangerously close to a fresh scandal," the countess said in a conspiratorial tone, more amused than worried. "Your daring journey with Miss Hammond and her outrageous habit of wandering about unchaperoned did not pass unnoticed, but surely you know that. You were seen together quite a few times, so expect some rumours here and there. I cannot help but wonder whether you have a particular talent for such things."

"I would call it a misunderstanding rather than scandal," he replied, equally amused, in the blunt manner they always employed when talking to each other since he was a little boy, and his mother was still alive. "Whilst I am aware of what Society's ladies are assuming regarding my relationship with Miss Hammond, I'm afraid their assumptions do not reflect the truth. Miss Hammond is not my mistress. She is my betrothed."

"A most bitter truth for most of them to swallow." The countess laughed, her face beaming with a wide smile. "I understand why there is no announcement yet since Miss Hammond is still in mourning, but you must allow me to congratulate you. You deserve some happiness."

Much as he enjoyed the countess' company, his presence at her house that night had another purpose than to discuss his private affairs or how daring his airship journey to Australia with Annabella was. He excused himself and took his leave, returning to the ballroom just as the Earl of Ledburry and Baron Hydenhollow were making their way towards the door.

He followed them from the distance, grateful that his title and station allowed him to go up the grand staircase without raising any eyebrow. On the first floor, he extracted the amplifier out of his waistcoat's pocket and inserted it in his ear, ready for the overwhelming cacophony of sounds assaulting his senses. After a few moments of adjusting to the acoustic onslaught, he focused on the loudest and closest voices, which he identified as belonging to the two Senior Lords.

The study. They are in the study.

Making sure no one noticed him, he crossed the corridor to the library – which shared a wall with the room where his two targets had congregated – and entered.

He installed himself into Ledburry's leather armchair with a book, his eyes on the pages, but his entire attention upon the conversation taking place in the other room.

"Those missing circuits were the diversion we needed to turn Wyverstone's attention away from our work," Ledburry said from across the library's wall, his voice low enough to be inaudible without the contraption. *"I made sure they will have a hard time finding them."*

"However, we still need to complete our own circuit if we want to have the humautomata ready on time," Baron Hydenhollow replied, discontent lacing his tone. *"I still believe it was a bad idea to remove Miss Hammond from her workbench. We need the finished prototype soon, and Quimby has yet to find a solution."*

Humautomata? Herdforthbridge thought. *What the devil are they planning to create? How many prototypes? For what?* He touched his ear with an instinctive gesture, waiting for the conversation in the adjoining room to continue.

"That was a necessary setback," Ledburry explained. *"You are well aware of how ruthless Wyverstone can be in his pursuits, so I had to set him on a different trail. As for Miss Hammond –"* A pause. *"I am quite certain that such an obstinate woman is working on her own, without my approval. Most likely, we will have those circuits soon."*

"Assuming she does indeed complete those circuits without our knowledge, how exactly are you planning to take them? I doubt Miss Hammond would just give us her work after what we have done to her. And we cannot break into Windstoneham's townhouse and take them."

Ledburry's sinister laugh echoed in Herdforthbridge's ear. *"I have my ways, and none of them requires Miss Hammond's presence. They actually exclude it."*

The duke froze, those words only confirming his deepest fear. If Annabella completed the bloody circuits, she would die.

"My laboratory has perfected the anaesthetic we need for the surgery," the baron said. *"Now we should be able to attach those*

brass parts to a human body – if we have Miss Hammond's circuits, that is. Until then, we need to keep the French missing cargo hidden, the English team stalled, and the Classified Affairs' attention on another matter while Miss Hammond finishes her work."

Hydenhollow paused for a few seconds to gulp a drink, then laughed and continued with a cheerful voice. *"It was indeed audacious of you to hide a trunk full of wires and cogs in a school, right under Wyverstone's brother's nose. So far, everything is going like clockwork."*

"As it should," the earl agreed. *"And I'm expecting news from France soon."* The thud of soles on the thick carpet. *"But now we should return to the ballroom before my wife starts searching for me."*

When the sound of their footsteps receded on the corridor, the duke left the library, and in less than ten minutes he was in his mechanical horse-drawn carriage, on his way to the Inspectorates to meet Jasper.

They would find the French's missing cargo that night.

12

Long after midnight, under the murky, yellow lights of the streetlamps, Westminster square lay empty and ominous, its cobblestones wet and gleaming in the thin drizzle. The massive red building of the Inspectorates loomed over the entire space, its windows unusually dark and silent, its outline concealed in the overall gloom. No shadow broke the stillness.

Almost.

Dressed in black trousers and a black shirt, his dark, untamed hair tied with a black leather ribbon, Jasper slid along the wall of the Inspectorates' eastern wing with the agility and stealth of a night predator, unseen, unheard. Avoiding guards and streetlamps, he reached a small service door tucked in a stone alcove inside the far end of the wall, abandoned years before, and took out the key Edmund had given him.

The rusty iron door opened with a jarring creak.

Jasper swore and remained still for a few moments, but he was too far, and the night too chilly for any guard to patrol that secluded area.

He crouched to enter the building through the alcove, careful to close the iron door behind him, and climbed up a narrow flight of windowless service stairs covered in mould and moss, the stifling air acrid with the pungent stench of rot and decay.

The top of the stairs led him to another small wooden door, which gave in under the pressure of his hands. He emerged on the third floor of the Inspectorates, at the end opposite from Ledburry's laboratory.

The overwhelming silence amplified the sound of his boots on the cold marble of the corridor, making him hold his breath and keep his lithe figure close to the wall while passing a few smaller laboratories bound to be relocated at the Engineerium's headquarters after the Engineers World Gathering.

He would not waste that chance. Everyone was dancing at the Countess of Ledburry's ball, even the earl's assistants, who usually spent long hours in the laboratory.

Five minutes and a demonstration of his lockpicking skills later, he was inside Ledburry's workspace.

A strong smell of carbolic acid and medicine assaulted his nostrils as soon as he entered the vast room that looked similar to a medical facility. Medical treatises, drawings, papers covered in strange formulae, and instruments filled the cabinets or lay on the workbenches. Under the light of his pocket lamp, through the glass windows of the furthermost cabinet, he recognised some of Annabella's brass parts, covered in a thin layer of dust.

Did they abandon Humautomaton? Jasper found the prospect rather odd, given the project's importance, but had no time for such musings. Aware that he would not find answers in the laboratory's main room, he entered Ledburry's private office.

Jasper leafed through the documents on the mahogany desk, but only found letters from Ledburry's peers, a medical journal, and a few books stacked on a pile of tracing paper sheets. He pulled out the sheets. If the Doctors Order's Senior Lord kept tracing paper, then he also ought to keep a bottle of tracing liquid. He opened a few drawers until he found what he was searching for.

He spread the sheets on the desk and poured half of the bottle over them. The paper absorbed the liquid greedily, turning yellow and revealing its contents. Anatomical drawings and annotations, most probably Ledburry's own research.

Except for the last sheet of paper, which only included a date and a few words.

The 10th of June, 1896. Fireworks celebrations.

Intrigued, Jasper took the paper to examine it under the warm glow of his pocket lantern.

"The 10th of June – the date of the Engineers World Gathering's grand opening," he whispered, trying to understand. "But why the tracing paper? Why must he hide a fireworks celebration with tracing paper?"

He returned the bottle of tracing liquid back into the desk's drawer, only to hear the muffled sound of glass on leather or textile instead of glass on hard wood. Curious, he crouched behind the desk and pulled out a thin binder containing several expense deeds. Jasper almost laughed, recognising the payment for Sheridan's lodging.

Edmund will be pleased to have this. Who knows what the other expenses might reveal.

He pushed the drawer with the back of his hand just as the laboratory's door opened and closed with a thud. Jasper froze, quickly assessing his options. In two strides, he would be behind the open door of Ledburry's office.

Herdforthbridge entered the smaller room before he could put his plan into action.

"What the devil!" Jasper let out a deep, long breath. "How did you enter?"

"Through the front door, of course," the duke replied, as if to remind him he was one of the most powerful men in England, whose presence at the Inspectorates no one would question, regardless of the hour.

He glimpsed at the binder in Jasper's hand but said nothing, choosing to answer Jasper's questioning stare instead. "I think I found out where the French's missing circuits are."

～

JASPER GAPED at the duke with an incredulous stare, repeating the information he had just received. "In a school? Under my nose?"

Master Hollingsworth's words from the other night suddenly emerged from his recent memories. *Her new assistant has proven to be quite an asset, regardless of the physical infirmity that many, unlike my daughter, would not have ignored.* He laughed, a bitter laugh at his own ignorance. Now it all made ghastly, sickening sense.

Sheridan. He is Rowena's new assistant. I should have known. I should have bloody known!

"It seems we made a habit of exploring Rowena's schools together, searching for villains," he added aloud, without a word about Sheridan. "Or stolen circuits. For the only place I can think of is her school."

"Precisely my thoughts," the duke agreed. "My carriage is waiting behind the mechanical waterfall. I suggest we leave the same way we entered and meet there."

A quarter of an hour later, Jasper climbed inside Herdforthbridge's mechanical horse-drawn carriage.

They stopped close to the former warehouse that hosted Rowena's school, and Jasper alighted. Herdforthbridge discarded his hat and evening coat and followed.

"How the bloody hell could someone bring and hide such a load here without anyone noticing?" Jasper wondered, taking in the large construction. "If the French's missing circuits are indeed here, I doubt Rowena is aware of that."

"The building has an underground passage that connects it to the docks," the duke explained while they explored the school's surroundings. "The passage ends in a cellar – a second, smaller cellar, built underneath the main one."

"A hidden cellar? Are you certain?"

"Perhaps you forgot that this building used to be my property before I donated it to Miss Hollingsworth," Herdforthbridge said without looking at Jasper, his attention on the cobblestones as if searching for something on the pavement. "Many warehouses such as this one had the same layout. Years ago, smugglers used these underground passages to bring their wares to the wealthy who paid for them. But the smugglers' business had dwindled considerably after the Reform, so the passages and secret cellars have rarely been used over the past ten years."

He turned to look at Jasper before continuing his curious search around the school. "The layout of the secret passages and double cellars was not exactly a secret. So I assume it was not that difficult for Ledburry and Hydenhollow to come up with the idea of using them. Of course, choosing Miss Hollingsworth's school was their best option, for no one would have thought to search there. Oh, here it is."

The duke crouched before an inconspicuous manhole whose texture and pattern were similar to the surrounding cobblestones, close to the school's service entrance – the former back entrance to the warehouse. He removed the lid, revealing a narrow tunnel that descended into darkness.

Herdforthbridge climbed down first, his clothes and hair damp with drizzle, Jasper's pocket lantern in his mouth. Jasper followed.

The short downward tunnel spilt into another narrow passageway that led towards the school, whose end climbed up to a wooden trapdoor. Herdforthbridge pushed it open, then shifted his weight upwards into the damp secret cellar.

Jasper climbed after him and took a quick look around. The small space was empty, except for a tangled pile of wires and brass cogs.

"What now?" the duke asked, staring at the troublesome French cargo. "What do we do with them?"

"I say we take them to my workshop and let Edmund decide."

A daring move. Jasper pushed the heap of metal with the tip of his boot. *Sheridan must have asked for a job at the school to keep an eye on these circuits. The second he realises they are gone, Rowena will be in danger.*

IN HIS STUDY at the Wyverstone house, where Herdforthbridge and Jasper had found him working in the dead of night, Edmund turned each page of the leather binder his brother had extracted from the inside pocket of his wet canvas coat.

"I shall go to the Inspectorates to check these deeds," he said, finally closing the leather folder and checking the timepiece he kept in the pocket of his waistcoat. "But I'm afraid they are not enough." He strode to the tall, wrought-iron framed windows, staring outside into the darkness of the garden, brushing off his forehead a few tendrils of hair that had fallen over his eyes and obstructed his vision. "Whilst these might be important evidence in a future trial, I cannot arrest a peer of the realm with only some receipts as evidence. I need more substantial proof to accuse Ledburry of sabotage or sedition."

"I assume confronting Ledburry and Hydenhollow is out of the question," Herdforthbridge said, his face pale in the dim light of the study. "You cannot say I have overheard their discussion. Even if you did, they would only deny everything and be more cautious, so we would lose track of their endeavours."

"Precisely," Edmund replied, turning to his two guests, his blue eyes tired but still sharp. "Taking back the missing circuits was a necessary compromise, as the English team could not resume their work without those. But we cannot afford to raise more suspicion."

He returned to the leather armchair behind his desk, leaning his elbows against the wooden top, his hands clasped under his chin. "You did well to take them to the workshop," he said, his lips curled in a tentative, exhausted smile. "However, you cannot reveal yourselves as the finders of the circuits. The less damaging option we have is for Jasper to bring those wires to the Crystal Palace and leave them at the French team's pavilion without being seen. We still have about two hours until dawn, which should be enough."

"Worry not, they will miraculously appear in the morning," Jasper said. "Besides, even if someone sees me, I am still one of the exhibition's overseers, so no one would question my presence." He stood, ready to leave. "Do you believe Rowena might be in danger?" he asked, his hand on the door handle, his voice tight. "I don't quite like that the French's missing circuits were hidden underneath her school."

"I doubt it, but I shall have some of my men keep a close watch on Miss Hollingsworth," Edmund said, easing some of Jasper's guilt and worry. "She was not involved in this affair, so no one would relate her to the circuits' disappearance from that cellar, of whose existence she was not privy. However, Ledburry is intelligent enough to associate the Classified Affairs to the suddenly found cargo and the binder missing from his laboratory." He rose and rolled down the sleeves of his white shirt, ready to leave for the Inspectorates. "Which means their next move will come sooner than we expect, and we must be ready for it."

The Engineering School made quite a different picture during
the night, Carmina decided, staring at the back wall of the large
building whose shape was but a shadow against the dark,
starless sky, a gloomy, sinister place rather than the busy,
cheerful institution it was during the day. In the subdued glow
of the streetlamps, much fewer than those lining the front wall
overlooking Rue des Écoles, the magnificent classical columns
and sculptures adorning the windows were almost invisible.

At the end of the building's western wing, hidden in a recess
inside the wall, Carmina found a small square-shaped opening
at the ground level, accessible through a narrow stone staircase
descending to the service entrance.

That was the window used for unloading coal into the
building, and the perfect place to infiltrate the school without
forcing doors.

Cursing her long skirts and making a mental note to scrape a
disguise next time, she slid through the soot-stained opening
and landed on a pile of coal inside the storage room.

Grateful for the black dirt covering her from head to toe,
Carmina left the storage room and emerged on the dark,
cavernous corridor below the school's ground floor level. Only a
few electric bulbs lit the empty passage, their light too dim for
her to distinguish anything further than two feet away.

Her boots made no sound on the floor's cold stones. She
crossed the western wing of the school, carefully checking each
lavishly carved door that lined the right side of the high walls. All
of them were unlocked, a sign they had no secrets to protect – a
small library, two study rooms, and a lecture hall. No laboratory.

Only a metal door towards the corridor's end, unadorned
and unassuming, remained closed when Carmina tried to
open it.

This must be it. The laboratory Quimby entered when Annabella was here.

She extracted her lockpicking set from a pocket of her skirts, chose the pin she needed, and crouched before the door, which gave in a tad too easily.

If it were that important, the laboratory would have been better secured.

The experiment room that looked nothing out of the ordinary and so much like the ones she had already visited on the ground floor only confirmed Carmina's suspicions. The space bore no evidence of Quimby's presence. Only glass containers, a few wires, and many jars with chemicals filled the cabinets and workbenches.

And yet, she was certain she was in the right room. But her answers were not there.

She was missing something.

When you are in a deadlock, approach the matter from another angle. The words of the late Earl of Wyverstone – her mentor – popped into her mind. She stood still in the middle of the room, letting her mind weave a new net of connexions and possibilities.

Miss Blackwell and Annabella came from the same direction as I did. Yet, if Quimby had appeared in front of this door from the opposite end of the corridor, there must be another door around here. But where?

Carmina clicked the door shut behind her, careful to lock it again, and crossed the last portion of the passage to a flight of stairs leading up to the ground floor. Tucked under its base was another door, smaller, with a round upper edge, painted in the same colour as the high stone wall, with no handle or lock to be picked.

It can only be unlocked from the inside. Which meant there was another way to reach that space.

She stared at the door's outline, barely visible in the darkness, assessing the possibilities.

Where is the bloody entrance?

The indistinguishable voices coming from the other side of the door stopped her in her tracks. Holding her breath, she hid in the darkest corner behind the stone steps and put the amplifier in her ear.

Suddenly, the muffled sounds became crystal clear.

A British accent and a French accent.

"Worry not. In London, everything is going according to the plan," the British accent said. *"At the moment, the English team is too preoccupied with your missing circuits and the stalling of their work to think of anything else."*

"But are you certain we've also diverted the Classified Affairs' attention?" The French accent sounded far less optimistic. *"We cannot afford that earl's interference if we want to see the results of our efforts at the Engineers World Gathering's opening. One slight delay, and it's all for nought."*

The British accent, which Carmina recognised as Benedict Quimby, snorted. *"There will be no delays. I am tired of living like a fugitive instead of occupying the place I deserve for my merits. But I intend to change this soon."*

A short pause. *"As for the Classified Affairs' Chief Inspector –"* He laughed. *"I have some surprises for him. And I assure you they are shattering enough to shake even an untouchable and cold-hearted man such as him and remove him from our way."*

For a few long moments, the only sound Carmina could hear was the beating of her own heart. But she would worry about Edmund later. For now, she was an agent of the Crown with a duty to fulfil.

Silence, then she heard the two men's steps receding behind another door that opened and closed. In what Carmina estimated as less than five minutes, they came out of the experiment room she had inspected earlier.

The dim light on the long corridor confirmed the men's identities.

Maurice Gervaise and Benedict Quimby.

In a split second, she made her decision. Abandoning her plans to search for the door to the hidden room, she followed the two men, hoping to find where Quimby was lodging. As soon as they disappeared up the main stairs to the ground floor, she hurried out of her dark corner back to the coal storage room – the quickest and safest way out.

Hidden in a dark spot behind the school's corner on Rue des Écoles, she watched them emerging through the school's main entrance, then parting ways.

Even better, Carmina thought, following Quimby from a safe distance, under the shelter of the night, careful to keep herself in the shadows. He passed Musée de Cluny, turned around the corner on Boulevard Saint Germain, and disappeared inside one of the buildings lining the street. Carmina counted the doors, then looked up at the dark windows, waiting.

"First floor, second window to the right," Carmina muttered a few minutes later when a patch of yellow light spilt out from the building. "Edmund, I found him. We finally found him."

COVERING his mouth with his hand to stifle a yawn after an adventurous night, Jasper walked around Rowena's school in Holborn for a casual inspection of the place in broad daylight. The surroundings kept no trace of his and the duke's visit the night before. The iron manhole covering the tunnel they had used to take out the French's wires and cogs was barely distinguishable from the pavement's flagstones.

With a satisfied nod, he entered the school and found Rowena in her office, writing in a ledger, her attention focused on the pages she was filling with her slim, elegant handwriting.

He smiled and watched her for a few moments, taking in the sight of her, of her black curls slightly caressing her shoulders, of the pale blue dress whose lace collar covered the base of her slender neck.

As if sensing his presence, she looked up from her papers and returned his smile. "I hear they found the French's missing cargo," she said, standing to welcome him. "Shouldn't you be at the Crystal Palace? Or celebrating with Ivy and the others?"

"How about you? Shouldn't you rest more? Now that you have a new assistant, I thought you finally decided to follow your physician's advice and protect your lungs. Your health is still fragile, yet here you are for almost the entire day."

"While I do appreciate your concern, I assure you I am a perfectly functional woman, and I would always choose my school over sitting all day in my drawing room at home doing nothing." A shadow darkened her dear face. "Besides, Mr Marlowe – my assistant – has requested a few free days to see to some personal affairs, so I have no assistant for a while."

If Jasper had any doubt regarding Sheridan being Rowena's assistant, her mention of the name he had already seen on the package containing Annabella's books confirmed his suspicions.

And he had just lost him again.

Which was not exactly unexpected since the man had no circuits to keep an eye on any longer.

"Will you be careful?" he asked, squeezing her hand, preparing to take his leave. "Please, Rowena, do take care of yourself."

At the Crystal Palace, the news of the missing circuits' reappearance was on everyone's lips. Suppressing a grin, he walked towards the French pavilion, greeting Fontaine with an innocent, surprised look.

"So you found them," he said, his tone matching the bewilderment on his face.

"Or rather they found us." The chief engineer of the French

team squinted at him with a doubtful stare, his arms crossed at his chest. "After such an extraordinary return, perhaps I should start believing in miracles. Don't you agree?"

His pointed gaze was a clear indicator of his suspicion regarding Jasper's involvement in the matter.

"Perhaps," Jasper said, pretending not to understand. "If you need help with those circuits, pray do tell me. Your team has yet to complete that automaton."

"How kind of you," Fontaine replied in a tone which Jasper placed closer to mockery than gratitude. "But I have already asked for help, and our school will send a technician." He lifted an eyebrow in a derisive smirk, running his thin, long fingers through his auburn hair. "As for help, if I were you, I would be more interested in solving my own family's problems rather than offering my help to others."

"Whatever do you mean by that?"

The Frenchman turned towards a wooden crate to retrieve a folded copy of the latest *Londoners' Journal*, which he shoved in Jasper's face.

Ignoring Fontaine's continuous efforts to annoy him, Jasper took the newspaper, only to turn ashen at the sight of the front page.

He excused himself and hurried towards the closest door, cursing under his breath.

13

———

Jasper ran up the marble steps of the Inspectorates' grand staircase to the second floor, ignoring all the people – clerks, engineers, and aviators – whom he usually greeted each time he visited the place, his breath quickened, his eyes bloodshot with rage, the exhaustion and need for sleep gone. As soon as he'd entered the building, he had been summoned to the proceedings hall to hear the Board's new verdict, but that could wait for a bit longer. Crossing the corridor to the alcove that hid the door to the Classified Affairs, he stormed into Edmund's office without bothering to knock.

His brother was just returning his teacup back to the small, gold-rimmed saucer, his face a blank, unreadable canvas. The latest issue of *The Londoners' Journal* lay open on his desk beside the teapot.

Jasper nodded towards the newspaper. "I gather you've read that heap of bollocks."

"I have," Edmund replied, his voice as collected as his expression.

"Then you understand I cannot let our family's name be dragged through the mud. I'm going to kill that bloody editor with my own hands."

Edmund's features turned from unreadable to annoyed, his forehead forming a few thin creases. "You will kill no one."

Jasper grabbed the newspaper and read aloud the title on the front page.

"*IS THE EARL OF WYVERSTONE TRULY THE PROTECTOR OF ENGLAND'S SAFETY?* I wonder whether we read the same thing."

"We did," Edmund said. "Unless you are not referring to the article that reveals Jade's past endeavours as the feared bare-knuckle fighter Blackhand."

"Damnation, this ain't about Jade! It's about you!" Jasper leafed through the newspaper until he found the article. "Listen here. *Whyever any decent Englishman should approve of the Earl of Wyverstone's actions? This esteemed personage chose to protect his brother from shame instead of revealing the truth – a truth that would have cast a dark shadow over young Jade Kendall Asher, who used to be an officer in Her Majesty's service. An officer in Her Majesty's service fighting in the slums of Whitechapel for the entertainment of the most sordid of London's inhabitants! Imagine the scandal if he had been found out! Which he had not, because of the earl's machinations. The Earl of Wyverstone, a man who puts his personal interests before those of his country, should relinquish his highly regarded position as the Chief Inspector of Her Majesty's Office of Classified Affairs, for he is certainly not qualified to protect the Crown and the country.*"

Jasper threw the Journal back on Edmund's desk. "For the love of God, I cannot understand how you can be so undisturbed when they bring such serious allegations against you."

Edmund poured a cup of tea for his younger brother and beckoned him to take the chair in front of his desk. "Hysterics do not solve the problem. They must have the information from Sheridan, who probably had kept it a secret for such a long time not out of fear, but to follow someone's instructions. Quimby's, most likely. This article might be a part of a larger attempt to keep my attention diverted. Or they are trying to tie my hands and force me to resign to render me powerless. In other words, I am quite the thorn in their side, so they need me out of their way."

Jasper remained silent for a few moments, dissecting his brother's words, rotating the cup on its saucer without lifting it, his eyes focused on the amber liquid.

"We should do something about this article," he finally said. "That bloody journal is still holding a grudge against us after their failed stunt with the articles about the Laevium Works, so they've become our enemies' weapon. This is why they published that nonsense."

"Their reason is irrelevant and doesn't change the fact that all of London now knows that Jade fought in the slums and I covered his activities. Going against that journal will not help the situation, so I'll do no such thing." He threw Jasper an icy stare. "And neither will you."

His tone made it clear that it was not a request, but an order.

Jasper sipped the warm tea, aware that he should not press the issue further. "At least now I understand what Sheridan was doing at the Journal's headquarters a few days ago. To think the bloody bastard tricked us into believing he wanted to consult the archives from ten years ago when he actually intended to provide information." He laughed – a bitter, harsh laugh. "I was a fool to waste my time inquiring about what happened on the 20th of April 1886, believing I would find out what Sheridan was after."

In an instant, Edmund's face turned ghostly pale, his blue eyes filled with a dread Jasper had never seen in his brother's expression before. He stood and put his hands on the mahogany desk, slightly leaning towards Jasper. "Tell me if I understood correctly," he said, a steely inflexion in his voice. "Edwin Sheridan researched *The Londoners' Journal*'s archives from ten years ago? More specifically, around the 20th of April 1886?"

"Indeed," Jasper replied, not understanding the strange look on Edmund's face. "Has anything happened that day? I made some inquiries and found nothing of importance, except the death of the Marquess of Windstoneham's eldest daughter. Though tragic, I fail to comprehend how that event is related to you."

Without answering his question, Edmund unlocked the cabinet beside his desk and took out a few papers, which he handed to Jasper. "I must leave London for a while, but I shall contact you when needed. These are the safety instructions for the test flight, which I count on you to schedule soon."

Jasper stared at his brother in utter confusion, without even a glance at the papers he was now holding. "Tell me you do not intend to resign or hide because of that article."

"No," Edmund replied, his cold voice and calculated composure back in place. "I intend to expose whatever conspiracy is brewing and protect those who are dear to me. This time without fail."

Seated next to Annabella on the first row of wooden benches in the proceedings hall, clutching the papers Edmund had given him less than half an hour before and wondering what prompted his brother's unusual behaviour, Jasper had a hard time concentrating at what Theophilus Hollingsworth and the Earl of Ledburry were saying. The only thing he registered was that, upon the Board's final decision, all of them were cleared to continue their work, and Ivy – who was absent from the meeting, as she could not attend on such short notice – to resume her activities as a pilot.

"What a disgusting snake, that Ledburry!" Annabella said

after the meeting while walking with Jasper down the corridor towards the Inspectorates' main entrance. "If it weren't for my project, I would have declined that bloody hypocrite's offer to return to his laboratory."

"You should still decline his offer and stay away from his laboratory for a while," Jasper warned. "That place is nowhere near safe."

She halted before the massive carved door, facing him with an angry look. "I would never cower in fear before that man. I shall return to the laboratory and finish Humautomaton."

Jasper tried to read the look in her fiery eyes. "Is there any way to convince you to stay away from that place?"

"No, it isn't," she replied, holding his gaze. "Ledburry tried to discredit me and allowed for my books to be stolen, so I do not trust him. I know how dangerous it might be to work with him again, but I am willing to take the risk for my project's sake." She opened the door, and they went out into the midday warm sun. "I find this entire affair strange. The French replace an excellent airship with an incomplete project. They ask us to bring some circuits from Paris. The circuits disappear, then reappear miraculously, and their project has yet to be finished. Instead of sending *L'Étoile* and following their initial plan, they go on with this lost cargo charade. As we speak, found cargo or not, they have no exhibit. To me, it looks like the French are not even interested in the Gathering, but in interfering with our work."

Jasper crossed his arms, a dark shadow clouding his face. Annabella's words made perfect sense – one he hadn't given too much thought before. She was right. The French showed no particular interest in an event where all the other countries brought their best inventions. They had changed their exhibit at the last moment, sent an incomplete prototype, and cared nothing about their project's safety.

Gilbert Fontaine was the only one who actually gave a bloody damn about the French exhibit.

His thoughts returned to the ghastly allegations against Edmund, made the very day when the circuits reappeared – or rather the very day they disappeared from their hiding place. Was that a coincidence? Jasper doubted it.

They fear him. They fear my brother and the Classified Affairs. It is him, not the circuits, they are interested in. But how the blazes are the French, Quimby, Ledburry, and their clique related? I'm missing something here. Something important.

"Enough about the French," Annabella said with an exasperated sigh, interrupting his inner monologue. "When are we having the test flight for the *Lady*?"

"In three days," Jasper replied. "On Thursday morning."

THE CHEERS FILLING the hangar at the news of the Board's decision brought a smile to Jasper's tired face and reassured him that they still had a chance to finish everything on time. After sending some of his men to the English pavilion at the Crystal Palace to resume their work, he had one last thing to do.

"Have you seen Ivy today?" he asked the remaining labourers who were about to return to their activities. "Is she at her berth?"

"No, Master Jasper, she's 'ere," one man replied, nodding in the general direction of the ceiling, before disappearing behind the other side of the airship's tall scaffolding. "She's up in the gondola with Hamilton."

Jasper climbed the iron ladder to the gondola's lower deck, halting halfway to take in the view. The late spring sun coming through the high rectangular windows cast the early afternoon's mild light upon the people scurrying around and the piles of metal scraps and wires spread on the floor. The place was bustling with activity, as if the pressure and uncertainty of the last few days had never happened.

He climbed the rest of the rungs and entered the piloting area, which resonated with Ivy's voice. "I am not jealous, you arrogant dolt! *The Skycradle*'s board is easier to use. I tell you, this piloting board still needs a few tweaks here and there."

Jasper coughed to announce his presence, hiding a grin. Those two's constant bickering never failed to amuse him.

"There's no need to be so fiendish with poor Hamilton now that you don't need his help any longer."

Ivy turned to face him, her bright, green eyes as wide as saucers. "Do you mean I can finally retake my place at the piloting board? Did they find the missing cargo?"

Jasper nodded.

"Who was behind this?" Avery asked. "Did you find out who took that pile of wires?"

"I'm afraid not," Jasper said apologetically. "They simply appeared at the French team's pavilion out of nowhere."

Avery lifted an eyebrow, a corner of his mouth curled in a sarcastic smile. "Of course, Lord be praised for His almighty miracles." He turned back to Ivy. "Well, now you can pilot your beloved *Skycradle* again, but having me as your navigator would be an asset for your airship. I would keep me if I were you."

Ivy nodded, her cheeks red with a violent blush. "Yes, I think I should very much like to keep you."

Avery laughed and ruffled her hair just as Robert Elmstone entered the gondola. He went straight to Jasper, ignoring the other two.

"The *Lady* is completed," he said. "But everyone wants to know what comes next. When are we starting the tests?"

Jasper swallowed the uncomfortable lump in his throat. "About that –" He swallowed again. "I'm afraid I need to check with the Office of Classified Affairs to –"

"Are you planning to do the test flight like you did the engine mounting?" the engineer asked in a harsh voice, his eyes dark.

"You lied and sent everyone for a day off only to work in secrecy. Tell me, Asher. Is this how you trust your people?"

Jasper opened his mouth to say something, but no word came out. The man was right to be furious.

"It's not just me," Elmstone continued. "You offended the entire team of engineers when you chose to mount the engines secretly, Classified Affairs' order or not. I won't accept the same treatment for the test flight. I want to be part of it."

A few moments of silence were the only time Jasper had to choose his answer. Elmstone had worked hard for months and spent days and nights at the hangar to see the *Lady* completed. He had the right to take part in the test flight. Who was he to deny him that?

"You are right," he finally said. "I'll add you to the Thursday morning test flight crew."

THE REPETITIVE CLIP-CLOP of the mechanical horses, which blended with the rumble of carriage wheels on cobblestones, registered in Annabella's mind the same way as the constant, obsessive tick of an old grandfather clock, hammering her ears and senses with a dull, unchanged noise. Through the half-drawn curtain of the window, she caught glimpses of London unfolding before her eyes in a mixture of colours and textures, buildings and people, daylight and shadow.

She moved her gaze from the bustling city outside to the tall, lean figure of Herdforthbridge comfortably seated on the upholstered bench in front of her. "Oscar, I know the way from the Inspectorates to my house. You do not have to escort me everywhere in your carriage as if I were Her Majesty herself."

The duke leaned towards her, his elbows on his knees. "I am trying to make up for our lost years, so it is only natural to spend as much time as possible in your company. It has never occurred to me that my presence could displease you."

Annabella lifted an eyebrow, but her face was beaming with a wide smile. "Do not dare insult my intelligence with such ridiculous tales." She cupped his cheek, her forehead touching his, welcoming his strong arms around her waist. "Please, trust me. I know what you think, but I assure you I am not in imminent danger. You have no reason to worry. Besides, you might want to hear that I can resume my work at Ledburry's laboratory, so I shall be protected from Quimby."

The duke's handsome face turned darker, a dangerous undertone clouding his blue eyes. He covered her hand with his, squeezing it lightly. "Such news only deepens my worries. Please, Annabella, try to postpone the completion of your work for as long as possible. Can you do this for me?"

Annabella pulled out from their embrace, leaning against the carriage wall in a swish of silk, clutching her reticule in her gloved hands, her eyes ablaze with anger. "No, Oscar, I cannot. I cannot stop my work just because first Jasper, and now you ask me to decline the offer to return to my official place in the Engineerium or postpone the completion of Humautomaton. That project is already too difficult to finish, so I cannot afford further delays. I must find the perfect frequency and voltage for my circuits to be used on humans without harming them. Your request is selfish and inconsiderate towards my work as an engineer."

"You don't understand!" The duke's thunder-like voice reverberated in the small enclosure of his carriage. "I would rather be inconsiderate towards your work now than attend your funeral instead of our wedding later."

Annabella stared at him, his unusual reaction sending shivers down her spine.

"This is not right," she said a few moments of stunned silence later. "What precisely are you hiding from me?"

"I am not hiding anything. But I am quite certain that the second you complete the circuits, Quimby will want to get rid of you. If you decide to continue, at least promise me you will trust no one, not even your colleagues at the laboratory. And especially not the Earl of Ledburry."

~

BESIDES THE EXCELLENT FOOD, exquisite fashion, and spectacular sunsets, Paris also had the most adequate thrift shops and street merchants for whoever needed clothes and accessories for a last-moment disguise – especially handy when the beneficiary of such items was an agent of the British Crown.

Pleased with her loot, which she carried in two bags in her arms, and mentally assembling her new outfit, Carmina returned to her lodging on Rue de la Sorbonne and climbed up the stairs to her rooms on the second floor.

She had at least two hours to rest and prepare her disguise before going out to sneak into Quimby's rooms.

With that thought, she turned the key into her small flat's door, but it remained stuck in the keyhole.

The door was unlocked.

Holding her breath, she let her bags on the floorboards, careful not to make any noise, and gripped the paralysis pistol hidden in the depths of her skirts' pocket. With the stealth of a predator and the agility of a cat, she pushed the door with her shoulder and slid inside the vestibule, noticing the door to the sitting room slightly ajar, a slant of golden natural light coming through.

She froze in surprise in the doorway, her heart drumming in her chest like some crazed engine at the unexpected sight welcoming her. In the small parlour, seated at the round cherry wood table, Edmund was sorting a pile of documents. He wore only trousers and shirt, without a waistcoat, his sleeves rolled up to his elbows, his right hand supporting his cheek. A few strands of his raven hair had fallen over his forehead in slight disarray. In the fading red glow of the sunset, his beloved face appeared even more handsome. He looked more like a man and less like the ruthless inspector who ran Her Majesty's Office of Classified Affairs.

She smiled at the rare image of the man. *Her man.*

It had never been easy, their love. More often than not, it brought heartbreak, compromise, longing, and stolen nights. But it also meant happiness beyond anything Carmina had ever felt, happiness so powerful that took her breath away and swallowed her whole, scattering all pain in the wind.

He lifted his head and welcomed her with a shadow of a smile. "You are here."

She took a few steps towards him. "*The Chief Inspector never does field work and always keeps himself out of danger's way,*" she chanted. "Something out of proportion must have happened for you to breach the most important rule of the Classified Affairs' protocol and follow me here. The other day I heard a conversation that quite clearly pointed at you as the target of Benedict Quimby and his acolytes, so they must have set some kind of plan in motion. I have been trying to reach you the entire day to deliver my report."

Edmund ran his long fingers through the dark strands of hair that covered his forehead, a bitter laugh escaping his throat. "Of course, I have expected that much. Yes, something happened, and it is all related to some campaign whose purpose is to vilify me. Jade's endeavours as a bare-knuckle fighter have become public information in London, and now everyone believes I am a corrupt official who used his influence in his brother's favour. And that is not even the worst of it."

He took her hands in his and cleared his throat, his words heavy and sour. "They wanted to find my weakness, and I'm afraid they succeeded."

The piercing gaze of his blue eyes squeezed Carmina's heart as she waited for him to explain. Outside, through the tall window, the last traces of sunset were slowly vanishing into the night and the mellow light of the streetlamps.

"You," Edmund finally said, letting out a long breath. "I'm afraid Quimby knows my weakness is you. And this is not all. I believe he knows who you are."

14

A long stretch of silence settled in the room as Edmund struggled to read Carmina's expression, to catch a hint of what she felt after reading the *Londoners Journal*'s article and hearing the news he had just delivered. But her face remained unchanged, the depths of her green eyes a realm impossible to decipher.

"I am to blame for this," Edmund said when she continued to stare blankly at the tall windows now darkened with the night outside. "Had you not been so important to me, you would have not become a target."

Carmina took a few steps towards the table, beckoning him to join her. The unreadable expression from before had turned into a strange determination he could not fathom.

"Regardless of the outcome, I would not change a thing," she finally said when they were both seated, facing each other. "I have always been aware that my real identity was a liability." A moment of silence. "I knew it from the very first moment the late Earl of Wyverstone came with the proposal that changed my life, giving me what I most yearned for – my freedom, in exchange for my service as an agent of the Crown."

She locked her eyes with his, and in that instant, he knew

she was aware of how her words had shaken him to the core. At last, after all their years together, she was prepared to tell him the entire truth. And his father seemed to have played an instrumental role in it, a role he had never informed Edmund about.

The room was dark, except for a few slants of murky light coming from outside. But none of them stood to light the lamp on the sideboard or the bulbs in the wall sconces.

"I often wondered how you staged your death and then opened the Cinnamon Dove, for Windstoneham was rather strict about his daughters' connections and pin money." Edmund broke the silence, his gaze caressing her figure in the mild darkness, revelling in the intimacy of the moment, in the new, stronger bond being forged between them. "But it never occurred to me that my father had anything to do with it."

"My death as Rebecca Beatrix Hammond and rebirth as Carmina Harcourt was His Lordship's idea," Carmina replied, her velvety voice close to a whisper, tight with the weight of her confession. "Back then, I used to disguise myself and sneak out of the Windstoneham house to explore London. Somehow, the earl found out about my eccentricities. He believed my skills could be helpful for the Classified Affairs, and I was desperate to escape the confining life in my father's house, so our interests aligned.

"He prepared everything for the night of my demise. For a powerful man such as him, finding a corpse to replace me must have been easy, especially during those first months after the Reform, when death was still an everyday occurrence in London's slums. Then he provided the funds for the Dove but gave me free rein there. The wretched life in the slums was not unknown to me. My clandestine outings had shown me enough of it, and I had tried to help as much as I could, unbeknownst to my father or my family. For that reason, the earl's proposal concerning the Dove was an opportunity I could not miss. I turned the place into a shelter for destitute women and trained them in the art of disguise and information gathering so that they could help me in my endeavours as an agent."

She rose and started towards the windows, her long skirts' soft swish the only sound in the room's stillness. As she stood facing the street outside, her profile a blend of shadow and light, one hand on the wooden frame, her hair gathered at her nape in a loose chignon, a few rebel strands fallen over her cheek, she looked mysterious, lost in a world of her own, and breathtakingly beautiful. Without turning to him, she continued, her voice strong with resolve.

"Until this day, I kept my vow to protect the secret of my becoming Carmina Harcourt, which no one except His Lordship and I knew about. But if our enemies have found out about the events from ten years ago, then I want you to know the truth from me, and not from the gossip page of a newspaper. I owe that to you. To us." She stopped for a moment, clenching her fists. "Edmund, I am aware of how dangerous my work is. Of how every single mission can end in my death or my discovery. And yet, I would not change a thing. You once made the wrong decision for my safety, but I would face any danger with you rather than be safe without you."

Edmund stared at her for a few long moments, transfixed by the overwhelming love gripping his heart, gutted by her blunt honesty. In a few strides, he closed the distance between them and wrapped his arms around her waist from behind, leaning over her shoulder. "Forgive me," he whispered, his lips brushing her earlobe. "Forgive me for leaving you those years ago. Forgive me for being such an imbecile."

Carmina turned to face him, her palm caressing his cheek, her green eyes holding his blue gaze. "Fear not. We cannot be certain that I am a target or that Quimby – or anyone else – knows who I am or what I am to you and the Classified Affairs. Perhaps we have no reason to worry." She placed a featherlike kiss on the firm line of his jaw. "But whatever comes, I am ready for it. We shall fight it together. Now I believe you might want to hear my report."

"I COULD ARREST Quimby this very evening," Edmund said after Carmina finished recounting all the details about her nocturne intrusion into the Engineering School. They had returned to the table, the lamp between them casting a yellow glow on their faces. A spicy fragrance of cinnamon and orange peel came out of the pot of fresh tea Carmina had just brewed. "But I am not willing to sacrifice whatever information we can gather about his activities here, so I shall take the risk and tail him for a while."

He rested his chin on his hand, doubt shadowing his eyes. "However, this entire story unsettles me. If they truly know who you are and who you are working for, then Quimby and Gervaise had set you a trap, and you are falling right into it."

"A more accurate description would be that they *think* I am falling right into it," Carmina countered. "Whilst they might be aware that Madame Hamel is a ruse, they cannot know I saw into this possible trap. However, the risk for Quimby to disappear again is real, so we need to move quickly." She rose, smoothing her dress. "He must be at the school, working with Gervaise, so I shall search his rooms."

"*We* shall search his rooms," Edmund corrected, attracting Carmina's astonished stare.

"I hope you do not mean you are coming with me."

"This is precisely what I mean," Edmund confirmed.

"The Chief Inspector never does field work and always keeps himself out of danger's way," Carmina quoted from the Classified Affairs' code of conduct. "This is our most important rule, and the first one His Lordship made sure I understood the moment he paired me with you for the Humautomaton case. The office losing its head is a risk we can ill afford, and your request is as outlandish as it is unexpected, especially given your obsession with following the protocol."

"Lately, I have come to realise that, at times, evading the protocol is more efficient," Edmund countered. "As the Chief Inspector, I should adapt when the situation requires it. This is why I am here."

"Still, we cannot risk losing you."

"Perhaps I should make myself clear," Edmund said, his voice back to the strict tone of the Chief Inspector of Her Majesty's Office of Classified Affairs. "This is not a *request*, but an order from your superior. I believe we should prepare to leave instead of wasting our time on such a useless conversation."

Carmina's lips curled into a smile. "Then help me out of these skirts. I need some more appropriate clothing for such an endeavour."

"*His windows are dark,*" Carmina announced in Edmund's ear through the amplifier. "*He is not at home.*"

She was walking a few feet ahead of him on Boulevard Saint Germain, dressed as a newspaper boy. Edmund followed her, his attention on distinguishing her voice from among the colourful sounds of the street. The late spring night air was laden with the subtle fragrance of flowers and the merry chitchat of the students, writers, and artists having a drink outside, close to the Sorbonne.

"*I'm breaking in,*" Carmina continued, walking towards the entrance to Quimby's lodgings. "*It should not take long.*"

"I would rather you let me do it," Edmund said. "We cannot be certain he is not here."

"*No, we cannot, but I know how to protect myself. Need I remind you why they call me the queen of disguise?"* Her light tone did not reassure him. However, she was right. Carmina was Classified Affairs' best agent when it came to infiltrating strange or dangerous places.

"All right," he agreed, his voice reluctant, watching her disappear inside the building. "I shall keep close." A moment of silence. "Be careful, Carmina. Please."

He planted himself at a table of a café nearby and ordered a drink, hiding his face behind the open French newspaper he was pretending to read, keeping a close eye upon the entrance to Quimby's lodgings. Regardless of the late hour, the café's small terrace was full of people, making it easier for him to blend among the lively little crowd.

In contrast to his perfectly calm exterior, dark rage surged through him when Benedict Quimby finally appeared from the opposite direction. Almost a year of useless searching when the former Senior Lord of the Engineers Order was hiding in plain sight, months of frustration amplified tenfold after each dead end, countless days and sleepless nights of strategizing and changing teams flooded his mind with the power of a mighty river, making his blood boil and maddening his senses. For a few moments, his only thought was to kill the man with his bare hands.

Which, of course, he could not do.

Recovering his wits in an instant, Edmund rose and walked around the corner of the building, keeping away from Quimby's sight.

"You need to leave," he whispered. "Our quarry is here."

No confirmation or other sound came through the amplifier. Perhaps she was too far, and Jasper's small contraption could not reach her.

He repeated his instruction, this time louder, his voice stern and commanding. "Carmina, you need to leave that place now. If you do not answer, I am coming after you."

"I had no time to leave the building, so I hid on the floor above." Carmina's voice was barely audible. *"I shall see myself out when Quimby enters his rooms."*

Edmund watched as the former Senior Lord reached the building, his stout figure and jovial countenance unchanged, walking as if he were not the Classified Affairs' most wanted criminal. Again, the impulse to come out and arrest the man overwhelmed him. He took a deep breath and clutched his fists to keep his composure. He never gave in to such impulses, and he could not afford more mistakes. Soon, he would arrest him. But not that evening. His intuition told him there was much more to the entire affair than simply catching Quimby, and he was close to finding out what.

In the past months, he had learnt that intuition was a powerful tool, which he should not dismiss. Not even when he had no clear evidence to support it.

When Carmina emerged from the building, he had reverted to the unperturbed Chief Inspector of the Classified Affairs, his momentary insanity gone.

She was carrying something, a small parcel he could not quite distinguish in the yellow light of the streetlamps and from where he was following her. About a quarter of an hour later, they congregated in her sitting room again. Two books, which Edmund identified as the parcel Carmina had carried from Boulevard Saint Germain, lay on the table.

"These are Annabella's books," Carmina explained before he could ask anything. "I was not sure whether to take them. But when I looked inside those books, I realised that leaving them there just to cover my traces was a luxury we could not afford. See for yourself."

Edmund opened one of the books, which was filled with Annabella's writing. And with Quimby's own drawings and detailed notes.

"Bloody hell!" He moved his incredulous stare from the pages back to Carmina. "These look like experiment results."

Carmina nodded. "They must have already tried their own *incomplete* circuits on a human being. Or on more than one human being. Which is precisely what Annabella has tried to avoid at all costs."

Edmund rose, the dark shadow in his blue eyes the only indicator of the torment inside him. Innocent people had suffered again because of his inability to find and stop Quimby. Innocent people might have died because of his incompetence. "Come. It's about time we looked into that laboratory you told me about."

NOTHING but the hollow thump of their boots on the stone floor broke the heavy stillness of the Engineering School's underground corridor, which they had entered through the coal trapdoor Carmina had used the evening before. They had decided against using the amplifiers, keeping them in their pockets instead. The echo in the overwhelming silence was enough for them to hear if anyone was coming.

The western wing was as deserted as it was dark. The sickly light of a few wall sconces barely lit their way towards the end of the corridor, but they were grateful for the darkness. The school's doorkeeper kept himself far from the building's innards and inside his wooden booth close to the main entrance door.

If their luck held, their presence would remain unnoticed.

Edmund crouched before the door Carmina had indicated and picked the lock under the meagre light of her pocket lamp, granting them access inside the laboratory where Annabella had seen Quimby.

"We should search for a trapdoor of some sort," Carmina said, her voice close to a whisper. "A door that would open a secret room or passage, different from this one. The place we need to reach has another door, which can only be opened from the inside. I saw Quimby and Gervaise coming out of this laboratory, so I assumed that the only way to get there was through this room."

Edmund took Carmina's pocket lamp. "We need to look for odd contours," he said. "As there is no visible door, the walls or the floor must hide an invisible one."

The floor was neat, with no other outline than the tiles' rectangular shapes, arranged in a pattern of small, interlocked diamonds. Nothing suggested a hidden entrance to a secret underground passage. Besides, he could hardly imagine someone the size of Benedict Quimby and Maurice Gervaise coming and going through a trapdoor in the floor. The mental image of the two men hoisting themselves up almost made him laugh.

No. They had to rule out the floor. He pointed his lantern at the walls. All were white and neat.

Except for one.

The wall opposite the laboratory door was adorned with a rectangular painted frame of golden wires, with three intermingled cogs in all four corners. The drawing looked rather like an ordinary ornament, only that the wires hid a very thin outline – the unmistakable contours of a door carved in the wall.

Pushing the hidden door from the sides proved useless. The bottom and upper edges were no better.

"This door ought to be actioned through a mechanism hidden inside an object around here," Edmund said. He had such a mechanism in his own office at the Inspectorates, which he used to open the trapdoor in the floor. "But which object?"

He checked the wall sconces while Carmina looked inside the cabinets. Nothing worked.

"Bloody hell," Edmund muttered, weighing in the entire room again. Nothing seemed amiss except a wooden mantel clock placed on a shelf behind the longest table in the laboratory. He went closer to it. "That thing looks odd. This room has at least three big brass clocks in the most visible places, yet they keep an old wooden relic where no one can even read the time properly. I wonder."

When he tried to lift the clock, it did not budge. He pushed it, and it slid forward. A crack followed, and they turned in the direction of the sound.

"The wall is moving," Carmina said. "You found the hidden door."

Edmund lifted the lamp. Ahead of them, a short flight of stairs led down to a narrow, darkened passage, which they crossed quickly. It ended with another short flight of stairs, whose uppermost stone step was wide enough to allow access to the small door on its top.

To their surprise, either in error or by design, it was unlocked. Edmund opened it, and they found themselves inside what looked like an experiment room.

The air was cold and damp, filled with a strong stench of rot and death. Carmina hugged herself and rubbed her arms, as if to keep safe from whatever monstrosity was going on in that place.

The pocket lamp revealed the interior, which was smaller than the other laboratory, with only one workbench in its middle. Wires, cogs and brass parts lay in disarray on the workbench and on the bare tiled floor. At the far end of the room stood a surgeon's table, covered with a bloodied cloth whose hem touched the floor. Above it, a few leather straps hung on the wall, next to a cabinet whose glass doors offered a clear view of the items inside – phials, syringes, and a locked brass box.

Carmina bent over the table and sniffed. "It reeks of blood," she said, an unusual tremor in her voice. "It must be still fresh. I wonder what the devil they did in here."

A shiver crept down Edmund's spine. But he had no time to think of that now. "Check those phials and see if you find anything worth taking. I shall try to open that box."

Several unsuccessful attempts later, the latch finally gave in under Edmund's lock pick and the lid sprang, revealing a pile of papers, which he put on the workbench.

"Poisons and anaesthetics, some of them lethal," Carmina said, coming beside him. "I took a few of the most dangerous ones in case we need such evidence later. What are those –"

She halted and turned towards the door, as the sound of boots on stone broke the silence. Edmund inserted the amplifier in his ear for a few seconds, listening.

"It's just one person," he announced.

"The passage is short," Carmina said, a shadow darkening her green eyes. "Whoever that person is, he'll be here in a moment. We need to hide."

"I have no intention to escape." A dark undertone laced Edmund's low, hoarse voice. "If it's Quimby, I shall arrest him the second he comes through that door. From what I could see, the documents in that box are the evidence I was looking for. There."

He nodded towards the surgeon table. They barely managed to slide underneath it and roll up the cloth a little, when the door opened. In the dim light of the newcomer's lantern, when the man bent over the brass box on the workbench, they could see more than his boots. It was not Benedict Quimby, but Maurice Gervaise.

A foul string of curses in French, promptly followed by loud thuds and the sound of cabinet doors opening and closing, and of glass smashed to pieces on the tiled floor of the room, indicated his discovery of the empty box.

Given the man's frenzied search, it was only a matter of time until he found the two English intruders. And the one thing Edmund could not afford was having his identity exposed in a foreign country, in a place he had no right to be, at a dubious hour, and without permission.

With a contorted move under the table, he extracted the paralysis pistol from his pocket and aimed.

"*Merde!*" Gervaise wobbled for a few moments before falling into an inert pile on the floor, his back at them. He broke into a hysterical burst of laughter, switching to English. "I know who you are, you deceitful little harlot! The English will not stop the progress of science, no matter their efforts or the pathetic spies they send to my school. Yes, I know you are a British spy. You were there the night they found Quimby's warship. He recognised you. Show yourself, you coward!"

Carmina exchanged a quick glance with Edmund, then nodded sideways, towards the centre of the room. He read her green eyes in an instant, nodding back in approval.

She came out from their hiding place and walked towards Gervaise. Counting on her to distract the man, Edmund slid out to search for the other door, his feet making no sound, his tall frame leaving no shadow in his enemy's field of vision.

"Quimby had the same speech before, mind you," she said, her voice steel, with an icy tint of mockery, appearing in front of him in her newspaper boy disguise. "He was as unimpressive as you are now. Just think about it. This place reeks of blood and death, so I have an idea about the activities undertaken on that table. One misplaced word, and the authorities will find out you are conducting illegal experiments. Needless to say, your career would be but a memory – a ghastly one, that is."

Gervaise's laugh reverberated in the small space with a sinister undertone. "I say, females are such gullible and idiotic creatures. If you imagined I used the school's resources without the authorities' knowledge, then you are far more of an idiot than the rest of your ilk. I wonder what our authorities will say when they'll hear we have a foreign spy in our midst."

Edmund stopped in his tracks, cold sweat crawling down his

spine. He gritted his teeth and clenched his fists, aware that he could not give in to his instinct and arrest the man. His authority did not extend over French territory, upon French people – regardless of how vile they were.

"Then complain to your authorities." Carmina's voice remained cool and even, her mocking smirk never leaving her face. "Do that, and you'll only risk a war France would most certainly lose."

"If you don't want war, then return the documents you stole."

Before she could answer, Edmund found the door, tucked beside the cabinet where they had found the box, painted in the same ochre colour as the wall. He pointed at his discovery, aware that she was watching him out of the corner of her eye.

Carmina lifted her arms. "You are delirious. As you can see, I have no documents. And I believe I stayed here longer than I ought to."

She turned her back at him and followed Edmund through the tiny door, ignoring the French invectives coming out of Maurice Gervaise's mouth in barely articulated sentences.

Soon, they found themselves beneath the staircase on the western wing's main corridor, darkness and quiet welcoming them.

THE USUAL EVENING hubbub had faded into silence when Carmina and Edmund emerged again on the pavement outside the Engineering School, dishevelled and dirty. The streets were deserted, as the cafes had long since closed for the day. Forgotten vestiges of the evening's entertainment, two drunkards slumbered against a wall, leaning onto each other, oblivious to the world around them.

It must be long past midnight, Edmund thought, extracting his timepiece out of his waistcoat's pocket to confirm.

Under the dim light of the streetlamps, the city had fallen asleep.

"We are only returning to your rooms to take Annabella's books, then we shall be on our way," he announced. "You go upstairs to pack, and I shall stop a cab. We should make haste."

Carmina nodded. "If they know who I am, they must also know where to find me," she said while they hurried towards Madame Blanchet's establishment. "We have less than ten minutes until the paralysis phial's effect fades, then Gervaise will either come after me or alert Quimby about the missing documents. However, we do not know what information they have about me."

"In such situations, I would rather assume the worst," Edmund replied just as they arrived at her place.

Soon, their hansom was driving towards Hôtel de Ville, Annabella's books tucked safely inside Carmina's travel trunk.

"Are you certain we are doing the right thing?" Carmina asked, her eyes locked with his in the mild darkness of the conveyance. "You haven't even tried to arrest Quimby."

"I'm not certain of anything these days. However, trying to arrest Quimby now would be a waste of my time," Edmund replied. "I'd wager he was the first person Gervaise visited after he recovered from the phial's effect, which makes it highly unlikely for us to still find him in his rooms."

The vehicle finally stopped, and they alighted on Rue du Temple in front of a building both of them knew too well. Edmund climbed the wide round stairs to the first floor, opening the door to a small flat – the same flat his father had rented for them during their first undercover mission in Paris, the same flat where they had become lovers, the flat of their oldest and dearest memories together.

He heard Carmina holding her breath, but she said nothing.

"I had expected difficult situations to occur, so I prepared an alternative," he explained, staring at her back, at the black curls that had come loose over the dirty fabric of her boy shirt. "I thought a second lodging would be more convenient than running around to find a hotel in case we needed to hide. As it turns out, I was right."

She turned her gaze from the window where she had first kissed him back to him. "This place has not changed at all. It froze with all our memories in it." Though cold and practical, he could detect a subtle softness in her voice. "But enough of that. We need to focus on the matter at hand." She pointed at the stack of papers Edmund had already placed on the table in the small parlour.

A corner of his lips curled in a hint of a smile. Count on Carmina Harcourt to keep her wits about her regardless of the situation.

Or the overwhelming memories.

He lit the lamp and divided the documents into two equal piles, one for each of them.

"What evidence do we need more than these?" Carmina asked a while later. "Look at this one."

She started reading from the paper she was holding. *I, Edwin Sheridan, hereby accept in good faith to become an experiment subject for the project Humautomaton, so long as my life is not in danger, provided that I receive a mechanical arm after the experiment's successful completion, at no cost, and with maintenance assured.*

"All the bills for Sheridan's lodging in Paris during the time he brought Quimby from England are here," Carmina continued, leafing through a stack of smaller notes. "And another contract."

She handed the document to Edmund. He read it quickly, his eyes becoming one shade darker. "Quimby pledged to make all his experiment findings available for the French authorities." He inhaled sharply and returned his attention upon his own stack of papers. Though tired after more sleepless hours than he could count, he was still alert. "Let's see what else we have."

Silence settled into the room while they continued leafing through the documents.

"This!" he said, breaking the late-night stillness. "This is what I hoped to find. I knew the risk of not going after Quimby the moment I saw him, but it seems I won this gamble."

Carmina lifted her head, startled. He could not blame her, as he almost never betrayed his emotions, and such elation was too far from his usual behaviour. But he was worn out and tired and close to finally uncovering what he had sniffed for months, and composure be damned.

He handed her the source of his elation.

A gasp and a look that he could place anywhere between stunned and horrified confirmed that the documents had the same effect upon her.

"This is insane!" she said, her voice once pitch higher than her usual tone. "If I understand correctly – and I should like to think that my brain is in perfect order – Quimby, Gervaise, Ledburry, Hydenhollow, and all the others who signed this paper are working to establish a United Confederation of Engineers, Chemists, Physicists, and Other Orders in England and the Continent, and replace the power in England with a technocratic one. This is no less than sedition."

Edmund nodded. "I knew Quimby had powerful accomplices, but I must admit I never expected a plot this wide and with such consequences. It looks like we found a treasure trove, and that is not all." He placed his pile of documents in front of her. "These are the answers to all my questions. Now everything starts to make sense."

Carmina leafed through the rest of the documents, the expression on her face changing constantly from bewilderment to downright anger. She read everything – the documents that tracked the moves of Annabella Hammond, Ivy Blackwell, and Jasper Kendal Asher, a clear instruction to silence the Earl of Wyverstone, the detailed plan of the gondotram accident in

Holborn. The back of the paper bore the stamp of the Engineers Order, classifying it as *Cancelled after the incident.*

"Bloody criminals!" Fury burnt in her eyes. "They rigged the wagon to produce potential subjects for their experiment."

Edmund beckoned her to continue reading. At the bottommost of the document stack lay the thorough description of a plan to remove the most important members of the Royal Family during their inaugural flight aboard *The Cerulean Lady* at the opening of the Engineers World Gathering.

Carmina stared at their findings for a long time, pondering. "Even with such overwhelming evidence, Ledburry is a peer of the realm, and his station offers him protection," she said when she finally looked at Edmund. "Arresting him and the likes of him is close to impossible. None of these documents can be regarded as high treason because no French authority signed them. Maurice Gervaise is a school dean, not a government official. Besides, we cannot accuse a foreign country's authorities without solid evidence, which we do not have."

She rose and walked towards the tall window, staring into the night. "Perhaps we should return to London and make sure the *Lady*'s test flight takes place without incidents. We cannot afford another *Golden Griffin*."

Edmund joined her, resting his hands on her shoulders. "Only Jasper and his three crew members know the date of the test flight, so we have no reason to worry. However, I have other concerns. None of these documents mentions how the French authorities are involved or how Humautomaton fits in this plot. I am inclined to believe that some crucial papers were left out of the brass box and hidden somewhere else."

Carmina turned to face him, his arms still on her shoulders. "What if our assumption is wrong? What if there are no other documents because the French authorities are not involved at all?"

He took out his pocket watch and left it on the table, then

started unbuttoning his coal-dirty waistcoat. "The idea occurred to me as well, so this is what I want to find out."

"Are we returning to London?"

He was aware of Carmina's eyes watching him intently. "No, not yet." He pulled his cotton shirt over his head with a disgusted grimace. It looked and smelled like a rag rather than a garment a decent man would wear. "Not until I have all the pieces on my chessboard. Tomorrow I shall visit an old friend who might provide the most important one." His blue eyes locked on her. "Now pray do throw those filthy tatters off your person. We need some sleep, and I have no inclination to share the bed with a street urchin."

She laughed and wrapped her arms around his bare chest, standing on her tiptoes to kiss him.

15

The dull light of the dawn overlapped with the electric bulbs and the lamps still lit on the tables and in the wall sconces, rendering their glow almost invisible. A tangled heap of wires lay in disarray on the main workbench and on the floor of the Doctors Order's laboratory, mingled with brass parts scattered all over the place, making it look like a battlefield rather than an experiment room. An acrid stench of burnt metal and smoke wafted in the air, defying the nostrils and the leather mask and watering the eyes of the only person in the room.

Annabella Hammond took out her goggles and her mask and inhaled deeply, oblivious to the pungent odour she was carrying into her lungs – and to the utter state of dishevelment she was in after a full night spent working at the Inspectorates. Underneath her filthy canvas apron, the black mourning dress she wore concealed the stains well, but her face and hair were an entirely different affair. Her carefully arranged locks had partially come loose, and her left cheek bore the traces of sooty fingers that had repeatedly tucked erratic strands behind her ear.

But who cared about such insignificant details when she had a victory to celebrate – and what a long-awaited one that was.

Between the voltmeter and the multimeter, her open notebook displayed the data she had been seeking for months. The right frequency, voltage, circuit length, and material. That night, she had finally reached *results*. She had sent word to Ledburry, regardless of the hour – and of Oscar's warning about the Doctors Order's Senior Lord. It was a risk worth taking, she had thought. She had worked for too many years on Humautomaton and needed to see it done. Besides, in all probability, Oscar had exaggerated a little, out of concern for her.

The Earl of Ledburry entering the laboratory stopped the train of her thoughts. "So it is finally done."

"It is," she said, her face beaming. "My circuits are ready for the final tests."

"Most excellent. The Chemists Order have already perfected the anaesthetic we need, so we can start the trials soon. I shall arrange with my hospital to provide a human test subject."

Annabella clenched her fists. Whilst she had shared her results with Ledburry, she did not trust him. "My condition remains. Our subject must *willingly* agree to take part in the trial."

The earl nodded. "I shall schedule the test surgery as soon as possible. Expect word from me in a few days."

"Damnation!" Jasper threw the newspaper across his workshop and hit the workbench's tabletop with both fists, forgetting about the food Mrs Carraway had left for him on the breakfast tray along with the blasted paper.

He was in no mood for breakfast. A thin veil of red blurred his vision, his head throbbing with the intensity of his rage. Slamming the workshop's front door behind him, he strode towards the Blackfriars Bridge skystation, too incensed to feel the cool wind that carried the smell of impending rain.

Disobeying a direct order from the Chief Inspector of the Classified Affairs Office had proven a terrible mistake. He should have followed his brother's strict instructions for the test flight. If he closed his eyes, he could still see Edmund's handwriting on the plain sheet of paper.

You are not to disclose the test flight date to other people than the three persons who are your crew for the aforementioned endeavour. Under no circumstances, regardless of the unexpected situations or requests that might occur.

Yet he'd chosen to dismiss Edmund's orders. His *superior's* orders. What was worse, Edmund had disappeared, and Jasper had no clue how to undo the damage he had so unwisely provoked.

All because he wanted to show his team that they could trust him. That he valued their work. He ran his hand through his unruly black curls.

What a fool I've been.

He found some space to read the bloody article again in the crowded gondotram on his way to the airharbour, his mind filled with thoughts of murder against the entire staff of *The Londoners' Journal.*

In the early hours of the day after tomorrow, all Londoners are invited to the airharbour to watch the test flight of Her Majesty's new, long-awaited airship, The Cerulean Lady. *We daresay such an event is not one to be missed, as the exquisite craft will proudly represent our country at the most prestigious engineering event in the world. What a surprise to see her shine before the official opening of the Gathering!*

At the *Lady's* hangar, Ivy and Avery welcomed him with an eyebrow raised and a confused expression.

"Have you finally lost your mind?" Ivy asked with a frown. "Why did you send the test flight date to the newspapers?"

"Hayes was here earlier, fuming like a steam train," Avery added. "Said we can't ask him to prepare the airharbour for a public event in such a short time."

"This is precisely the problem! The test flight was not supposed to be a public event!" Instead of subsiding, Jasper's anger had increased tenfold. "I did not send such information to the newspapers. How stupid do you think I am? Where the bloody hell is Elmstone?"

Robert Elmstone appeared in his field of vision before Ivy or Avery could reply. Oblivious to the other men who had stopped working to watch his outburst, Jasper strode to the engineer, grabbed his shirt and planted his fist on his jaw with all the strength he could muster.

Elmstone spat, reeling from the blow. "Care to tell me what I did to deserve that?"

"You leaked secret information to that blasted journal, this is what you did, you bloody cur!"

"I'm afraid I have no idea what you are talking about. Perhaps we should talk when you are in a less agitated state of mind and –"

Jasper gripped the man's shirt and collar with one hand. "Listen here, you rot! You were the only one outside my test team who had this information, which I revealed to you yesterday. And you gave it to that filthy scandal sheet!"

"I was not aware that the date of the test flight was secret information." Elmstone's unperturbed tone made Jasper want to punch him again. "I believed that the people had the right to be informed. And I still believe that regardless of the pathetic fits you throw."

"You have overstepped your boundaries and betrayed my trust," Jasper hissed. "I hope you received good compensation for what you did, for you are not in the Engineerium's employ anymore. Leave at once."

The engineer opened his mouth to say something, but left the hangar without another word.

"What are you going to do? Ivy asked, concern shadowing her face. "Will you choose another date for the test flight?"

Edmund would have known. Where is he? Where the bloody hell is he?

"We'll proceed as planned," he finally said, his shoulders sagging under the weight of his decision. "Attracting the public's hostility right before the Engineers World Gathering would be an ill-advised idea. We'll fly the *Lady* the morning after tomorrow."

A NIGHT of restful sleep after too many tiresome days had managed to dissipate the haze that had clouded Edmund's mind. Added to that, the freshness of the bright late spring morning sharpened his senses and lifted his spirit, making him more aware of his surroundings and more certain about the course of action he had decided to take.

He arrived at Place des Vosges early enough to still find his host at home, and late enough for his visit to be considered appropriate. Monsieur Antoine Laforet, the French Republic's Officer for Secret Affairs, lodged at No. 21 in the red brick building that lined all four edges of the city's oldest and, arguably, one of the most fashionable squares. Carmina followed at a short distance. Dressed as a respectable Parisian lady, she was walking around the square with her parasol open and her eyes upon the entrance where the servant was just closing the door after receiving the unexpected guest.

One slight nod in her direction, then Edmund climbed the stairs to his French counterpart's private study.

"Wyverstone, I am rather surprised to see you here." Laforet, a tall, thin man in his late forties with an austere countenance and a slightly receding hairline, welcomed him in heavily accented, grammatically perfect English, a worried frown creasing his wide forehead. "I do hope you happened to be in town and thought of visiting an old friend. Though, knowing you, I'm afraid it's quite the opposite. You are in town because something happened. Something important enough for you to seek my assistance."

Edmund took the glass of cognac he was offered, grateful for the direct approach so typical for Laforet. "Are you familiar with the United Confederation of Engineers?" he asked, watching the French's spymaster reaction to his question. He had been trained to read the slightest expressions, as was the case with the almost invisible lift of an eyebrow which came and went in the span of a second, the only sign of surprise on his host's face.

Yet the man said nothing.

"You should know that it would be in your best interest –" A pause. "In our countries' best interest not to hide anything, for I am in the possession of quite compromising documents, which are already on their way to London. You have two options: help me and avoid a diplomatic disaster or decline my request for help and risk a war France would lose."

Edmund took a slow sip of the amber drink, waiting for the other man's answer, betraying nothing of the uncertainty and restlessness he felt. He had taken a daring wager, one he was not certain he would win.

"When the English came up with this plan, I opposed it," Laforet finally said, his expression as unreadable and collected as Edmund's. "Strongly, bitterly. I opposed it because I was fed up with wars and useless death and loss, of which we'd had too much. But the prime minister dismissed my arguments as cowardice. He believed that it would be a chance for France to rise again and show her power to the world. Of course, nobody dared contradict the most powerful man in the country."

He started pacing around the study, his hands clasped at his back, his glass of cognac forgotten on the edge of his mahogany desk. In the bright light of the morning invading the room through the tall windows, his short blond hair looked almost white.

"The English wanted to create a powerful alliance that would replace the old order with a new one," the French spymaster continued. "That meant the reign of technology instead of the aristocracy. I was the only one who did not want France involved in such a conspiracy."

"You should have told me," Edmund said. "You should have sent word to the Classified Affairs, and we could have worked together to stop this insanity. Sedition is quite a serious offence."

"I could not betray my country," Laforet replied, his sharp voice leaving no room for argument. I am allowed to have a different opinion, but not to disobey orders."

"And what made you disobey orders now?"

"You are already in the possession of the very information I have been ordered to protect, so I have no choice but to help you," the French spymaster replied. "What are your intentions?"

Edmund let out a breath he did not know he was holding. He had always respected Laforet for his brilliant mind, for the way he could turn a dire situation in his favour.

"I shall destroy that nest of vipers and arrest everyone involved from the English side," he said. "But I'm afraid I cannot arrest a peer of the realm with what I have now. I need real evidence of sedition. Which brings me to the main reason for my visit."

Laforet stopped pacing, leaning against the wall near the window. "I can provide the evidence you so much need. But it comes with a cost."

Of course. Just as expected from Antoine Laforet.

"My country will not be held accountable for anything. I'll give you Maurice Gervaise as the only scapegoat, and that will have to suffice. I want no unnecessary turmoil in France."

"Agreed." Edmund knew better than to try to persuade the French spymaster further than the compromise he had just secured. A rather fair one, given that France could not continue the sedition plan without English help. "But I have one more request. I need your help to catch Benedict Quimby. I doubt you want such a dangerous man lurking on French territory. As I recall, I have already asked for your assistance in that matter."

"Fear not, Wyverstone. Benedict Quimby will be delivered to you soon." He installed himself in the leather armchair behind the desk, his face still as unreadable as a blank sheet of paper. "I cannot give you the evidence of our government's involvement directly, for that would be treason. But you might find some interesting items in the Foreign Archives, in the underground vault of the National Archives near Hôtel de Ville. Search on the fourth shelf, box 247."

"Thank you." Edmund rose and walked towards the study's door, stopping for a moment before opening it. "Oh, one more thing. If you want the French team not to lose face at the Engineers World Gathering, you should send *L'Étoile* to London."

The Frenchman nodded in agreement, and Edmund saw himself out.

"What shall we do next?" Carmina asked after he finished his account, her lace-gloved hand daintily placed in the crook of his arm. To any unsuspecting onlooker, they passed as just another couple enjoying the beautiful weather in Place des Vosges.

"How about a lovely promenade around Hôtel de Ville, my lady?" A mischievous grin brightened his face, promptly attracting Carmina's suspicious gaze.

"Of course, my lord. So long as I am informed about the specificities of such an endeavour, which I suspect are not exactly of romantic nature."

Edmund stopped for a moment, his eyes locked with hers,

his amusement gone. "We need to find a way to break into the Foreign Archives' building, for tonight I must perform a thorough search in this illustrious institution."

~

A FEW HOURS and a thorough inspection of the National Archives' exterior later, Edmund and Carmina were back to their rooms, reluctantly admitting that the building was a rather unbreachable fortress. The air vents were far too high to be accessible from the street. The windows of the cellar and coal rooms, secured with thick iron bars, were not an option either.

"I doubt we missed anything." Carmina followed Edmund to their bedchamber, stopping at the entrance to the dressing room. "We searched every inch of that building, and, as I see it, the only way to get inside is through the front door."

"Which is exactly what I shall do. I shall use the front door, mingle with the people inside, find a spot to hide and stay there until nightfall when most of the building will be empty."

"*I*?" Carmina asked, watching him rummage through his travel trunk. "Not *we*?"

"Yes, I." Edmund extracted a few pieces of clothing that would have made his valet cringe in despair and started undressing. Black trousers slightly too short, a cotton shirt and a waistcoat in colours as dull as London's weather, and a coat a few years out of fashion, quite the opposite from the perfectly tailored garments he usually favoured. "You must return to England, so I shall arrange for your immediate departure with the first passenger airship bound for London."

Carmina walked into the dressing room. "Why did you come to Paris?"

He stilled, his shirt half down his bare torso. "I had planned to join you when you found Quimby. But the article in *The*

Londoners' Journal made me change my mind and come earlier to make sure you were safe."

"So you would understand if I did the same," Carmina said as he continued with the appalling trousers. "For this precise reason, I am staying with you."

"No, you are not." Edmund's sharp voice signalled a non-negotiable order from the Classified Affairs' Chief Inspector. "You must bring the documents to London and hand them to Herdforthbridge, in the unlikely but not completely impossible case that anything happens to me. I cannot risk both of us being caught, and the documents taken from us. You possess the necessary intelligence to understand the enormous consequences of such a scenario. It would mean disaster not only for the two of us but also for the Classified Affairs and probably for England."

"Then let us return together." Carmina came closer, helping him into his coat. "We already have plenty of evidence."

"We have plenty indeed, yet not enough. I need clear evidence of sedition. Otherwise, I cannot arrest Ledburry and Hydenhollow. I am too close to that piece of evidence, and I do not intend to leave until I have it. If I cannot arrest those two traitors, the Engineers World Gathering risks turning into a disaster, with the Royals' lives under threat."

"Let me do it," she said, her green eyes pleading. "I shall infiltrate the Archives, and you take the documents to London."

"Carmina, this is my own battle, and I must fight it myself." He cupped her cheek, a bitter smile blossoming in a corner of his lips. "Besides, I missed field work."

She nodded. "All right. I shall return to London tonight. But you must promise me you'll not let yourself murdered on foreign lands."

Edmund didn't reply. He held her in his arms for a few long moments, relishing in the comfortable silence, in the subtle cinnamon fragrance of her skin, in the peace of those stolen seconds before the final act of his too long a performance began.

Less than half an hour later, they were on their way to the airharbour, the documents safely tucked inside Carmina's corset.

"My flight for London is at seven in the evening," she said, glancing around at the passengers roaming about the airships moored across the vast expanse of land. "I'll manage. You should be on your way."

Dressed as a province clerk no one cared about, Edmund entered the imposing building of the National Archives through the front door, mingling with the crowd of people, walking purposefully until he found a secluded alcove behind a small wooden door near the service stairs. He crouched there and took out his pocket watch.

They would all leave soon.

CARMINA WIPED the otherwise clean porthole beside her seat with the back of her hand, staring through the oval glass at the busy expanse of the Paris airharbour, whose end vanished into the distant red sunset. She watched as the other passengers climbed the metal steps to the berth's landing, without actually seeing anything, her mind travelling to an unsafe, unwanted territory.

Return to London and protect the documents. She was well too aware of the consequences of not following a strict order, of risking the success of a mission. And yet –

Her intuition screamed at her not to go, humming in her head louder than the voices of the airship's crew announcing the take off for London. In less than five minutes, it would be too late.

The documents felt rigid against the thin fabric of her

chemise underneath her corset. What she was about to do would have consequences. Her decision meant disobeying a direct order from the Office of Classified Affairs' Chief Inspector, perhaps even putting her country in danger. So be it. At least she'd have no regrets.

Something is not right. The French would never allow Edmund to leave with compromising evidence against them. They would never let him leave the Archives alive.

And no matter his training and skill, he was alone.

Protecting England's spymaster came first, no matter her orders.

Extending a mental apology to the rest of the passengers who would need to wait until they were cleared for departure again, she pulled her travel trunk from under her seat and hurried towards the airship's closest door and out on the berth.

When the airship finally left the airharbour to carry her passengers to London, Carmina was already on her way back to their lodgings on Rue du Temple.

Unlike her rooms at Madame Blanchet's, a speakerbox had been installed for their convenience on the sideboard in the parlour. Keeping her trunk close to extract the garments for her disguise with one hand, she dialled the London airharbour's code with the other.

"Good afternoon, Mr Hayes. Would you be so kind as to let me speak with one of your engineers? It's Miss Harcourt for Mr Kendall Asher." Her sweet voice promptly sent Hadrian Hayes to the *Lady*'s hangar without any other questions.

"Send Miss Blackwell with *The Skycradle* to Paris and ask Herdforthbridge to make the arrangements with the airharbour," she instructed as soon as she heard Jasper's voice at the other end of the line.

"I might think about it if you explain what the devil is going on." A mixture of confusion and anger laced his tone.

"I have little time for explanations," Carmina said. "Pray,

trust me and do as I ask. I need *The Skycradle* here in three hours."

Jasper let out a long, frustrated breath. "All right. Do you need me as well? Or the duke? Should we come with Ivy?"

As tempted as she was to accept, she could not do it. Jasper had to prepare for the test flight, and the duke would marry her sister in a few days. She had no right to risk their lives for her own choices.

"No," she said. "Miss Blackwell and her assistant would be enough. Instruct them to moor at the airharbour and wait for us."

"For *us*? Edmund is with you, ain't he? Why didn't he make this request himself?"

"Because he could not," she said, her voice tight. "Edmund is just about to break into the Foreign Archives of the French Republic."

16

Herdforthbridge said nothing. Seated in the comfortable leather armchair behind the desk in his private study, he listened to Jasper's almost incoherent account of his speakerbox conversation with Carmina Harcourt, trying to extract a dose of meaning from his visitor's inarticulate rendition.

Jasper stopped pacing about the room, halting in front of the duke. He took a deep breath, while Herdforthbridge waited for him to finish.

When he spoke again, his voice was back to normal. Almost. "Breaking into another country's archives is a serious offence. One that could lead to a diplomatic conflict. I hope you understand that."

"Edmund knows what he is doing," the duke said, content that Jasper's coherence had returned to some extent, along with the possibility of rational dialogue. "He would not undertake such a risky endeavour unless he is searching for something important. Some evidence of sedition, perhaps?"

"I'll go to France with Ivy." Jasper resumed his pacing about the study, wringing his hands, his voice trembling with something the duke recognised as dread. "My brother is in danger. I need to save him."

"I doubt Edmund needs saving." The duke rose and opened the glass door of the cabinet where he kept the brandy decanter. "Drink this. It should help with bouts of hysteria." He filled a snifter and handed it to Jasper. "Edmund will not have Jade's fate. Your erratic conduct is out of place."

He waited until Jasper regained his composure before he spoke again. "You have your own assignments to attend to. The *Lady*'s test flight is the day after tomorrow. You'll see to that, and I'll arrange for Miss Blackwell's flight to Paris." He glanced at the mantel clock. "And I should do it now. I fear time is not in our favour."

FROM THE WINDOWLESS corner where he was hiding, Edmund could not see whether it was day or night. He took out his pocket watch and checked the time at the light of the lantern he carried inside his coat along with a paralysis pistol.

Half past eight. The clerks should be gone by now.

Or at least most of them.

No sound came from the other side of the door. Edmund inserted the amplifier in his ear and listened intently for a few more minutes to make sure no one was around, before emerging on the dimly lit corridor.

Keeping the paralysis pistol at hand, he followed the mental map he had memorised while crossing the hallways and public halls hours earlier, careful to avoid the rooms whose doors were open or ajar. He was aware of the activity still going on in some offices of the National Archives, and of the risk his presence entailed. But he had already gone too far to change his mind or strategy.

The round marble stairs shielded by an intricate wrought iron banister snaked downwards in complete darkness. Edmund cursed inwardly and descended below the ground level, one hand on the railing, all his senses alert.

When he reached the last step of the staircase, he lit his pocket lantern, casting a barely visible glow in the cold, empty vault. An old former prison actively used during the Revolution, the Archives' arched basement kept a strong smell of ancient stone and rusted metal. Several doors lined the long walls, each with its own label.

At the opposite end of the gallery, the smallest, most unassuming door marked the entrance to the *Archives des Affaires Étrangères*. Finding the door had been easy. Picking the lock, however, proved a more difficult endeavour than Edmund had expected. He worked slowly, his attention divided between the cumbersome task and the gallery, halting whenever the faintest noise pierced through the overwhelming silence.

Several failed attempts later, the door finally gave in, and the room revealed itself under Edmund's lantern. Ornate wrought-iron shelves and cabinets lined the walls, each filled with metal boxes arranged in perfect numerical order. A row of plain wooden desks and benches crossed the space through the middle. Above the shelves, the electric bulbs set into wall sconces complemented the long candelabra hanging from the vaulted ceiling over the desks.

Box 247, the French spymaster had said.

Edmund pulled out the rectangular case, grateful for the orderly arrangement of the shelves' contents, and extracted the only item he found inside. He frowned, wondering whether Laforet had ridiculed him or set a trap, only to realise that the thick document he was holding included the information he needed.

He read the same paragraphs twice, in both French and English, as if to make sure the sentences glaring at him in black ink were not the product of his imagination.

At the bottom of the page, the signatures of the French prime minister, the French Minister of Development and Technology, Benedict Quimby, the Earl of Ledburry, and Baron Hydenhollow sealed the document.

Edmund leafed through to the last pages of the agreement.

Images of *The Golden Griffin* and the broken gondotram in Holborn returned from the depths of his memories. But he had no time for idle thoughts. Time was running out.

He folded the papers and tucked them inside his coat, starting towards the door.

The screech of a metal door opening stopped him in his tracks, allowing him only an instant to shove his lantern into a pocket and hide behind a shelf before a murky glow lit the room again.

"Well, well, I should congratulate myself." A loud masculine voice reverberated in the vaulted room, a voice which Edmund recognised as belonging to Edwin Sheridan. "Who'd have thought I'd tail the fearsome British spymaster without making myself noticed? Or maybe you ain't that good. Doesn't matter. That French imbecile thinks he helped you but helped me instead. You're trapped in here."

Edmund bit his lip, trying to ignore the debilitating pain inflicted by the augmented sound. No matter how much he needed to hear the noises outside, if he wanted to keep his sanity, he had to take out the contraption.

He froze with his fingers on the small device as the amplifier carried another sound inside his ear. *"Edmund, are you still here?"*

Damnation! Why can't you, for once, do what you are told? Why are you not in that bedevilled airship to England? Why the bloody hell are you here?

But he had no time to argue. He had to send her away before Sheridan spoke again and she heard and realised what was happening.

Before Sheridan found him.

Edmund opened his mouth to whisper something, but no words came out, his mind quicker than his lips. He could not dismiss her like that, not when they worked as a team again. As equals.

Together, they might have a better chance to win the mad game his mind had just concocted. From where he stood, he saw Sheridan's revolver. Six bullets at most. He only had to lure the madman into a merry chase and make him waste all of them. Then he could confront him directly. Instinctively, he clutched his paralysis pistol, which he could not use from such an angle and distance.

He coughed and took one step into the room, prompting Sheridan to pull the trigger. And miss.

Five bullets left.

Sheridan pointed the revolver in the direction Edmund had lured him. "Your Lordship, I was eager to meet you again and settle our old debt. Pity it will be the last encounter you and I will ever have."

‍～

W‌ITH HER LONG black curls spilling over her back from under a white cotton bonnet, wearing a simple blue dress, and carrying a basket of freshly baked bread, no one took Carmina for anything other than a young bakery girl. When she arrived at the French National Archives, it was already night. The building stood silent and dark, with only a few windows lit.

Some clerks were still working regardless of the late hour. She had counted on that.

Putting on her most innocent smile, she entered and found herself face to face with a large man in his early thirties.

"This is not a place for young girls to visit," he said, his eyes inspecting her from head to toe. "At night, day or any other time. Leave."

"But, monsieur, you can't do this!" Her eyes were brimming with unshed tears. "My mistress sent me with these." She removed the cotton towel, letting the fragrance of fresh bakery waft around them. "Said it's for the brave people who work for us and our country until late. They deserve a loaf of fresh bread." She tore a piece and handed it to the doorman. "See for yourself how good it is."

The delicious taste of fresh bread, in addition to her green eyes staring imploringly at him while batting her eyelashes, had the desired effect. A few minutes later, she was descending the round staircase to the arched basement of the building, frantically searching for the entrance to the Foreign Archives.

If he was still inside, he would have his ear amplifier with him.

"Edmund, are you still here?"

Silence.

"Edmund, if you are here, answer me. Please."

The same overwhelming silence, broken seconds later by the unfamiliar voice of a man.

"Your Lordship, I was eager to meet you again and settle our old debt. Pity it will be the last encounter you and I will ever have."

Carmina stilled, aware of the danger Edmund was in, of the limited time she had before the doorman realised something was amiss and started searching for the brazen bakery girl, and of her need to understand what was happening. She followed the direction of the voice until she discovered the door to the Foreign Archives.

Edmund's voice carried through the amplifier into her ear. *"Do you have the slightest idea what you involved yourself in?"* He sounded calm, as if he had everything under control. *"Your irrational quest for revenge could put the entire country in danger."*

"I don't give a bloody farthing about a country that treated me like rot in a slum's court. After I lost my arm because Your Lordship decided in my place it was the best thing to do, I led a vermin's life. Do you have the slightest idea what a vermin's life is like?" A bitter, sinister laugh. *"You don't. These people pulled me out of the gutter and gave me a new purpose, so I'd serve them rather than the country. With a bit of luck, they will even give me my arm back. Though I grew tired of waiting for the Australian chit to finish her bloody work."*

"Quimby and his ilk are only using you," Edmund said, betraying no trace of fear or apprehension. *"You are nothing to them. They will discard you the second they decide they have no more need of you, which will happen sooner than you imagine. I have discovered their plot and sent plenty of evidence to London. Evidence of high treason that the office will use no matter what happens to me. Or perhaps you fancy replacing the life of a vermin with no life at all."*

The noise of a bullet exploded in Carmina's ear, making her wince with sharp pain and fear. Then the sound of metal hitting metal, and the other man's voice, whom she had identified as Edwin Sheridan. *"Bloody hell!"*

Carmina let out a breath she didn't know she was holding. *He missed. Edmund is safe.*

But they were too deep in the underground for anyone else

to hear. If she didn't distract the man, if she didn't help, Edmund's chances were slim. From the little information she could infer about what was going on inside, he could not use his paralysis pistol.

"I don't care about your damned evidence. Or about what those toffs are plotting." Sheridan's voice grew louder. *"I don't care to understand. I only want one of those mechanical arms and revenge against the man who destroyed my life. Fair enough, ain't it? But they are dragging on with their mechanical limbs, and I've lost my patience, you know? So I decided to take my revenge first, then wait for the toffs to finish their bloody experiments with those opium eaters."*

Carmina wiped her sweat-covered palms on her cotton skirts. *Experiments? Opium eaters?*

Another bullet. This time, followed by the sound of splintered wood.

Another miss. And Edmund's voice, as cold as ever.

"It would be in your best interest to surrender." A short pause. *"I have the power to help you – provided that you cooperate, of course. You should give me that revolver before you do something that might put a rope around your neck."*

Sheridan's reply came in a hoarse tone, half mockery and half annoyance. Missing his target again must have distressed him. *"You keep your power, and I keep my revenge. I lived these past years only to watch you die by my hand, to open your belly and see your guts spill in the gutter. Your Lordship, you can't hide forever behind those bloody shelves. And when you come out, I swear on the Devil's own name you won't leave this place alive."*

Carmina breathed deeply, trying to calm herself.

She had to find another way to enter and distract Sheridan, who had a revolver and enough patience to wait for Edmund to emerge from whatever place he was hiding.

But no stone in the pavement moved, no brick in the wall

gave in under her palms, no other door stood close. There was only one way to get in.

Or *storm* in.

Her hand steady on her paralysis pistol, she pushed the door open with a loud metallic screech that made two things happen at the same time.

Edmund leapt from behind a tall shelf, no doubt to avoid Sheridan's attention – and revolver – turning upon her.

Sheridan pulled the trigger with the precision and viciousness of a man thirsty for revenge.

Carmina froze, her weapon sliding from her hand as Edmund dropped his paralysis pistol and fell on his knees, a grisly red stain darkening the left side of his waistcoat.

"No!" Carmina's voice echoed in the vaulted room, hollow and broken. "No! No!"

She ran towards the spot where Edmund lay crouched on the floor, almost reaching it before she fell in front of him, her limbs numb. In a blurry corner of her peripheral vision, a tall man who only had one arm was pointing her paralysis pistol in her direction.

Edmund stretched to grasp his own pistol, but Sheridan kicked it out of his reach, sending the last phial of Carmina's pistol into his leg. "Now, now, this is even more entertaining than I thought." His chilling laugh reverberated within the high stone walls. "How thrilling to have both of you here. Pity you won't live long enough to see the pretty surprise I prepared for you in England."

He stood before Edmund, towering over him. "I wanted to kill you right away, but now that your strumpet is here, I changed my mind. I'll kill her before your eyes. Slowly. And you'll feel every second of it."

Squatting near Carmina, he grabbed her hair and dragged her to him until her head was on his knees. "But I want her to feel something too. Wouldn't be fun to kill the chit knowing that blasted serum stopped the pain." He put the paralysis pistol on the floor and extracted a knife out of his coat's pocket.

Hatred darkened his eyes as he stared at Edmund, his hand at Carmina's neck. The blade traced a thin line on her skin from her jaw to her collarbone, leaving a trickle of blood in its wake. "She can feel pain here."

"Touch her again, and I swear on my father's grave it will be the last thing you will ever do." Edmund's hoarse voice trembled with dread, his composure wavering.

"Trouble is, Your Lordship, you can't threaten me. As you are now, you can't do anything but watch how I kill your lover."

Carmina bit her lip, mockery and defiance glittering in her green eyes. "You have exactly fifteen minutes to kill me, so you can only be that slow. Let us see how you fare."

"Brazen female!" The blade crossed her neck again, just above the collarbones, this time slightly deeper. Bright red blood smeared her skin.

Carmina clenched her teeth. She would not scream. And she would not die there. Not like that. Regardless of how mad that madman was.

Her eyes locked with Edmund's, and she understood how hard he was trying to cling to the last thread of sanity he possessed. He could not break. If one of them broke, they would die.

"Let her leave, and I shall help you escape. You stand no chance against the Classified Affairs."

"Your Lordship, it's too late for negotiations. I don't recall any negotiations when you decided to maim me. You and that bloody doctor of yours. This is my answer to your proposal." Sheridan's blade left a new red trail, this time on Carmina's cheek, down to the corner of her mouth. Blood covered half of her face and neck.

She swallowed hard, trying to ignore the pain. She would not scream. She would not show fear.

"Leave her alone, you damned bastard! It's me you want! Leave her!"

Sheridan's thumb traced an imaginary line underneath Carmina's eye. "Your Lordship, perhaps you would like to see how I pull out her eyes."

"Take your filthy hand off her!" Edmund screamed, the last trace of his composure gone, dark fear clouding his blue eyes. His black hair was plastered on his damp forehead and cheeks, dishevelled and wet with sweat. "Somebody! Is there no one left in this bloody building?"

"Your Lordship, no one will hear you. These dungeons are too deep and too far from the guards. But I'll give you her eyeballs as a keepsake. Until I kill you as well, that is."

Carmina's heart sank. They could not die like that. How many minutes since he had shot them? An eternity had passed already. And it was her fault. Had she not lost her temper when she saw Edmund falling before her eyes, they would have already been out of there, with Sheridan captured.

She saw the glint of Sheridan's knife coming to her face, heard Edmund's desperate scream. And instinctively closed her eyes.

That could not be the end. And yet –

She counted the seconds. One, two, three, four. No blade touched her.

In the silence that followed, Carmina slowly opened her eyes again. Above her, Herdforthbridge was holding Sheridan's arm in an iron grip, his blue eyes smouldering with rage.

"I apologise I came so late to the party. Though I must admit, I do not fancy such grisly social functions."

They had been too engrossed in their ordeal to notice the duke enter through the door Carmina had left open.

Sheridan stared at him with a bewildered look. "Where the devil did you come from?"

"I only use front doors," Herdforthbridge said in the despising tone he always employed with anyone who dared challenge his status and power. He turned to Edmund, flexing his fingers. "I punched my way here. Good exercise, that. I knocked the doorman senseless, but I suppose he will recover soon. We don't have too much time. Minutes, I would say."

He glanced around to have a quick grasp of the situation. "As I see, I have to choose between taking the two of you or this bloody cur out of here. I consider myself a rather strong man, but I cannot carry three people."

One fist in the gut sent Sheridan to the ground. "My valet will chastise me for this, but I believe you spurted enough vile for one night." The duke removed his perfectly knotted silk neckerchief and tied it around Sheridan's mouth, one knee firmly pressing the man's arm. "Now for the last touch." He collected Edmund's paralysis pistol and sent the phial into Sheridan's shoulder. "I shall alert the doorman about the intruder in their basement. After we leave this place."

"Rope," Carmina said. "You'll find a coil of rope in the pocket inside my skirt. Take it and tie that man lest he disappears as soon as the phial effect vanishes.'

"No," Edmund said. "Take Carmina and Sheridan. You cannot let him escape. I'll follow you back to London."

"I shall assume that your wound made you delirious," the duke said while grabbing the thin rope and tying Sheridan to a desk.

Supporting both Carmina and Edmund and dragging them out of the building in their still inert state, past the still unconscious doorman, proved a more challenging undertaking.

Once outside, Herdforthbridge pushed them into the

carriage that was waiting for him. He turned towards the coachman, one foot on the conveyance's step. "Go wake up that guard inside and tell him they have an uninvited guest in the basement, which he must deliver to the authorities. Then come back here and drive straight to the airharbour as fast as you can."

Minutes later, they were on their way to the Paris airharbour.

Carmina moved her fingers tentatively, then her legs. The phial's effect had started to recede. "I'm sorry. I bear the guilt for tonight's debacle. I should have not barged in like that. I should have let you act as you saw fit."

"You acted upon the first rule of the Classified Affairs, as any agent would have," Edmund said, his hand touching her cheek. "*The Chief Inspector never does field work and always keeps himself out of danger's way.* You wanted to protect me. I cannot blame you for following the code of conduct."

A corner of her lips curled in a bitter smile. She hadn't acted as an agent, but as a woman. And he knew that. Yet he still wanted her as his agent.

When they arrived at the airharbour, Herdforthbridge was already informed about the developments in Paris and the documents Carmina and Edmund had found. "With the evidence I have, I can arrest half of the Orders' Senior Lords," Edmund concluded. "Now I only need to catch Quimby with the French's help and protect the *Lady* from an attempt against Her Majesty's life. Without annulling the entire event."

The Skycradle's dark outline against the night sky brought them a sense of peace. Soon, they would be home. They alighted from the carriage, Edmund holding Carmina close to him, an arm wrapped around her shoulder protectively, without bothering to hide any longer. With the other, he held her scarf pressed against his wound.

"Your Grace, Your Lordship, Miss Harcourt!" Ivy Blackwell was perched over the berth's railing next to Avery Hamilton, watching them with wide eyes. "Have you escaped some battlefield?"

"Miss Blackwell, would you be so kind as to take off for London at once?" the duke said. "And pray do bring us some carbolic acid and bandages. Lots of them."

~

"That sorrowful set are making sure I cannot arrest them. I did not expect them to move so fast, which is rather an alarming development." Edmund folded the newspaper he had been reading until a moment ago and put it on the small coffee table in Herdforthbridge's breakfast room, a gloomy expression on his otherwise unreadable face. His physician, Carlisle, whom he had summoned in the dead of night, had dressed his and Carmina's wounds and assured them they were only superficial lacerations.

They had arrived in London past midnight, and both he and Carmina had spent the night at the duke's townhouse to avoid waking up their own staff at that hour and in their wounded and dishevelled state. After their mishaps from the night before, they had awakened to equally unpleasant news.

Edmund paced around the small parlour, his elbow propped on one hand and his chin on the other, his face still pale. "If one newspaper praises Ledburry and Hydenhollow as the leading scientists of the country, others will certainly follow. And since I am everyone's favourite villain after that article in *The Londoners' Journal*, arresting Ledburry and Hydenhollow would only bring even more hate upon my head. But a bloody article won't stop me from doing the right thing."

Herdforthbridge took the newspaper and opened it again, reading aloud. "*Without a doubt, Humautomaton will change medicine as we know it today. This ground-breaking discovery, for which all of us should be grateful to their lordships the Earl of*

Ledburry and Baron Hydenhollow, will restore hope to all the hopeless men, women and children who lost a limb and, thus, had their lives upended. We are not wrong to say that the laboratories of the Doctors Order and Chemists Order are the saviours of these unfortunate people."

"Saviours of these unfortunate people," the duke repeated. "This is bad. Seeing those two elevated to saints in the public eye is nothing short of disgusting."

"Annabella couldn't have chosen a worse moment to complete her damned circuits," Edmund said. "Had her work been still in progress, the newspapers would not have been filled with news about Humautomaton and praise for Ledburry and Hydenhollow."

Herdforthbridge ran a hand through his golden curls. "I did try to stop her, for her own safety. But you know how stubborn she can be, and I respect her enough to not interfere with her work." His forehead creased in a frown. "However, it was rather surprising to notice that the article failed to mention the Engineers Order and Annabella's name. Which is odd, given that she was the brain of this experiment, and the Engineers Order started the project. Not the Doctors Order or the Chemists Order. This doesn't sit well with me."

"A smart move, that one," Edmund said, leaning against one side of the tall window overlooking the street. "I believe the article's intention was not to praise Humautomaton, but to cast an angelic light upon Ledburry and Hydenhollow after exposing me as a corrupt official. Turning those two into heroes will make it considerably harder for me to arrest them, even with the incriminating documents I've brought from Paris."

"There is more to this," Carmina said, returning her empty teacup to the saucer. "The Engineers World Gathering is the most anticipated event in the country, on the Continent, and far beyond. London is already ready for it, and a large public is expected to attend. In such circumstances, a scandal involving peers of the realm who are so esteemed in the public eye would scar the event, and England would risk being held accountable by the participating countries for not solving its problems before the Gathering. Especially since we had a full year to do so after Quimby's war airship had been discovered." She looked at Edmund. "I believe you should not arrest them now lest you'll create a stir I am not fully certain you can contain."

"All right," Edmund agreed after a few moments of heavy silence. "I have no intention to throw London into chaos. But I must take all necessary precautions to thwart whatever plot they have concocted for the Gathering." He started towards the door. "I must leave now. Urgent matters to attend to at the Inspectorates. Starting with finding those explosives they intend to use."

"You should go home and rest, as Carlisle suggested," the duke said. "That wound is not exactly a scratch."

An unexpected knock at the door didn't leave Edmund time to answer. Herdforthbridge's valet, Jervis, appeared in the parlour, a newspaper in his hand.

"Pardon me for the intrusion, Your Grace, but I thought you might want to see this," the man said, handing him the paper. "A special edition of *The Londoners' Journal*, which might trigger quite a scandal if not handled quickly and promptly."

The duke eyed him with a contemptuous look without taking the newspaper. "This newly found inclination of yours towards Society's gossip almost forces me to reconsider your staying into my service. I believe I have made you aware in no uncertain terms and more than once of my repulsion towards such matters. Particularly towards that journal."

"Your Grace, scandals are of no interest to me. But since this is about His Lordship the Earl of Wyverstone, I thought Your Grace and His Lordship would want to read."

Herdforthbridge grabbed the newspaper and started reading

the article his valet had indicated, his face turning all shades of livid as he progressed.

When he finished, he passed it to Carmina. "This time, that scandal sheet went too far. Such an attempt to vilify Edmund against Ledburry and Hydenhollow is unacceptable, especially since it drags the good name of my future wife's family through the mud. I shall make sure they will not spew such filthy lies again."

No muscle moved on Carmina's face while she read. Her green gaze betrayed no emotion as she put the journal on the tea table, its black letters visible to everyone.

In our relentless quest to be the most reliable information source for our esteemed readers, we are faithful to our promise to bring to your attention our latest discoveries regarding an important personage in charge of our nation's safety. But first, we must reveal another piece of astounding news, this time about the eldest offspring of the late Marquess of Windstoneham. For years, the family has been mourning the untimely loss of their beloved daughter, whom they thought dead in an ill-fated carriage accident. What would Lady Windstoneham say had she found out Miss Rebecca Beatrix Hammond was alive? What would Her Ladyship say had she found out her eldest daughter has extended her patronage upon an infamous house of ill-repute, relinquishing her respectable name and going under the sobriquet of Carmina Harcourt? What would Her Ladyship say had she found out Miss Rebecca Beatrix Hammond has been involved for years in an illicit liaison with the Earl of Wyverstone?

Carmina spoke at last. "No, duke, these are not lies. I truly am Annabella's sister."

Herdforthbridge gaped and tried to say something, but no sound came out of his open mouth, his shocked gaze holding Carmina's.

"They even used our full names," Edmund said, anger burning in his eyes. "Worry not. I shall try to stop this news from spreading."

"Please, do not." Carmina rose and smoothed her skirts, her voice calm. "I have always been prepared for this day. Besides, every household in town must have read that newspaper by now. No respectable member of London's Society would miss a special edition of *The Londoners' Journal*, would they not? Now I must take my leave. I need to return to the Dove."

17

From where he stood at the entrance to the Inspectorates, Jasper saw his brother alight from the mechanical horse-drawn carriage and walk the few steps left towards the building with a slight limp, his face tense and ashen.

"When I found the door to your office closed, I hoped you wouldn't come at all," Jasper said, standing to meet Edmund. "You shouldn't be here. Carlisle recommended a few days of rest if you want your wound healed."

Edmund frowned. Whether it was a grimace of annoyance or of pain, Jasper couldn't say. "Perhaps I should release my physician from service for blabbering useless things to everyone around me."

"You shouldn't have left as you did." Jasper followed him inside the building, walking slower than usual. "I had no way to reach you when I needed your help."

Edmund's every step across the main foyer was a fight against pain. He turned to Jasper. "I had no choice."

"I'm sorry," Jasper said, careful to lower his voice as they passed the people entering or leaving the building. "It's my fault that the test flight day became public knowledge. I should have been more cautious."

"I doubt anything will happen during the test flight," Edmund said while they were going up the stairs to the Classified Affairs' office on the second floor. "They intend to destroy the royal airship when Her Majesty is inside, and not before. But I shall not allow that."

Jasper glanced at the dull daylight coming through the tall curtainless windows, at the thick clouds blanketing the sky with the promise of rain. "Everyone is now debating whether a corrupt official such as the Earl of Wyverstone is fit to protect the country. It is all a trap, and this morning's article in *The Londoners' Journal* is enough proof of that."

Edmund stopped in front of his office's door to unlock it. "I hate it that they dragged Carmina through this mess. I hate to see her life and secrets exposed in such a manner. They harass her because of me."

Jasper understood his brother's frustration. Carmina Harcourt was one of the most discreet and private people he knew.

"What are you planning to do?" But his question remained unanswered. They entered Edmund's office, only to freeze in the doorframe.

Fear not, Wyverstone. Benedict Quimby will be delivered to you soon. The French spymaster's words took a whole new meaning in Edmund's mind.

"Bloody hell," he muttered. "They *did* deliver Quimby to me. Quite literally."

On Edmund's leather armchair behind his desk, arms hanging inert and eyes wide open in an expressionless stare, sat Benedict Quimby.

Dead.

～

A NOTE LAY on the desk, with only one sentence written on it.

"*Disposable material*," Edmund read, staring in turn at the dead man's cadaverous face and the small piece of paper in his hand.

He returned the note onto his desk and proceeded to do a quick inspection of the lifeless body of the former Senior Lord of the Engineers Order.

"Poison," he said after a short while. "Perhaps something from the Chemists Order's laboratories."

"This affair is turning nastier by the hour." Jasper stared at Benedict Quimby with a grimace of horror and disgust. "To murder that bloody bastard and plant his blasted corpse in your office is quite a clear statement."

"It is," Edmund agreed. "Now I understand why this morning's article omitted the Engineers Order and Annabella's names. She completed the circuits, so she became disposable material as well. Their message is clear. If she does any wrong move, she will be next. They blackmail us to keep themselves safe until their plot succeeds and the actual ruling system is overturned."

"Greedy bastards!" Jasper clenched his fists. "They seem to forget how difficult it was for the Reform to pass. And now they risk destroying everything the Orders have accomplished in the last ten years."

Everyone in England knew about the heated debate that had lasted for almost a year and changed the former ruling system eleven years before. Society had been divided, with many aristocrats opposing the proposal of a joint rule shared between the Royals and the Orders, for the sake of the country's technological advancement. The Marquess of Windstoneham had been among the fiercest opponents of the infamous bill, while Benedict Quimby, the Earl of Ledburry, Baron Hydenhollow, and Theophilus Hollingsworth had been among its fiercest supporters. In the end, the advocates of the technocratic monarchy had won, and the High Orders of

Sciences and Crafts had been born under the auspices of the Royal House, much to the delight of the aristocrats geared towards scientific experimentation and discovery.

"If you arrest them, you risk Annabella's life."

"I know." Edmund's voice was eerily calm. His pensive gaze settled on the droplets of rain crashing into the window. "The only way I can arrest Ledburry, Hydenhollow, and their sorrowful set is to find real evidence I can relate to their assassination plot against Her Majesty. If I have something to support the information in the documents I found in Paris, those traitors are mine."

"I can be of help," Jasper offered.

"No. You need to prepare for tomorrow's test flight. Half of my agents are already scurrying about London in search of undeclared large quantities of explosives. Herdforthbridge and I shall join them soon."

Jasper's blue eyes widened. "You? Doing fieldwork? That's against the Classified Affairs' rules."

"Everything I have done as of late was against the rules," Edmund said, unperturbed. He turned to look at the ghoulish delivery again. "Now, I believe we should clear up this morbid mess."

Herdforthbridge leafed through the papers his solicitor had prepared for his upcoming nuptials without really reading, his mind addled after the events of the previous night and following morning, trying to organise everything in neat compartments in his brain and understand what was at stake and the course of action he had to take.

A brief walk would help him clear his thoughts, he decided.

He stood and started towards the door of his private study at the exact same moment when said door opened and Annabella entered with the swiftness and chaos of a hurricane in a swish of black silk, with his butler in tow.

"My lady, please allow me to announce –"

"That would be all." The duke signalled his butler to leave them alone, which the man promptly did.

Herdforthbridge needed just one second to assess the situation. No matter how rebellious she was, Annabella would not risk smearing her mother's good name by marching into his house unchaperoned. Unless –

She read the bloody article.

Annabella looked straight at him, shaking with anger, her eyes throwing daggers. "Did you know?"

"Yes and no."

"Oscar, for the sake of our future together, I need you to tell me the truth. I am in no mood for games or vague replies. You are Wyverstone's best friend. I doubt you don't know who his mistress is."

For a few long moments, Herdforthbridge thought about his answer, appraising what he could lose or gain from it.

No, no more secrets between them. If he wanted her trust, he needed to offer trust in return.

"I am well acquainted with Carmina Harcourt," he finally said. "But I never was privy of her past. I believe Edmund was the only one who knew who she really was." He paused for a few more seconds, to prepare himself for what he was about to say. "As for our future together, I am ready to tell you everything. My truth. For there will be moments when I need to be away on duty. I am an agent of the Crown, working under Her Majesty's Office of Classified Affairs. Wyverstone is not only my friend. He is my direct superior."

A mixture of confusion, bewilderment, and incredulity darkened Annabella's eyes. She clenched her fists into the fabric of her skirts, then released them again.

"Is this why you joined us on our journey to Australia?" Her voice trembled. "Were you the one who took Francis' drawings and gave them to Wyverstone?"

"Yes." Herdforthbridge saw her face turn ashen. But he would not lose her. Not when there were no more secrets, no more lies between them. "However, it was only a pretext to see how you fared without me. I had wished to discover you led a miserable life without me in Sydney, just as I had led a miserable life without you in London. What I discovered instead was how much I still loved you. Please, Annabella, never doubt that. Never doubt my feelings for you."

"I trust you, Oscar," Annabella said, the darkness in her eyes gone. "I am here because I need you to take me to the Cinnamon Dove. To see Rebecca with my very own eyes."

The duke shivered, appalled by the outlandish request. "Absolutely not! Do I need to explain in clearer detail what kind of establishment the Dove is?"

"I do not care about what kind of establishment the Dove is! If you are not willing to help me, I shall go alone. Is that a better option?"

Herdforthbridge ran a hand through his hair and let out an exasperated sigh. "Devil take me, Annabella! You are the most aggravating woman I have ever met. All right. I shall take you to the Dove."

CARMINA STOPPED for a moment to gaze at the patch of dreary sky visible through the windows lining the narrow corridor that led from the Dove's main wing to her private quarters. The rain always calmed her nerves, and now she needed peace and composure – and some good sleep. She had been afraid to return to the place she called home, but her fears had proven groundless. Everyone had welcomed her as they always did after her days of absence, as if nothing happened, as if they had not read the article revealing her past as the Marquess of Windstoneham's daughter – though she was certain they had. In everyone's eyes, she was still Madame. Her girls were more concerned about the bandages around her neck than about her aristocratic lineage.

She let out a breath of relief before opening the door to her private study and finding Hazel crouched on an armchair in front of the elegant mahogany desk in the centre of the room, her eyes red and puffed and still glistening with tears.

Carmina hurried to her most trusted assistant, her own worries forgotten for a moment. "What is the matter? Has anything happened to your mother?"

Hazel's sobs intensified, her entire body shaking, words coming out in stuttered sentences, broken and barely intelligible, back to her old accent. "No, Madame, it ain't me mom. It's me fault. I should've told you about me bastard of a brother. If I did, maybe you could've protected your secrets. I ain't worthy of your kindness. You have every right to banish me. Jasper told me who gave you those scars. I know it was me brother."

Foreboding gripped Carmina's chest. Or it was just fatigue, but it didn't matter. The day had more revelations in store for her. She pulled her chair closer to Hazel's and waited for her sobs to recede before speaking again. "I shall not hold you accountable for another person's wrongdoings. You have shown your loyalty to me, and I still trust you with my life. Regardless of the story you have to tell. But I shall ask you to tell me the truth."

She listened as Hazel recounted the hidden part of her life in Whitechapel, which included her brother Edwin, how he had recently inquired about His Lordship the Earl of Wyverstone and visited *The Londoners' Journal*'s archives, and why Hazel chose not to say anything for fear of alarming her Madame uselessly. But she had been a fool to believe he was harmless. All that time, Sheridan had been digging into Madame's past, and now it was too late for any of them to do anything to repair the damage.

Carmina remained silent for a while, trying to assimilate the newly acquired piece of information, staring intently at the drizzle outside as if it held the answer she was searching for. "Everyone is entitled to their secrets," she finally said, gently resting her hand on Hazel's shoulder. "I can only assume you had good reasons to keep your brother's existence a secret, just as I kept my real identity a secret. I am glad we had this conversation, which I see as a further bond of our mutual trust and friendship."

Relief washed Hazel's face. "Thank you, Madame. I'm grateful for –"

The door flew open before she could finish. Annabella Hammond and the Duke of Herdforthbridge entered the room, ignoring the doorkeeper's attempts to announce them properly.

Understanding Carmina's order from a glance, Hazel hurried out of the study and dragged the doorkeeper with her, kicking the door shut.

Annabella stood still in the middle of the room, her eyes wide with shock.

"Rebecca," she mumbled, staring blankly at Carmina as if to make certain she wasn't a trick of her vision. "Almighty Zeus, so it *was* true. All of it was true."

Ten years had passed since she had last talked to her sister. Ten years since they had last been in front of each other as they were that afternoon in her private study at the Dove. Carmina should have been scared. Terrified.

Yet she only felt a strange sense of relief. Her mind drifted briefly to unwanted territory, wondering what it would be like to have at least an ounce of her old life back. A life where she could embrace her mother and sister again. The mother and sister she had been watching from afar, aware that she could never approach them, that she was dead to them, that giving them up was the sacrifice she had to make to gain her life of independence.

"How could you?" Annabella's harsh tone interrupted the dangerous turn of her thoughts. "How could you do such a horrible thing to us?" Her voice trembled with anger and another emotion, which constricted Carmina's heart.

Hurt. Disappointment.

"Coming here was a most unwise idea," she said, showing nothing of the turmoil inside her. "This is no place for a well-bred lady."

"Given that Mama and all of London's Society know about you and this establishment, it's a bit late for such magnanimous considerations, is it not?" Annabella countered. "I never believed you could be so selfish, thinking of nothing and no one but yourself."

"I shall not try to make excuses," Carmina said. "But I shall ask you not to judge things you cannot understand."

"Then let me tell you what I understand." Annabella's voice could cut through steel. "I understand it has never occurred to you what the consequences of your decision would be for Mama. For me. You never thought of that, have you?"

Carmina walked with slow steps to the window, clasping the curtain's red velvet and staring at the rain outside for a few moments, before turning to face her unexpected guests again. "I have. I have long thought before deciding to take such an extreme measure. In the end, I had to leave because I was choking in that house. You were right. I was selfish. Between my freedom and my family's grief, I chose the former. I believed that your grief would pass with time, while my life would have ended in a place where the only future for me would have been a husband of our father's choice." She glanced at the duke, who stood at Annabella's side without a word, his hand gently squeezing her shoulder. "I never worried about you because I knew Herdforthbridge loved you enough to not stifle your spirit."

"We've always had each other against Father." Annabella took a few tentative steps towards her, stopping halfway. "We would have fought together."

"I know. But the prospect of my freedom was too tempting when the opportunity was presented to me. I shall not ask for forgiveness, for I have never regretted my choice."

"Opportunity –" Annabella rested her hand on the nearest armchair, her gaze never leaving her sister. "I should have imagined someone helped you with this mad idea of yours. Who was it, Rebecca? Who helped you do something so cruel? Mama almost fainted when she read that article this morning. She refused to believe it was true and her daughter could do this to her."

Carmina turned her gaze back to the window for another long minute to hide the emotion she could no longer contain. Annabella had every right to be angry with her. She had done something terrible and unforgivable to their mother, who had always protected them the best she could. The countess did not deserve such cruelty. "While I cannot reveal the circumstances of my staged death, I have always regretted the suffering I have brought upon you and Mama," she finally said, without facing her sister for fear she would break. Each word she uttered lifted a tiny drop of the heavy burden she had been carrying for the past ten years. "But I've learnt to live with this guilt, for I had no choice. It was the price I had to pay for my freedom."

For the first time since their impromptu arrival, the duke spoke. "Now that everything is out in the open, what do you intend to do?"

"Honestly, I do not know," Carmina replied, her green eyes

still staring at the rain outside. "I had no time to think about that yet. But I shall keep the Dove. The people here need me."

Annabella sank into the armchair she had been leaning against until a moment before, her lips curled in a mocking smile. "Poor Mama," she said, her voice bitter. "With two daughters of such questionable reputation, she can never show her face in polite Society again. One ran away on her wedding day all alone to Australia, while the other has been living in disguise in a house of ill repute as Wyverstone's – As Wyverstone's –"

But she could not bring herself to utter the word.

"No, Annabella, you are wrong." Edmund, who had just arrived, joined Carmina beside the window. "Your sister never was my whatever improper word your inventive mind has summoned. To me, she is someone I have always loved and respected, the only woman I have ever wanted. I would marry her this very moment if she had me, and all of Society can go to hell for all I care." But he didn't wait for a reply. His eyes turned one shade darker as he looked at the three of them. "Alas, we should leave family matters aside for a while and handle a far more urgent matter."

"Which is?" Annabella asked.

Edmund's reply came promptly. "Which is preventing the grand opening of the Engineers World Gathering from turning into utter disaster."

18

Everyone kept silent for a long while, trying to digest the new piece of information England's spymaster had shared, looking at each other with grim expressions.

Annabella rose suddenly and started pacing around the room, one gloved hand at her temple. "It is my fault again," she mumbled to no one in particular, tucking a perfectly arranged black curl behind her ear. "I keep making mistakes, and other people pay a hefty price for them. Quimby's death is the latest of my unforgivable errors." She turned to face Herdforthbridge, who was watching her, his blue eyes dark with concern. "I should have listened to you and Jasper. But I was stupid enough to dismiss your fears and let my pride get the better of me. I completed my circuits and played right into their hands."

Carmina waited for her to settle back into her chair before she spoke. "This is not the time for guilt and apologies. We must act."

Annabella stared at her sister, her eyes wide as if she had just discovered something important. "I was too angry to pay too much attention before, but those bandages around your neck and the scar on your face strike me as odd. And now you talk about how we must act, with the collected tone of someone who knows what she is doing. You are not only Wyverstone's lover. You are his agent as well, are you not?"

Carmina exchanged a quick glance with Edmund, then nodded. "Yes. I am an agent of the British Crown." She turned to the earl again. "You must allow me to join you and Herdforthbridge when you search for the explosives."

"No," Edmund replied in his no-room-for-arguments voice. "I need you to keep a close watch on Ledburry."

"I can do that," Annabella interfered, attracting the others' baffled gaze upon her.

"No, you cannot," Edmund said curtly. "For two reasons. First, you are not an agent, and I would never put a civilian in danger. Second, right now you have at least a pair of eyes commissioned to tail you and watch your every move, so you must play stupid. You should help Jasper and Miss Blackwell with the final tests for the *Lady*." He paused for a few moments. "But you could tell me something. Do you know of some secret testing facility for the Humautomaton? Have you ever heard anyone in Ledburry's laboratory talking about that?"

"What?" Annabella's expression was genuinely puzzled. "No, I know of no such thing. I told the earl in no uncertain terms that my conditions are not negotiable. Our test subjects must be provided by hospitals. They must choose to take part willingly, and not be coerced into accepting. To my knowledge, we do not have a date and test subjects yet."

Edmund rose, glancing at the mantel clock. "I need to return to the Inspectorates. You should see to your tasks as well. We have work to do, and too little time left."

Annabella stared at Carmina reluctantly, her eyes two dark pools of unspoken questions.

"I promise we will have a proper talk after this ugly affair is over," Carmina said. "The three of us. You, Mama and I."

"I shall take you to the airharbour." The duke offered his arm, which Annabella took with a hesitant nod.

"Wait." Carmina stopped them just as Herdforthbridge was about to open the door, prompting her sister to turn to her again. She extracted two books from her desk's top drawer and handed them to Annabella. "I retrieved these from Quimby's possession. I believe they are yours."

Annabella grabbed her precious books and murmured a bewildered thank you before the duke escorted her outside the room and the Dove.

Edmund stayed.

He pulled Carmina in his arms, his fingers a soft caress on her nape. "Are you all right?"

She breathed deeply, inhaling the familiar, beloved scent of him. "I'm not quite sure. Things kept happening today, too quickly for me to sort them out. The foundation of everything I've built for the last ten years is shaking, and I'm scared. I do not think I'm fully ready for this." She lifted her gaze and placed her hand on the firm line of his jaw, staring at the unfathomable blue depths of his eyes. "*I* should ask *you* if you are all right, which I suppose you are not, if I am to infer from your pale complexion and how you struggled to look as if your wound were nothing."

He pressed his hand over hers against his cheek. "I am not here to talk about my wound. When Herdforthbridge called to tell me he was bringing Annabella to the Dove, I left Carlisle to perform the post-mortem at the Inspectorates and hurried here." His expression turned more serious. "I meant every word. Now that your real identity and our relationship are public knowledge, I see no reason to hide and love each other on borrowed time. I think we should marry."

For a moment, Carmina forgot how to breathe. The day kept bringing unexpected developments.

"You know I cannot give up the Dove. They need me."

"I never asked for such a thing," Edmund said. "You can

continue your activity as the Dove's benefactor. And as an agent. Marrying me does not mean curtailing your freedom."

She just stared at him, astonishment and hope dancing in her green gaze.

"You do know how that would reflect upon you, do you not?" she finally said. "I am an outcast, much more so than my sister. Unlike me, Annabella has never linked her name to a house of ill-repute."

Edmund laughed, a low, hoarse sound. "I am past caring what Society thinks of me. Perhaps you should be reminded that I am their favourite villain at the moment. The corrupt and depraved official working for his own benefit instead of the country's."

Carmina wrapped her arms around his neck and pulled him to her, their lips almost touching, her voice a whisper, barely audible over the soothing sound of rain rasping at the windows. "If I have a chance to a life with you, I shall take it."

A MURKY BLEND of insufficient daylight coming through the windows and electric glare coming from the bulbs lined alongside the hangar's walls swathed the *Lady's* blue envelope in an almost ethereal glow, her golden patterns and letters shining over the dreary scenery below. The hubbub of the workers' shouts and engine buzz had turned into background noise, easy to ignore.

She was beautiful, Annabella thought as she stood at the base of the tall scaffolding, her head craned upwards to gape at the magnificent structure. The most beautiful airship she had ever seen.

Through the glass of her magnifying lenses, she read again the letters on the gondola, which she herself had painted not long before. Golden foil had been applied over her elegant handwriting, turning the *Lady's* motto into a work of art.

Ea Caelium Superabit.

She will conquer the skies.

But will she? Will she really conquer the skies?

"Annabella, what the blazes!"

Jasper's loud voice made her jump out of her skin. Startled by the sudden interruption, she turned to him with a dumbfounded look.

"You haven't heard a word I said in the past ten minutes, have you? Asked you about five times to go up and open the pods to help me check the bloody engines."

Of course, he was angry and had every right to be so. "I'm sorry. I was not ignoring you. It's just that my mind was elsewhere."

He sighed and directed his gaze towards the envelope, as if to decipher the reason for her rapture. "I understand what a shocking revelation Carmina's identity ought to have been to you. But at least for today and tomorrow, please help me. Help *us*. Be here and act like an engineer. I know it's selfish of me to ask this of you, but I am certain you will have plenty of time to solve your family matters after we see the *Lady* safely in the sky. Can you do that?"

Annabella removed her goggles and let them hang around her neck, her attention fully on Jasper. By the looks of it, he hadn't slept for days, spending most of the time at the hangar. He was right. They had to see the *Lady* safely in the sky.

"It was not my sister but my guilt that was plaguing my mind," she said. "Everything, even Quimby's death, happened because of me. Because of my pride. My damned pride urged me to complete the circuits, although you and Oscar warned me against it. Now –" She stopped to steady her breath. "Now I became a blackmail weapon in their hands."

A reassuring smile brightened Jasper's tired face as he pulled his canvas cap over his black, unruly curls with an automatic gesture. "We should trust my brother."

We.

Annabella returned his smile. She had Oscar, Jasper, and the others – people she could trust. And Rebecca had made a miraculous, albeit unsettling, reappearance in her life. She didn't feel alone anymore.

Yet, a terrible dread gripped her heart. What if it was too late to undo the damage she had caused? What if Wyverstone did not find the explosives he was searching for?

"How can we make sure Ledburry won't attempt to sabotage the *Lady* tomorrow?" she asked. "Like Quimby did with the *Griffin*?"

"He won't," Jasper said, his confidence bringing an ounce of comfort to her troubled mind. "If he wants to murder Her Majesty, he needs the *Lady* intact. Besides, I've checked every nook and cranny of this airship, and tonight I'll stay here to keep watch." His face beamed with a boyish grin. "See? You have no reason to worry. Now, will you *please* help me check those engines?"

Annabella nodded and climbed up the mobile ladder to the first engine pod. She opened the hatch and entered, but she could hardly focus on her task.

I cannot just whine and wait for others to undo the effects of my own errors. I need to act.

The day dragged on among the engine pods and a myriad of other tests. By early evening, her work at the hangar was done.

She joined Jasper, Miss Blackwell, and Avery in the gondola. "I fear I must take my leave," she said. "I am unwell and in need of rest."

"Do you want me to escort you home?" Avery offered.

"Certainly not. Make your sore self useful and stay with Jasper at the hangar."

Outside, the rain had stopped, leaving a heavily clouded sky in its wake. A strong smell of tar, fuel, and metal filled the air darkened with the billows of soot coming out of the nearby factories' furnaces.

She took the first hansom cab in the line outside the airharbour. "The Inspectorates," she instructed the driver.

As expected, Ledburry was still in his laboratory. She strode purposefully to his workbench.

"Lord Ledburry, we need to talk."

HALF PAST SEVEN in the evening.

Carmina slid the elegant, gilded watch into the pocket of her gentleman attire's waistcoat and paced along the third floor again from one end to the other with an important air, as she had been doing for more than half a day, observing who entered or came out of Ledburry's laboratory. But nothing suspicious came to her attention, with the notable exception of the complete lack of visits from Baron Hydenhollow, a regular of the laboratory.

Perhaps she should just leave and report to Edmund.

But just then, Annabella emerged in the corridor, striding towards the door she had been watching.

What is she doing here at such an hour?

She turned on her ear amplifier just as Annabella walked into the room.

"Lord Ledburry, we need to talk. I'm here because I need help, and you are the one who can provide it."

MUSTERING an extensive amount of anger had been easy. All Annabella had to do while sitting in the hansom on her way to the Inspectorates was to focus her entire attention on Rebecca's lie, on the discovery that she had misled all of them into believing she was dead when she was, in fact, loitering around and doing dangerous things without the slightest remorse or consideration for her family.

After half an hour of pondering upon her sister's lie, Annabella didn't even need to channel her willpower to look authentically enraged when she entered Ledburry's laboratory, all fired up. She *was* authentically enraged.

"I would like to know when I can test my work for Humautomaton," she explained when the earl had no reply to her preamble.

Ledburry lifted his eyebrows in surprise, but only for a second. "Miss Hammond, I fear I cannot tell when a hospital will approve my request and send test subjects. I encountered more difficulties than I expected. People are rather reticent toward technology when it comes to their own lives."

"Then devil take them!" Her heartfelt expletive triggered another surprised expression on the earl's face. "I have waited enough. If need be, I am willing to adopt more unconventional methods. I shall not be the mockery of that lot. My sister, Wyverstone, and even Oscar. How can I become his wife when he diminishes me like that? All of them kept secrets from me." She started pacing about the room, clenching and unclenching her fists with a nervous, repetitive movement, then stopped abruptly in front of Ledburry's workbench, leaning towards him, her hands planted firmly on the tabletop. "I want to show them what I can achieve. Without their help. I want to show them I can be an engineer without being at their mercy."

The silence following her heated tirade stretched for several long moments. Or perhaps minutes? Half an hour?

Annabella's bodice suddenly seemed too tight, blocking all the air from her lungs. Her heart was racing, wondering whether Ledburry would take the bait. Once, she had convinced Theophilus Hollingsworth to give her an airship for her mad journey to Australia. But cunning Ledburry was not good-natured Master Hollingsworth.

She held his appraising gaze without wavering, until the reply finally came.

"Tell me, Miss Hammond, how far are you willing to go to acquire the recognition you crave?"

"As far as necessary," she said, her resolute voice matching the fiery spark in her eyes.

Another long moment of silence. Another assessing stare from the Doctors Order's Senior Lord, as if he were still in doubt.

She didn't flinch.

"I might have a solution for the Humautomaton tests," Ledburry said. "But I need to trust you completely. Which I fear I cannot."

No, she would not lose. She was too close.

"First and foremost, I am a scientist," Annabella said. "I have been working on this project for too long, and I am well aware that, on certain occasions, ethics comes second to scientific development and discovery." She pressed a gloved hand on her temple with an affected air, moving her gaze from the earl to his workbench. "Besides, the betrayal of those whom I have considered my friends and family was enough to stir me towards that less orthodox path I would have otherwise avoided."

"Very well." Ledburry grinned, as if he had just won an important battle. "You will have the role you deserve. Now, my dear Miss Hammond, I shall ask you to be my guest in a place you will most certainly find captivating."

EDMUND CLENCHED HIS TEETH, ignoring the searing pain as he soaked a fresh bandage in the carbolic acid solution Carlisle had left for him. Slowly, he loosened the dirty cloth that circled his torso, revealing an ugly, almost blackened gash that seemed to have become larger than it had been a few hours before. The bullet had not touched any vital organ, yet the bloody wound looked much worse instead of starting to heal. His physician had urged him to rest, which he was aware he should do, but he had no time for such mundane activities. Rest would come later.

He glanced outside. Dusk had already turned into night, and Westminster square spread deserted and ominous, the drizzle falling in a thick curtain of raindrops under the yellow light of the streetlamps. In front of the Inspectorates, the perpetual tumbling of the mechanical waterfall was but a distant sound, hardly audible through the glass of his office's windows.

Where the hell is Herdforthbridge?

As if summoned by the Earl of Wyverstone's thoughts, the door opened, and the duke strode into the room. He took the chair across from the desk, waiting for Edmund to finish dressing his wound.

"You look terrible. Cadaveric, to be precise, though I believe you already know that. With all Carlisle's efforts, healing is quite impossible if you intend to loiter about London's warehouses in search of explosives. We should postpone our search for another day. Preferably for when you are feeling better."

"Do not dare diminish me," Edmund said in a harsh tone, without looking at him. "For as long as I can stand, I shall see to my duty. I shall hear no more of this ridiculous talk about rest and how terrible I look."

"Whether or not you want to hear it does not change the facts." Herdforthbridge stretched his legs and crossed them at the ankles with an unperturbed look. "You should reconsider your involvement and send your brother instead. Lately, he and I seem to make a rather efficient team."

"Absolutely not." Edmund buttoned his waistcoat again, hiding all traces of his medical intervention from a few moments before, then wiped his sweating brow with the back of his hand. "Jasper needs to keep watch at the airharbour."

The duke lifted his arms as if admitting to a lost case and rose, coming closer to the desk where Edmund had spread a detailed map of London. "All right, then. Where do we start?"

230

19

From the stuffy confines of the hansom cab, Annabella tried to make out her surroundings without much success. Ledburry choosing such an unassuming conveyance instead of his perfectly polished, emblazoned mechanical horse-drawn brougham or his steammotor had alerted her, but at least confirmed she was on the right track in her unusual pursuit. Still, those streets were oddly unfamiliar to her. Where were they? Holborn? Clerkenwell? She couldn't say.

The driver seemed certain of their destination, although Ledburry had uttered no word. He had climbed inside with just a nod towards the man who sat on the box at the back of the cab. Was he one of the earl's minions in disguise? Most probably.

It was too late for her to retreat. And yet, regardless of the apprehension gripping her chest, she was aware she would not have retreated even if she could. Undoubtedly, half of her fears were just the effect of the ominous night looming over the poorly lit streets with their crumbling buildings.

She almost sighed with relief when they finally reached an area she recognised. The vehicle turned into Charterhouse Street, only to get lost again in a maze of lanes off Smithfield

Market, before stopping in front of the low-arched entrance to a court.

Ledburry alighted and held out his hand, helping her climb down. The court was dark and empty save for a broken cart propped against a raw brick wall and a wooden washtub with a dolly inside. A foul smell of rotten fish and urine crinkled Annabella's nostrils. She lifted her gaze to the surrounding walls, but nothing moved. All windows, some left with just the frames, were as dark as the cloudy sky above.

The earl strode to the furthermost wall opposite the court entrance and pushed a small wooden door, which an untrained eye would not have noticed, nodding towards Annabella to follow him inside a long, narrow vestibule that opened into a larger room.

Instinctively, Annabella pressed her hand on her stomach as soon as she entered, fighting the nausea that churned her insides when she recognised the unmistakable odour of an opium den, concentrating her vision on Ledburry's back, trying not to lose her focus. Out of the corner of her eye, from the beds accommodating two, even three desperate creatures in search of oblivion, thin clouds of fragrant smoke drifted towards the cracked ceiling.

No one paid any attention to her or Ledburry. The earl crossed from one end of the room to the other, ignoring the sorrowful scenery around them, and pulled a ragged curtain of indefinite colour.

Annabella followed him inside a small, round alcove with no furniture. A second curtain of indefinite colour covering the walls hid another door.

The Doctors Order's Senior Lord unlocked it and lit a pocket lantern, revealing a flight of wooden stairs descending into the building's innards. Annabella had a thousand questions, but she kept them to herself. Careful not to close the alcove's door completely, she climbed down the steps behind Ledburry until they reached the bottommost step, in front of an old arched door. The earl lifted the wooden bolt lock and opened it, their destination coming into her terrified view.

She blinked, trying to adjust her vision to the raw light of a cellar large enough to be equally a prison and a surgery room, an iron grate dividing the space to serve both functions. Behind the grate, several men and women lay in the same opium-induced state of semi-consciousness she had seen in the room above the stairs.

Without waiting for Ledburry's instructions and oblivious to the sickening smell of opium blended with the stench of flesh decay and blood, Annabella rushed to the grate and gripped the iron bars to have a better look at the poor lot sprawled on the cold stone floor, realising the full horror of the place. Maimed bodies in various stages of gangrene, barely alive, filled the small, prison-like space. Most of them missed at least one limb, the wounds where a leg or an arm – or both – had been severed gaping wide, stained with the foul dark colour of infection.

She turned around to observe the rest of the cellar on her side of the grate. Blood everywhere. On the stone slabs of the floor, on the walls, and on the only metal workbench that occupied the centre of the room. Canvas aprons and leather gloves hang on the walls. In a large box on a nearby table, knives and scalpels lay carefully arranged according to the size of their blades. Next to them, bloodied and broken syringes filled another container.

This must be Ledburry's property, and that opium den above gives him test subjects no one would ever ask about. Unfortunate creatures whose lives mean nothing to no one. This bastard maims innocent people here in the name of science!

Channelling all her willpower to remain calm and collected, looking as if assessing the place, she finally turned to the Doctors Order's Senior Lord, her tone distant and neutral. "Are we performing the tests here?"

"We are," Ledburry confirmed. "I have worked on a few experiments myself, but I fear I had no success. Yet. You are here to change that."

"Opium is not enough," Annabella said matter-of-factly. "We cannot work without a strong anaesthetic."

"Which, fortunately, we possess." The earl offered her a blood-curdling smile. "Hydenhollow has perfected the substance we need."

"And where exactly is Hydenhollow?" Annabella hoped he would not see through her attempt to postpone her predicament. "He should be here to help us."

Ledburry dismissed her worries with a wave of his arm. "The two of us should be enough, for the baron has more important business to attend to tonight. Besides, Hydenhollow does not know about this place. Alas, he still conducts himself upon some rather archaic notion of morals and insists the test subjects must fully agree to participate." He discarded his coat, rolled up his shirtsleeves, and pulled an apron from the wall, then turned to face her. "Now, my dear Miss Hammond, shall we begin?"

CARMINA COULD NOT RECALL another moment when she was that grateful for her choice of disguise. Surely, a young gentleman on his route to perdition ought to be more convincing than a newspaper boy or a street sparrow, which were her more regular personas.

"I asked what the bloody hell you want. If you keep staring like a calf, we'll throw you out, toff or not. This ain't a pub or a brothel."

"I want –" She breathed deeply, a sad smile lifting the corner of her mouth before her green gaze settled on the annoyed man who seemed the opium den's foreman. "I want to forget. And

Lord Ledburry sent me here. Said this was the best place for people like me, in search of oblivion."

"You are acquainted with His Lordship?" The man lifted his eyebrows, visibly startled. In all probability, Ledburry didn't usually send him young men willing to waste themselves.

She nodded.

"Make yourself comfortable," the man said, pointing at an empty bed in the far corner of the large room. "Wait there until I prepare something for you."

As soon as he turned his back at her, she started to search for Ledburry and Annabella. Her amplifier carried no trace of their voices, which meant they had either left using some other exit or gone downstairs in a room hidden from the rest of the guests.

The latter made more sense than the former, Carmina decided, striding to the other end of the main room. Soon, she found herself inside a curtained alcove, whose door had been left ajar.

She closed it behind her and went downstairs in the darkness, feeling her way alongside the wall, too afraid to use her pocket lantern. Her amplifier came to life, carrying fragments of conversation into her ear. Letting the sound guide her, she reached the floor and another door, which hid her sister and the earl.

"No, Miss Hammond, we are not waiting," Ledburry's voice thundered. *"I should like to have our first Humautomaton completed by dawn."*

∼

Annabella tied the strings of her canvas apron with excruciatingly slow movements while her mind was trying to concoct an escape route. She could not remain trapped there. Her discovery of Ledburry's opium den and improvised surgery room was completely useless unless she got out of that hellish hole and let Wyverstone know about it.

No, she could not stay there. And yet, she could not just leave and risk innocent lives. A glance in the direction of the makeshift prison sent a shiver down her spine, her heart constricting with the heavy grip of guilt. She was the cause of that disaster, albeit indirectly. Those people sprawled on the cold stone slabs would soon die of infection if she did not help them. Escape would have to wait.

"I need clean sheets," she said, striding towards the surgery table. "A lot of them."

Ledburry opened a cabinet mounted close to the grate that divided the space and extracted a pile of white linen. Annabella spread one of them on the tabletop, her eyes wide in horror at the sight of the brass fragments, rags soaked in blood, and burnt wires thrown carelessly underneath the table.

She turned to face Ledburry, her worst fear confirmed. "You didn't only maim those people to turn them into patients. You have tried to attach the brass parts to their bodies, have you not?"

"*Maim* is rather a strong word and quite unseemly for our great endeavour, don't you think?" the earl said. "As soon as you completed your circuits, I wanted to see how they worked. Not as expected, unfortunately, so I realised I must be missing something."

Her dark gaze drifted around the room. "Lord Ledburry, may I ask how many people died here?"

The Senior Lord of the Doctors Order replied as if his answer was the most natural thing in the world. "Miss Hammond, no number of deaths is too big for such a scientific advance. I thought you were aware of that basic fact when you came to my laboratory to request my help."

A chill stabbed Annabella's chest as she realised the extent of her error. The man was too cynical to abide by common sense. He would spare no one to see his own work done. Not Quimby, not her.

Disposable material. Wyverstone had told them about the note he'd found in his office, along with Quimby's expired body. If Quimby was disposable material, then so was she.

Suddenly, everything made terrifying sense. He had never tried to hide the way to their destination while they were in the hansom cab. He had never denied his not-quite-scientific activities in that opium den. And that was because he had no reason to fear she would disclose any of his secrets. Ever.

The truth dawned, clasping its icy tendrils around her throat, choking her.

Ledburry never trusted her, like he'd led her to believe that night. Everything had been an act to lure her into that forsaken place where he needed her expertise and no one would find her, and she had played right into his hands. The earl only needed her to show him how it was done. He needed to know how to use her completed circuits. As soon as he had that knowledge, she became disposable material herself.

He would never let me out of here alive.

Cold panic blocked the air to her lungs, her brain frantically searching for a solution to leave that room before it was too late. She tucked a loose black lock behind her ear and tried to steady her breath.

A long moan coming from the other half of the room interrupted the train of her thoughts, prompting her to turn again towards the improvised cage.

Annabella's heart sank. Those people were trapped there without the luxury of an escape plan. Without the luxury of their own reasoning, which Ledburry had so cruelly deprived them of.

Why would my life be more precious than theirs? I have no right to seek escape when these men and women are only collateral victims of my own mistakes. Of my own involvement in Humautomaton.

The least she could do was to save them from certain death and give them new limbs. She would make her experimental surgery succeed, even at the cost of her own life.

Trying not to think of what awaited at the end of the medical procedure, she took a deep, calming breath, gathered her hair in a tight chignon at her nape, and arranged knives, scalpels, bandages, carbolic acid, and wires on the small tool table, then pulled a trunk of brass parts beside it. She strode towards the grate and chose her patient – a middle-aged woman whose left arm was severed from the shoulder.

"You will help me prepare her for surgery," Annabella said in a resolute tone, all her doubts gone, concentrating on the task she was about to perform. "And I shall need Hydenhollow's anaesthetic. Then I am ready to begin."

"Very well, Miss Hammond." The earl's voice almost sounded like laughter. "I am thrilled to see your skill. And learn."

No! Carmina almost screamed when she realised Annabella had just signed her death warrant.

Good Lord, can you not see you are falling into his trap? Finish the surgery and you will die!

But she could not utter the words aloud and had no way to convey them to her sister.

The amplifier continued to carry Annabella's voice in her ear. *"It took the combined efforts of three Orders and the Classified Affairs to convince Her Majesty that Humautomaton is an extraordinary project that would benefit many people. Regardless of her support for science, if she finds out about the experiments in this room, the consequences will be dire."*

"*No, Miss Hammond, you are wrong,*" Ledburry's voice

sounded amused. *"Soon, Her Majesty will cease to be a concern for us. Just wait until the Engineers World Gathering."*

"Why would I believe that? Is anything going to happen at the Gathering?"

The earl grunted, visibly displeased. *"Nothing is more appalling than an overly inquisitive lady. We should start that procedure before the poor woman expires on the table."*

The sound of two pairs of boots stepping on stone. Then Annabella's voice again. *"Wyverstone and Herdforthbridge must be looking for me. It would be unwise to stay here for too long."*

Ledburry's burst of laughter sent a shiver down Carmina's spine. *"Your duke is too arrogant to even think of setting foot inside such establishments. As for Wyverstone –"* A pause. *"He is hardly a problem. A bullet hit him with Hydenhollow's latest poison, which is now spreading through his accursed body, and the only antidote is safely kept upon the baron's person. That meddling bastard is dying and doesn't even realise."*

Carmina froze, her hand on the amplifier, crushed under the impossible choice she had to make.

Stay and try to save her sister. Or leave and try to save the man she loved.

SWEATING and hardly able to concentrate, Edmund wiped his brow with the back of his hand, brushing aside a few wet strands of hair that obstructed his vision. The bloody wound ridiculed him, challenging his willpower with every slight movement of his body.

Outside, the drizzle had increased in intensity, crushing into the windows with a repeated, monotonous thump, the only sound in the dark, deserted square.

"None of the old smuggler tunnels leads to Westminster, so I would safely rule those out," Herdforthbridge said, still perched over the London map spread on Edmund's desk. "I doubt they would keep a considerable load of explosives in a place too far for convenient use."

Edmund nodded. "They could only hide the gunpowder or whatever explosive close to Westminster Square, where Her Majesty will make her appearance for the public. And the closest place I can think of large enough to accommodate barrels of explosive is –"

The loud, metallic toll of the Westminster clocktower's bell reverberated over the square, startling both him and the duke, making them turn to the windows.

Edmund finished his sentence as he rose from his chair and started towards the door. "– the clocktower. Hollingsworth's trap might have caught a mouse."

20

Running in pouring rain had never been such a harrowing undertaking for Edmund, his wound sending jolts of sharp pain with each step he took. The blasted gush wasn't even deep. It should have been healing, yet it kept aggravating him, and the timing could not have been worse. At least he was not alone. If anything happened to him, Herdforthbridge would finish what he had started.

Edmund hurried up the clocktower, counting the steps to keep his mind away from the accursed pain, until they reached the entrance to the clock faces.

As expected, they found the door bolted.

"Let us see what we have inside." The thrill of anticipation made him forget about the wound for a few moments. That door would only lock if someone unaware of Hollingsworth's trap stepped inside the clock faces room.

He lifted the wooden bolt from its metal hinges, guided by Herdforthbridge's pocket lamp, and pushed the old wooden door open.

The narrow corridor stretching alongside the four walls of the tower was deserted. A chilly wind pushed a thin veil of rain inside, through the open window of the wall facing the river.

"I believe we arrived a tad too late," the duke said, pointing his lantern at the square of dark sky.

Edmund strode towards the opening in the clock face. "Damnation!" He perched over the frame, his eyes on a small airship disappearing in the distance. It was impossible to see her clearly in that blasted weather, but he could tell that her course had started from the tower. "I cannot believe we have been bamboozled like this!"

"Or maybe not." Herdforthbridge moved the light from the window to the nearest wall, revealing two barrels. He lifted the lids and sniffed. "Gunpowder. We found it."

Edmund frowned, staring at the containers with an unfathomable look. "No, this cannot be right," he finally said. "These two barrels cannot be the load we are searching for. It was all too easy. The perpetrators must have known about Hollingsworth's trap, else they couldn't have had an airship ready to pick them when the trap bolted the door." His eyes darkened with anger. "If these bastards believe they can fool me, they are dead wrong."

The duke secured the lids back on the barrels. "Whilst your theory makes perfect sense, it leaves us with nothing. What do we do now?"

"We need to find the next closest spot to the square," Edmund said. "Other than the tower."

He leaned against the window facing the Inspectorates, staring at the deserted square through the pouring rain, watching the perpetual movement of the mechanical waterfall.

The mechanical waterfall.

His sudden, hysterical laugh attracted the duke's curious eyes upon him.

"By God!" Edmund turned to face Herdforthbridge again. "All this time, I had the answer right under my nose, but I was too blind to see it. The only other likely spot to prepare an attack against Her Majesty is the mechanical waterfall. I've been staring at it day after day. I should have realised it sooner."

He strode towards the door, only to halt as a fresh, sharp stab of pain caught his breath. He inhaled slowly, grateful that the duke waited for him to recover without a word.

Soon, they were out in the square again, racing in the direction of the mechanical waterfall.

The enormous construction, a strange mixture of red brick, iron, and glass adorned with an equally enormous round clock on its top, harnessed the immense power of water to turn it into an energy source for the Inspectorates. It was one of the first – and still one of the most daring – engineering projects built after the Reform, a silent proof of the wonders that were to come in the new technological era awaiting England after Her Majesty had signed the decree, eleven years before.

They went down a flight of iron stairs to the back entrance, a rusty door only the machinists used. Edmund extracted a thin metal pick from his coat, ready to work on the lock, but Herdforthbridge pressed the handle and pushed.

The door was unlocked. Cautiously, they proceeded down the narrow iron passage through a maze of copper pipes, gauges, and wheels, guided by a faint light coming from the maintenance room, careful not to make any noise.

Someone was in there. Edmund stopped and inserted the amplifier in his ear, beckoning the duke to do the same.

"I expected ten and counted nine. How do you explain that? Both of you are as drunk as sailors. No wonder you lost your load on the way."

A vicious smile played on Edmund's lips as he recognised Baron Hydenhollow's voice. He might catch a mouse after all that night.

"Yer Lordship, I swear on me mum's grave we brought ten. I don't know fer the life of me where the last one is."

Edmund nodded towards the maintenance room's door and

made a sign the duke understood too well. Whoever was inside, they would take them by surprise.

They closed the distance to their destination in a few strides, and Herdforthbridge kicked the door open. In the rectangular space filled with cabinets and tools, whose left wall was lined with barrels identical to those they'd found in the clocktower, stood the Chemists Order's Senior Lord and two other men who could fit anywhere between dock workers and ruffians. All three turned towards the intruders with wide, startled eyes.

Before any of them could react, the duke planted his fist under the burlier man's chest, sending him to the floor in spasms of pain, while Edmund summoned all the power he still had in his body to perform the same move on the other ruffian, under the baron's terrified eyes. A few moments later, the two hoodlums, who were already drunk, lay safely incapacitated by the effect of the paralysis phials promptly discharged by the duke into their legs.

"I would not do that if I were you." Edmund's voice, low and menacing, stopped the baron from his attempt to leave the room. "Baron Hydenhollow, I believe you have quite a few explanations to give, for I cannot fathom what business the Senior Lord of the Chemists Order would have in a place only used by the waterfall's machinists and engineers, at such an impossibly late hour. Fortunately, I have plenty of time to listen, and the Classified Affairs office is conveniently close."

"Miss Hammond, if you are so concerned about the wretched life of this poor woman, you should better make haste. If we don't disinfect the wound and attach the brass arm, she will die before dawn."

For one moment, Carmina forgot how to breathe. The ugly affair was turning uglier by the minute.

She had to trust Edmund and his thorough experience with

poisons. By God, she knew too well what training with the late Earl of Wyverstone meant, how mercilessly England's former spymaster had prepared his son to take his place, including administering him small amounts of poisons to get his body used to them.

No, Edmund was not one to die easily. She would stay with her sister.

Still, extracting Annabella from that hellhole had to wait. If she acted too quickly, an innocent woman would die. While her sister and Ledburry performed their surgery, she would concoct a plan.

Crouched on the last step of the wooden stairs in the darkness, Carmina waited, hearing no other sound than the curt instructions given by either Annabella or the earl from time to time.

Pass me the carbolic acid solution.

I need to calibrate the voltmeter.

I finished cleaning the wound. I shall proceed to attach the brass arm.

Short scraps of conversation came and went through her amplifier, as Annabella and Ledburry were too focused on their task to talk. Time was dragging painfully slowly, with no way to know how long it had been since the medical procedure started. If it was half an hour or three hours, Carmina couldn't say.

But it was enough for her to come up with a plan. A most daring one. The only one possible.

"*I am done,*" Annabella's voice finally proclaimed. "*I attached the circuits to the nerves, and the brass arm is stable. We should wait for a bit, though, to make sure she is all right.*"

Her sister's announcement was the signal Carmina had been waiting for, which prompted her to creep up the stairs. She had not a second to waste.

Soon, she opened the door to the alcove, then pulled the curtain and returned to the main room of the opium den. Trying to ignore the heavy odour, she searched for the man in charge of the place.

"You!" He glared at her. "I thought you took your gentlemanly arse out of here."

"As it happens, I was with Lord Ledburry. He requires you in the room downstairs," she said, her voice as serious as her expression. It was a gamble – one she wasn't so certain she'd win. She couldn't know whether the man knew about the scientific pursuits from below the stairs.

But she had no time to ponder the possibilities or think of alternatives.

The man's eyes widened. Then he frowned, staring at her with a suspicious gaze. "His Lordship never lets anyone in that room. Why would he call for me all of a sudden?"

She shrugged. "My good man, how would I know? He told me to hurry and bring you down there. I think it's about the lady he brought with him."

The amount of detail should suffice to gain the man's trust. And it did.

He started towards the alcove, Carmina following closely behind, trying not to look at the decrepit walls and the more decrepit people sprawled in various degrees of waste about the room.

The man lit a pocket lantern and climbed down the stairs, then pulled open the wooden door to Ledburry's makeshift laboratory, or whatever that atrocity was.

A second was all Carmina had. When the door opened, attracting the dumbfounded looks of both Annabella and the earl upon the unexpected guest, she beckoned her sister from the doorstep.

Come here! Please!

That one, desperate sign was all Annabella needed. Without looking around, without turning back, she grabbed her skirts and darted out of the cellar, past her captor, as fast as she could. Then both women pushed the door and bolted it.

"We don't have too much time," Carmina said. "Let's get out of this godforsaken place."

A few minutes later they were out in the street, running in the downpour to halt a hansom cab.

"Wait." Annabella stopped abruptly before stepping inside the vehicle. "You cannot expect me to just follow you blindly. Whilst I am truly grateful for your help, I don't recall having made your acquaintance. Did Oscar send you?"

"No," Carmina replied, this time in her usual voice. "It's me. Rebecca. We need to hurry. Please."

She hadn't uttered her own name like that in years. It sounded strange and wonderful, like a long-forgotten caress.

Though startled, Annabella climbed inside the hansom without another word.

Carmina gave the address to the driver, then joined her, praying to all gods she wasn't too late, and Edmund was still alive. "Having those bastards locked in there will buy us more time," she said after she settled on the bench next to her sister. "Enough to see them arrested. Those poor sods intoxicated with opium are too far gone to understand what happened, and I doubt any of them knows about Ledburry's secret laboratory, which is too deep to properly convey any screaming – for I don't doubt that either the earl or the other one will scream for help."

Annabella inhaled deeply, then let out a long breath. "I am dead tired and have no idea where I am or where we are going, but I need to tell you something. About Wyverstone."

"I know, and he won't die," Carmina said curtly "We are on our way to the Inspectorates. To Edmund's office. If we are lucky enough to still find him there, we shall report what happened tonight, and he will finally have enough solid evidence to arrest Ledburry."

He would not die. She couldn't let herself think otherwise,

else the last thin thread of her sanity would break. For a few moments, neither of them said anything, their eyes on the dirty window and the rain outside.

"Are you happier like this?" Annabella's sudden question made her turn to face her sister again. "Leading such a dangerous existence, risking life and limb for Queen and Country?"

Carmina almost smiled, her face barely visible in the mild darkness of the hansom. "Were you happier in Australia?"

"In a way, yes." Annabella's dark eyes were distant, as if recalling a faraway past. "But not entirely. A part of me had always longed for home."

"Here. You have your answer."

When they arrived in Westminster, the red brick building of the Inspectorates loomed dark and foreboding over the deserted square.

Please, be alive. Edmund, be alive.

Carmina ran up the marble stairs to the second floor and opened the door to the Classified Affairs' office without knocking, with Annabella in tow.

Edmund was there and alive, with Herdforthbridge and Hydenhollow, standing near the crackling fire in the hearth.

His beloved face was almost white and his blue eyes were tired and hazy. But he was alive, and she could finally breathe.

All three men turned towards them.

"You look like the devil," Herdforthbridge said, glaring at Annabella with a mixture of profound worry and anger. "I should very much want to know where the blazes you have been."

For the first time that evening, Carmina truly saw her sister. Her hair had half come undone over her shoulder in an undefined tangle of wet locks. Black smudges covered her cheeks and forehead. Her dress and canvas apron were soaked with rain and blood.

"Judging from your appearance, both of you have gone through some rather messy ordeal, which I am most interested to hear about later," Edmund interfered before Annabella could say anything. "Now, I believe you need some rest. And a pot of warm tea. I shall call for some. The fire will help you dry your clothes."

But he only managed a few tentative steps towards the speakerbox on his desk, before collapsing in an unconscious heap on the floor.

～

"He is alive," Herdforthbridge said in his typically collected tone after checking Edmund's vitals. "Barely, but he is alive." He rose. "Carlisle must be still in the mortuary with Quimby. I shall fetch him, else His Stubbornship will die. I urged him to go home and rest, but my plea fell on deaf ears."

"Don't bother bringing the physician here, for it is not the wound but the poison in his body that's killing Wyverstone," Annabella announced, attracting the duke's baffled look upon her. "Apparently, he was shot with a bullet that had been treated with the Chemists Order's latest concoction. But fear not. We have the antidote." She turned to cast a murderous glare at Hydenhollow, looking like a warrior freshly returned from battle, wet to the bones, dirty and reeking of blood, and utterly dishevelled. "You! What a happy coincidence it is to have you here when we most need your presence, is it not?" She held out her hand. "Do not make me ask for that blasted antidote twice."

Her harsh tone made Hydenhollow take a few steps back, his stout frame hitting the tall bookshelf opposite Edmund's desk. "Miss Hammond, I see you are quite distressed, and perhaps your cognitive function has been somewhat affected. I assure you, I have no idea what you are talking about."

But the duke was already towering over the shorter man,

eyes dark and menacing, his low, hoarse voice a promise of imminent danger. "Is it true? Have you lot had the insane idea of poisoning *the Chief Inspector of Her Majesty's Office of Classified Affairs*?"

The way he uttered Edmund's full role and importance in that intense voice, emphasising each word, made him even more terrifying.

"I don't – I swear –" The baron stuttered, cowering under Herdforthbridge's intimidating presence.

"Ledburry has already told Miss Hammond everything," Carmina said, her expression betraying nothing of the torment inside her. "We have no time for this. Give us that antidote."

Hydenhollow extracted a phial from a hidden pocket inside his coat. Without looking at the others, he kneeled next to Edmund and uncovered his wound, then poured the phial's contents on it. "He should come to his senses soon," he said. "Just wait."

And they waited, Carmina holding him, his head on her lap, gently caressing his forehead. Finally, he opened his eyes and grunted. The pain had subsided, he announced, though he still felt dizzy, so while he recovered his strength, he would very much like to hear a detailed account of the events that brought the two women to his office in such a state.

When Annabella finished her story, during which Herdforthbridge repeatedly glared, clenched his fists, cursed, and swore to skin Ledburry alive, outside was already dawn.

"At least I saved that woman's life," she concluded. "And, by the looks of it, Wyverstone's – or so I hope."

"Lord Wyverstone will recover completely," Hydenhollow said, looking intently at the intricate carvings on Edmund's desk, his hands shaking. "He seems to have an abnormal resilience to poisons. An ordinary person would have been dead by now." He turned to Edmund with a sudden move and jolted from the chair where he sat, his face a hollow image of dread. "But I have never planned to use this poison to murder you! When Ledburry told me what he did, it was too late."

He started pacing about the room, in an advanced state of agitation. "The chemical that poisoned Lord Wyverstone was not intended for murder, but to be used in my laboratory as a base for a stronger anaesthetic. It had medical purposes!"

"Did you know about the opium den in Clerkenwell?" Carmina asked. "Were you aware of the experiments Ledburry was conducting there, also for *medical purposes*?"

The baron shook his head. "No. I did not know of such a place." He turned to Annabella with imploring, watery eyes. "Miss Hammond, you must believe me! I was waiting for us to perform the tests only when the hospitals and our patients agreed. Just like you."

Still pale and not fully recovered, though looking certainly better than the previous evening, Edmund returned to his desk. "Hydenhollow, I've had enough of your hysterics for one night. Pray do have a seat and calm your nerves. I should like to return to our previous discussion, for I have yet to hear a proper explanation regarding the rather large deposit of gunpowder we found inside the mechanical waterfall."

The baron turned paler than his questioner. "About that, I –" Another long silence followed.

Edmund laced his fingers and leaned his elbows on the desk, his expression giving nothing away. He waited. "Well, the matters are quite simple," he finally said, his voice icy cold. "At the moment, I do not need a thorough account. I am in quite a hurry to pay a visit to your friend Ledburry, who is currently detained in Clerkenwell. For now, admitting to your plan to blast *The Cerulean Lady* with Her Majesty inside would suffice."

The baron's face went from pale to ashen.

"All your incriminating documents from the French Archives are in my possession," Edmund went on. "The only thing you could obtain would be a slightly more merciful sentence, which is not possible unless you admit and cooperate." He slid a sheet of paper, pen, and ink across his desk, in Hydenhollow's direction. "Write your confession. You do agree that deportation is preferable to hanging, do you not?"

The baron wrote, while repeatedly running a sweaty hand through his hair with a mindless gesture, then returned the signed paper to Edmund.

"This is all I know," he said, his voice trembling. "I signed those documents because I truly believed in England's future as a technocracy. We could have accomplished so much, and now it all came to nought."

"Her Majesty was too indulgent with your ilk." Herdforthbridge almost spat the words. "You lot had more freedom than you deserved, and believed you could run amok undetected, all in the name of science. Using science to secure your own power and privileges is disgusting."

"There's one more thing you need to know," Hydenhollow said, ignoring the duke. "I have another concern regarding those barrels."

"Which is?" Edmund asked.

"One barrel has disappeared. We used two of them in the tower as bait, and all the rest should have been inside the mechanical waterfall's maintenance room. Yet one is missing. I counted nine, but there should have been ten."

"Who else knew where you hid the gunpowder?"

"Ledburry, Quimby, and Quimby's henchman, Edwin Sheridan."

Edmund's eyes turned a few shades darker. "Last I heard, Sheridan was in French custody."

"He returned from Paris yesterday."

A heavy silence followed the baron's announcement. Edmund rose and strode to the window, his gaze on the mechanical waterfall. The thick clouds had dissipated, leaving a patch of blue clear sky over the square in their wake.

The sky of early dawn.

"So that was Sheridan's plan," he finally said, turning back to face the others. "Now that Quimby is dead, he has no master anymore and can exact his revenge. And if he could not kill me, he would kill those close to me. My only brother. One gunpowder barrel disappeared just before the *Lady*'s first flight. I was terribly mistaken. The only thing truly in danger right now is the test flight. This is why he planted spies in Jasper's team to find out the details." He examined his pocket watch. "Soon, people will start gathering at the airharbour."

"My hybriship is moored at the Inspectorates. I can fly to warn Jasper," Annabella offered. She was a dirty mess, but at least her clothes had dried.

"I'm coming with you," the duke said.

Edmund nodded. "And I shall follow as soon as I can. But first I need to see what that opium den is all about and arrest Ledburry while he is still there."

He watched as Annabella and Herdforthbridge were about to leave, a hint of a smile on his otherwise inscrutable face. "Annabella Hammond," he said in an even tone.

She turned.

"You did an excellent job."

THE GREEN AND brown uniforms of the Classified Affairs' corps were not only a dreaded but also a rather unusual sight, especially in neighbourhoods too little prone to such grand state matters as sedition, betrayals, and assassination plots, which would justify their presence. Therefore, it was no wonder for Edmund, Carmina, or anyone else in their party that all the windows, broken or not, of the decrepit lodging houses were adorned with heads of all hair colours, ages, and states of filth, watching curiously the men descending upon their court in Clerkenwell.

Edmund found the opium den in the same state Carmina had left it a few hours before, the people sprawled on the cots too oblivious of their surroundings to react, some of them sleeping, others looking at the intruders with blank, unfathomable eyes. The overpowering odour and the opium smoke filling the space had no means to escape the windowless walls.

Carmina pulled the curtains to the alcove and hurried down the stairs. Edmund lifted the bolt and opened the cellar's door.

Annabella's story had not prepared him for the true horror of the makeshift surgery room. Blood and rot everywhere, filthy people agonising behind a rusty grate, crumpled sheets of linen imbibed with carbolic acid and blood, a crate whose contents looked eerily like a pile of discarded limbs.

He had believed he was used to all kinds of horrors. He had seen all kinds of horrors.

Yet he felt the urge to be sick.

In the middle of the room, perched over an unconscious woman who ought to be Annabella's patient, Ledburry was far too engrossed in analysing the surgery result and taking notes to even notice their presence, far too obsessed with the project to care about anything else, a terrifying smile plastered on his face, his eyes barely visible through the dirty lenses of his glasses.

Madness. The man was mad.

"Lord Ledburry, Senior Lord of the Doctors Order," Edmund's voice thundered in the stone confines of the cellar, startling Ledburry. "I am arresting you for high treason, sequestration, conducting illegal experiments, and plotting with foreign governments against the Crown." He turned to his men. "Make sure all the people here receive proper care. Take to the Inspectorates every single man and woman you find in the room above. Depending on their state of consciousness, send them either to the medical ward or the interrogation room. I have plenty to discuss with them."

∿

IVY LOOKED up with a wide grin while walking towards the cruise airship area of the airharbour. After a night of incessant rain, clear skies were a most welcome change. Especially on the day when they would fly the *Lady* for the first time. The air was crisp and almost clean, without any trace of the thick fog that too many a time kept her on the berth in the morning.

Her delight ought to have been plastered all over her freckled face, for Avery Hamilton displayed one of his so very annoying smirks, most likely on her account. As usual, he was the embodiment of *pompous*, all airs, striding at ease, his hands in his pockets, his black, shoulder-length hair tied with a leather ribbon, his every move natural and graceful.

The insufferable oaf, she thought, feeling her cheeks burn in the same shade as her hair.

A handsome, kind-hearted, highly efficient oaf, nonetheless.

Until he opened his mouth.

"That grin of yours can swallow this airharbour whole," he said, his voice carrying the hint of laughter, as it always did when he teased her. "If you are so enthusiastic about the test flight, why are we bothering with the technical checks for *The Skycradle*? We aren't using her today, so we could go straight to the hangar."

Ivy glared at him. "How many times must I tell you that this airharbour has *rules*? One of these *rules* clearly states that all airships docked here are required to do their flight checks each morning and evening, no exceptions."

They climbed the metal steps to *The Skycradle*'s berth. The door opened before Ivy could unlock it.

"How strange." She stepped inside and walked towards the

255

piloting area. "I never leave my ship unlocked. And what's with this smell?"

"Ivy, wait!" Avery warned, the tease in his voice gone, but she didn't listen. She took one more step and stopped, staring at the trail of black powder crossing the entire length of the gondola.

"Rats and caterpillars, what is this? And why does my airship reek of kerosene?" But Avery caught her arm and pulled her behind him before she could check.

He kneeled and sniffed, then rose and took her hand in his. "Gunpowder. We are leaving *The Skycradle* this instant."

"No, you're not, and yes, that's gunpowder," a voice coming from behind them said. "You both know what gunpowder does, yes? Blows up inconvenient things and disobedient brats. So you'd better do as I say. If you don't want to blast, that is."

They turned around in the direction of the voice, still holding hands, Avery's warmth and strength a safe anchor in a sea of unexpected dread.

"But you are Lady Hollingsworth's new employee," Ivy said, her green eyes wide with confusion at the sight of the tall, black-haired man short of an arm. "Daniel Marlowe. What do you want from us?"

He was standing near the ladder connecting the gondola to the envelope. A rope soaked in kerosene crossed the ladder's rungs, from the gunpowder trail and up into the hull. Where the gasbags were.

Ivy's heart almost stopped. Gunpowder, kerosene, and hydrogen. A most nefarious combination.

"One spark is all I need to set your *Skycradle* aflame," he said. "If you don't want her to blaze, fly her to the lake."

Where people are gathering for the Lady's test flight, Ivy realised with horror.

Avery let go of her hand and clenched his fists, starting towards the unwanted guest.

The man they knew as Daniel Marlowe lit a brass lighter

and crouched near the black powder trail, blocking their way to the door. "Do something stupid and you'll die."

"You can't be serious," Ivy said, her voice shaking with fear and anger. "You can't mean to interfere with the test flight."

"I ain't here for conversation. Fly the bloody ship. Now!"

21

By all gods who had ever graced the pagan pantheons, he was going to throttle those three.

Jasper returned his timepiece into the pocket of his canvas coat, his mood increasingly darker. Though he had expected their presence at least half an hour before, Annabella, Ivy, and Hamilton had yet to arrive.

A night spent keeping watch at the hangar, the scandal around Edmund, and the terrifying realisation he had been terribly close to losing his brother did not help.

He could manage his people, who were waiting near the *Lady*'s scaffolding. He could also provide them with the final instructions for the test flight. But he could not manage the test flight alone.

For bloody once, everything had gone as planned. Nobody had tried to rig the ship. The hangar had been closely watched by Edmund's undercover agents, who made sure no stranger came within a foot from its walls and doors. Only for his most trusted mates to muck it up, loitering devil knew where instead of coming to the airharbour.

Cursing under his breath, he strode out of the hangar to look for them, but the throng of people walking towards the lake obstructed most of the view.

An engine roar caught his attention just as Rowena Hollingsworth's steammotor entered the airharbour's wide lane, passing the crowds and stopping in front of the hangar's main entrance, where she alighted with her father.

She was as beautiful as the clear summer sky, her hair a cascade of black curls under the yellow straw hat, her dress a patch of pale blue underneath her driving coat.

For the first time that morning, he smiled, lost in the vivid gleam of her eyes. "You are early," he said, watching her slender gloved hand adjust the driving goggles around her neck.

"I could not wait," she said, her face beaming. "I had to see you before the flight. To tell you how proud I am of you."

The way she looked at him squeezed his chest and made him wish he could be more to her than just her *dearest friend in the world*. It would be so easy. All he had to do was reclaim his status, which he had relinquished after Jade's death, and return within Society's bosom.

But he could not. He had already made his choice.

His blue gaze moved from her face to Master Hollingsworth. Being besotted was a luxury he could ill afford. "Much as I'd like to share your enthusiasm, I can't. Annabella, Ivy, and Hamilton haven't arrived yet, and I can't fly the *Lady* alone. I wonder what those three are thinking, to be so late."

"Jasper, look, here they are!" Rowena pointed her parasol in the direction of the cruise airship area. "*The Skycradle!* If Ivy is flying, Mr Hamilton should be with her. Oh, and isn't that Miss Hammond's hybriship approaching the airharbour? Have you prepared some parade before the test flight?"

A shiver crept down Jasper's spine as he followed Rowena's gaze. Whatever *The Skycradle* and *The Resilience* were doing hovering over the airharbour when their pilots should have been at the hangar ages ago, it didn't bode well.

Something had happened.

"Perhaps you should like to take a look while we make the final preparations," he said, beckoning them to enter. "Will you wait here for my return?"

"Of course, dear boy," Master Hollingsworth said, having deciphered the troubled glance Jasper had sent him in the brief moment when Rowena wasn't looking.

I don't know what happened, but it isn't good. Stay here where you are safe.

As soon as Theophilus Hollingsworth disappeared inside the hangar with his daughter, Jasper ran towards *The Skycradle*, oblivious to the noise of engines approaching.

Edmund's steammotor stopped beside him. "Get inside," he shouted.

Jasper did. "What the devil is going on? Why are you here?"

Edmund's pale countenance remained inscrutable, his voice even. "To end a story that is already too old for my tastes."

From *The Resilience*'s small gondola, Herdforthbridge watched with relief the airharbour's skyline coming closer and closer. Only a few puffy clouds shadowed the clear, blue sky, their edges trimmed with the sun's red-golden glow.

A perfect day for showing the royal airship to the merry assortment of men, women, and children of all stations eagerly waiting to see her gracing the skies.

As they hovered over the crowds of people making their way towards the entrance and beyond, he moved his gaze back to Annabella. Deep, blueish circles smeared the pale skin under her dark hazel eyes. Her black hair was as tangled as a crow's nest, loose locks falling in disarray over her shoulders and cheeks. Her black dress seemed to have gone through war, reeking of blood, the hem caked with dried mud.

She was as wild and savage as a sonata.

A tempest of a woman. Beethoven's seventeenth sonata.

As he watched her steer the airship, her attention entirely on the piloting board, he could almost feel his fingers dancing upon a set of invisible piano keys.

The aggravating woman had been working for days and days on those blasted circuits of hers, with little sustenance and even less sleep. She had spent an entire night in a madman's den, saving someone's life and risking her own while gathering important information that would finally allow Edmund to arrest the Earl of Ledburry.

She ought to be exhausted.

Yet it had taken less than half an hour of precise piloting from her part to get them to the airharbour. She'd never wavered, never shown how fatigued she actually was.

He smiled, his chest swelling with a happiness he'd thought forever lost. One more day and that utterly mad woman, that utterly wonderful woman, would be his wife.

"I shall guide *The Resilience* to the *Lady*'s hangar, and you will climb down the rope ladder to talk to Jasper." She turned her dark gaze from her levers and gauges to him. "As soon as I find a berth, I shall join you. Jasper must be mad at me by now."

"Please be careful," the duke said. "Missing your wedding again would be rather anticlimactic."

She laughed. "This time, I would not miss it for ten trips to Australia and another ten to the Arctic." Then her smile was gone, and she was staring at him with the intent gaze he knew too well. "Oscar, you should learn to trust me more. I know what I'm doing."

He closed the narrow distance between them, lightly squeezing her shoulder. "We are here to warn Jasper, but we have no idea what is going on. This is not a matter of trust but of self-preservation."

Annabella didn't answer, focusing instead on entering the

airharbour's sky space. She fiddled with a few commands on her board, but stopped just as she was about to take the turn towards the hangar.

The Resilience remained still in the air for a few moments, while Annabella squinted through the glass pane. "I am very curious to know why *The Skycradle* is flying when she should not."

The duke pulled the goggles over his eyes and looked in the same direction, spotting the unmistakable outline and colour of *The Skycradle* flying towards the lake.

"Is there any chance for Miss Blackwell to have relinquished her participation in the test flight?" he asked.

"Absolutely none. Miss Blackwell should be at the hangar, not in *The Skycradle*." She brushed a stray lock off her brow. "If she is flying her airship instead of helping Jasper when he most needs us, I can only conclude that, like in our case, something happened. At least I have you with me. I hope she has Avery with her."

Without another word, Annabella set *The Resilience* on her course towards Miss Blackwell's airship.

The duke turned to her, studying her profile. "This is not the way to the hangar. Care to tell me about your plans?"

"I cannot know until I reach Miss Blackwell. But I feel it's important to get to *The Skycradle*. After what I've learnt in the past hours, I fear she might be in danger."

Loud cheers erupted from below, as the people on the airharbour's grounds waved and shouted frantically.

"Good God, these poor chaps believe they are watching a parade," the duke said, aghast. "They think your hybriship and Miss Blackwell's *Skycradle* are part of some aerial display."

Annabella grinned. "Then who are we to shatter their hopes? Let us offer them what they wish to see."

To the audience's delight and Herdforthbridge's horror, Annabella swirled *The Resilience* a few times in the air before flying so low she almost touched the ground. Then she was up in the air again, reaching *The Skycradle* close to the lake, above the rows of seats filled with people watching in raptures.

They were already close enough to see *The Skycradle*'s trapdoor opening, and a container being lowered down, suspended in a nest of rope.

"Here we have our missing barrel," the duke said, cold dread lacing his voice. "If we don't stop the blast, these people will die a terrible death while believing they are watching some kind of spectacle."

"Crowds of terrified people running idly would not have helped me carry out my plan," Annabella argued.

He eyed her suspiciously. Her ideas were always bold and, most of the time, downright dangerous. "And your *plan* is?"

"To avert the explosion, which I can do if I direct the gunpowder barrel into the lake."

Of course, another mad idea of hers. "And how exactly do you intend to do that without setting your hybriship on fire?"

"Miss Blackwell is in danger, and I am the only one who can help her," Annabella said, her voice grim. "But first, I shall lower the ladder so that you – What the devil!" She leaned her forehead against the front window to see better. A steammotor had stopped below the hanging barrel, and someone alighted.

"Get out of there, you imbecile!" Annabella shouted, waving as frantically as the people on the benches, aware that her voice could not reach that far. "Get out of there!"

"He won't," the duke said, looking through the magnifying lens of his goggles. "The imbecile is Edmund."

Ivy Blackwell's heart was beating as loudly and erratically as a malfunctioning airship engine.

She wiped the thin sheen of sweat off her brow with a quick

move of her hand, her gaze stuck on the familiar object approaching against the blue, almost cloudless sky.

Miss Hammond's hybriship.

Coming towards them, unaware of the danger.

Ivy clenched her teeth, gritting them so hard she could hear the noise in the back of her brain.

Rats and caterpillars! How do I tell her to leave?

Still in front of her piloting board, keeping *The Skycradle* above the stacked rows of benches just as the lunatic had ordered her, she turned her head towards the main space of the gondola, her heart shrinking. With an expression she could not read, Avery was holding the brass lever of the pulley that kept the rope nest suspended, the gunpowder barrel tangled in it. Coatless, his shirtsleeves rolled up to his elbows, his strong arms tensed, he was watching her. Kneeled beside him, the lunatic kept his brass lighter too close to the rope for her comfort.

If I hadn't accepted Avery as my assistant, he wouldn't have been here now. He could die because of me.

The thought of him dead took all the air from her lungs, choking her. She had to do something. But what?

"I don't know why you are doing this, and I don't really care about your reasons," Avery said to the lunatic in his eerily calm voice that usually preceded a storm – or a brawl. "But those people who are watching us did you no harm and don't deserve such death."

"What makes you think I give a damn about them?" the lunatic said. "But I do give a damn about that weird airship coming right at us. We must do something about her, yes?"

The loud cheers reached through the trapdoor from the benches below. Their audience had no idea about the danger looming above them.

Neither had Miss Hammond. And now that she had a better view through her magnifying lenses, neither had His Grace the Duke of Herdforthbridge, who was with her in *The Resilience*.

Ivy wiped her brow again. So many innocent people could die in a moment. People whom she held dear. Whom she *loved*. She could not allow that.

As soon as his business there was finished, the lunatic had said, the three of them would fly to Paris. After blasting a gunpowder barrel over the airharbour for no reason! The man was insane.

Her hands trembled on the edge of her board. The few tendrils of auburn hair that had escaped her braid had curled with sweat. Her body was shaking underneath the petticoats and leather corset of her aeronaut ensemble. Her wet chemise was plastered on her skin.

She was not afraid.

She was *terrified*.

Being terrified was loathsome. But succumbing to such terror was much worse. She would never forgive herself.

She smoothed the pleats of her knee-length overskirt to calm her nerves, inhaled deeply, and started towards the open trapdoor, where Avery and the lunatic were crouched.

"Where do you think you're going?" the lunatic's voice thundered in the gondola. "Take another step and you'll be the first to die."

Avery's handsome face turned ashen. "Ivy, please," he said, his dark gaze an unspoken plea. "Don't do anything stupid."

She nodded, halting midway between the piloting area and the two men, aware of the black powder spread at her feet. Just one sparkle and *The Skycradle* would – But no, she would not think of that.

"I'll stay here, all right. But I *will* speak. I have something to tell that lunatic who captured my ship."

Jasper jumped off Edmund's steammotor, slamming the door, hardly believing what he saw. He looked above, shielding his eyes with his hand, as if to ascertain that a gunpowder barrel was indeed hanging over hundreds of people, that the airship hovering over his head was indeed *The Skycradle*, and the terrifying sight wasn't the result of his overwrought mind.

He blinked. The image did not disappear.

"And now what?" he asked, coming beside his brother, his hands in the pockets of his long canvas overcoat to hide the alarming degree of their trembling. "By God, if he sets that rope on fire –"

"I must attract his attention upon my person," Edmund said, moving a few steps closer to the patch of grass below the barrel. "But first, we need to find out if Miss Blackwell is unharmed and if she is alone up there."

Jasper nodded and put the amplifier in his ear, trying to catch the sounds coming from the airship above.

"Ivy, please. Don't do anything stupid."

"Hamilton is with her," he announced, letting out a breath he didn't know he was holding. He ran a hand through his tousled black locks, sending his cap to the ground. Bloody hell, he had no means to reach her.

Then Ivy's shaky voice stopped him in his tracks.

"For the past ten minutes, I've been wondering whether my parents felt the same terror I feel now when they realised they were going to die. Whether I'd have the same end as they had, blown to pieces in an airship explosion." She stuttered, on the brink of tears. *"And you know what? I don't want to end like this. I don't want to die! I want to live and fly my airship until I grow old!"* Her voice broke in a flood of tears, and Jasper swore, wishing to inflict a slow and painful death upon Edwin Sheridan. *"And I hope that someone, somehow, will save me."*

Her words from the night of their first flight together, one year before, surfaced from the quagmire of his memories. *I never ask for help because I have no one to turn to.*

We'll save you, he thought, his heart shrinking, understanding how scared she was. *We'll save you. You are not alone anymore.*

Ivy's voice again, this time more resolute through her tears. *"But even if no one comes, I can't let you have your lunatic way. I won't cower in fear. No one will die today because I was too afraid to face a madman."*

What the devil was in that mind of hers? He could easily imagine Ivy provoking Sheridan with her impulsive recklessness. He had to get her out of there before it was too late.

Annabella's hybriship had almost arrived within the amplifier's range. And the idea suddenly came to him.

"If he saw us, and I wager he did, Herdforthbridge will use my amplifier," Jasper said, turning to Edmund. "I'll try to communicate with Annabella through him. But we should send these people to safety. We don't know when that madman decides to blast the barrel."

"We have no time for evacuation." Edmund started walking in the opposite direction from the lake. "It would only create panic and chaos. But if I go, Sheridan hates me enough to follow me blindly just to kill me."

"I expected a more intelligent idea from England's spymaster," Jasper said, prompting his brother to stop. "For this once, I have a better one."

He returned the amplifier to his ear, just in time to hear the duke's voice.

"Asher, can you hear me?"

"We must take the barrel out of here," Jasper instructed, his voice cool and resolute. "I need Annabella to lure *The Skycradle* above the lake, where I'll handle the damned rope. And quick. Can she do that?"

"Just watch me," Annabella's voice confirmed.

"Your idea could send those two to their deaths," Edmund said when his brother paused his amplifier. "You will tell them to stop."

Jasper didn't budge. "You've changed," he said. "A little while ago, you wouldn't have wavered. Between hundreds of people and one of your agents, your choice would have been clear."

"I've changed," Edmund agreed, to Jasper's surprise. He lifted his gaze up to where *The Resilience* was flying. "Those two are to be married the day after tomorrow. I do not fancy sending them to their graves instead of the altar."

Jasper flinched, but only for a moment. "Trust her. Besides me, Annabella Hammond was the only other child Master Hollingsworth had ever accepted as his apprentice. He'd chosen her for a reason, and that was her quick mind. We are powerless down here. There's nothing more we can do without further risking Ivy's life. Annabella can pull this off. They will live."

The Resilience's trapdoor opened under Annabella's command. Miles and miles of rope ladder cascaded through the gap and into the air.

"Climb down!" she shouted to a dumbstruck Herdforthbridge. "Hurry, Oscar. Please!"

The aggravating woman had finally taken leave of her senses.

"Care to explain what exactly you are doing?" he asked, though he already knew the answer.

She cupped his face, piercing him with her dark gaze. "You must leave this hybriship. I cannot save Miss Blackwell and Avery if you are here."

The madwoman was preparing for the very likely possibility of death. *Alone.* And that was the one thing he could not let her do.

He would always blame himself for not following his impulse to take the first steamship to Sydney after she had left him. Making the same mistake twice was out of the question.

He did not move an inch.

She exhaled sharply, her voice a symphony of exasperation. "Good Lord, Oscar, what am I to do with you?" Her hand rested on his cheek, soft and warm. "I must drag that barrel away from here, an activity I cannot pursue with you on board. While I am rather proud of my skills and what I can do with this airship, there are still certain risks. I cannot gamble with your life, you see? If you care about the safety of those wretched onlookers who are waiting below for some stunt or about the lives of Avery and Miss Blackwell, you will climb that precious, exasperatingly beautiful frame of yours down that blasted ladder and let me do my work."

It was never supposed to be like this.

He pressed his forehead against hers, trying to keep his voice light. "You, wild creature, do not think, even for a second, that I would just leave you to your own devices. I am perfectly aware that you are perfectly capable of flying your hybriship to Australia, the Arctic, or the devil knows where, and running away from our wedding again, which I cannot possibly allow. I shall stay with you and make certain I have my bride. Stop pestering me and tell me what we need to do."

Her brilliant eyes widened, and she beamed as understanding dawned. "Damned man, how I love you! If that is your wish, we shall face this together, then. Trust my skills, but do not blame me in the afterlife if I fail."

Goggles hanging around her neck, leather gloves clutched in one hand, she kissed him. A brief kiss, but hard and wild, as if it were their last.

When she pulled away, Herdforthbridge returned the amplifier in his ear, only to jolt in pain as a loud crash and thud almost left him deaf through the small contraption.

Annabella clutched his arms, her eyes questioning. She could not say anything, not when her voice was so close to the amplifier.

"You bloody cur! Don't say I didn't warn you!"

They rushed to the gondola's front window. "Something must have happened in *The Skycradle*," the duke said, concentrating upon distinguishing the sounds coming out of Miss Blackwell's airship from the general noise of the crowds below. "I think that was Sheridan's voice. Cursing. Perhaps Miss Blackwell's passionate speech distracted the man, and Hamilton took advantage. If I'm correct, he must have hit him."

And Edmund's voice over the noise. "I shall try to dislodge the barrel as you reach it. Then you'll take it to the lake. Tell Annabella to make haste."

Annabella hurried behind the piloting board before the duke could tell her anything, turning cogs and pulling levers. He took the contraption out of his ear and joined her. "What are you doing?"

"This is our chance." She pulled her goggles over her eyes. "I count on Avery to apply his expert beating upon that bastard. And on Miss Blackwell to change *The Skycradle*'s course."

As she spoke, *The Skycradle* was indeed changing her course, flying in the opposite direction from the lake.

"Excellent!" Annabella shouted with a triumphant grin. "Most excellent!"

She started to change *The Resilience*'s own course to follow Miss Blackwell, but stopped suddenly, her hand rigid on the main steering lever. One glance and the duke understood. The magnifying glass of their goggles offered them the terrifying spectacle of a thin coat of fire engulfing the rope that held the barrel.

"When the fire reaches the gunpowder, it's over." Annabella's voice was ice cold. "But the rope is long enough to give us a slim chance, and I'm going to take it."

She accelerated, keeping her course straight towards the barrel.

"How much time do we have?" the duke asked, his heart thumping wildly.

"Mere seconds," Annabella said, flying full speed towards their target. Her airship was small and fast and a wonder of a vehicle.

Below them, he saw Edmund aiming his revolver. The bullet, shot with the precision expected from England's best trained agent, cut the rope, sending the container on a fast drop towards the ground.

The cord's end glowed, its red blaze advancing rapidly.

Edmund's bullet had aimed too high, and the flames had reached past the cut. The bloody barrel kept falling while the bloody rope kept burning. In a matter of seconds, the area around the lake would be ablaze.

"Oscar, brace!" Annabella shouted as she suddenly lowered *The Resilience* to receive the troublesome cargo in the space between the left envelope and the gondola. The small hybriship shuddered at the impact, making the duke lose balance. But she held and continued with the same speed towards the lake.

"Please enlighten me." Herdforthbridge returned to Annabella's side. "Are we by any chance carrying an almost burning barrel full of gunpowder with us?"

"We are," she said, then she looked at him, and he read everything in her eyes.

The barrel could explode any second. Whilst they had reached the lake, they might not make it to the water. Miss Blackwell and Hamilton were safe, Edmund and Jasper were safe, the crowds were safe.

But they were not. If the barrel exploded above the lake, the only thing it blew to pieces would be their hybriship.

"If we die here, I want you to know I have no regrets," he said as she pulled and pushed more of her blasted levers, whose function he did not understand. "I love you and all the chaos you brought into my life."

"I have no regrets either," she said, fiddling with one more cryptic button on her piloting board. "I love you and all the order you brought into my life."

As she uttered those words, which might very well have been the last ones he would ever hear from her, the two envelopes retracted, dislodging the barrel.

Container and hybriship plunged into the lake's water almost at the same time, the collision's force sending Annabella and Oscar to the gondola's floor. Everything went still except for a loud, distant thump, and Herdforthbridge wondered whether they perhaps had died.

He heard Annabella's breathing close to him and realised that the loud, distant thump was not the gunpowder exploding, but his heart. Suddenly they were up on the lake's surface, gliding on the envelopes.

They were alive.

He pulled her to him, still sprawled on the hard wood of the gondola's floor, and kissed her.

"You mad, wild creature!" He laughed, crushing her in his arms. "Your brilliant mind saved us. This incredible vehicle you invented kept everyone alive."

The Resilience reached the shore to the sight of hundreds of people standing, waving, and shouting, the benches a spot of colour against the clear blue sky. A light wind carried the fragrance of spring tinged with the airharbour's strong odour of tar.

He smiled. The world was right again, and the day felt warmer and brighter.

"These people don't realise how close they were to disaster," Annabella said, her beautiful, smudged face beaming. "At least we offered them quite a spectacle, which they will believe was part of the test flight."

Herdforthbridge jumped on the shore and helped her alight from the hybriship on the patch of grass where their friends were waiting. Edmund, Jasper, Miss Hollingsworth and her father, Miss Blackwell, and Avery Hamilton.

The duke went to Edmund. "What about Sheridan?"

"We have him," he said. "He is in the custody of the Classified Affairs' Corps. So is Ledburry."

Carmina Harcourt emerged from behind the others and wrapped her arms around Annabella. "Thank you," she said, her trembling voice a whisper only Annabella, Edmund, and the duke could hear. "Thank you for being alive."

To make the Classified Affairs' Queen of Disguise cry was quite a feat, Herdforthbridge thought, almost amused. Carmina Harcourt, one of the best agents the Crown ever had, always cool, composed and imperturbable, was actually sobbing.

"If I said we had enough excitement for the morning, I would be wrong." Jasper glared at them, his arms crossed at his chest, pretending to be in one of his usual fits of anger – something which the duke might have believed had it not been for the smirk curling the corner of the younger Asher brother's mouth. "It is about time we returned to the hangar. We have one *Cerulean Lady* waiting for us."

EPILOGUE

London, June 1896

"Whilst it pleases me to no end that the new workshop suits your tastes, I am here to remind you that we must take our leave lest we shall be late to the Engineers World Gathering's grand opening."

At the sound of that low, thick voice, Annabella Bashford, the Duchess of Herdforthbridge, turned just in time to see her husband stepping into the room, tall and achingly handsome, the sun coming through the windows playing in his golden, shoulder-length curls. Her heart racing, she started towards him, a wide smile on her face.

He had set a workshop for her as a wedding gift, in his former music parlour adjacent to the conservatory. Wide and well-aired, with tall windows covering the most part of the walls, it exceeded her wildest expectations for a workroom. In a harmony of wood, metal, glass, and brick, the cabinets and shelves, the tables, and the workbenches were provided with all the instruments and implements she needed for her experiments – voltmeters, multimeters, cogs, wires, gauges, chosen most likely with Jasper's help and expertise. Sheets of paper and tracing paper, pens, quills, and other drawing tools filled the drawers of her desk. Gloves, goggles, and canvas aprons were neatly folded inside a cupboard close to the central workbench. Massive pots of luxurious plants decorated the corners of the room and the empty spots alongside the walls. More plants were hanging from the high ceiling in between rows of long wires that supported electric bulbs.

Her own space, which this dear man who knew her so well, and for so long, had prepared so carefully. Less than two weeks had passed since their small wedding at Herdforthbridge's townhouse in London, and she had never been happier. Or more complete.

And that was their first public appearance as a married couple.

"Oh, but I am so ready," she said, her eyes gleaming. "Ready to provide all of London Society with excellent gossip material, that is. Just imagine!" She changed her voice to dramatic effect. "Poor Herdforthbridge, look at him! How completely besotted he must be to let his wayward wife continue with her tinkering and fly airships instead of entertaining guests and paying morning calls."

He laughed wholeheartedly, a glint of mischief in his blue gaze. "I do not know about that, but I can ascertain at least that our difference in attire will make us the most bizarre couple at the event."

Her Oscar looked dashing in formal attire, wearing his perfectly tailored, perfectly spotless clothes with his usual grace and elegance, tall and beautiful in black and white, with just a hint of that wild, untamed part of him, which he had discovered in himself during their journey to the Australian colonies and which she loved so much. Whereas she –

She proudly wore her aeronaut ensemble. The long canvas

overskirt had replaced the black silk of her mourning dress. On the dark brown leather corset that kept in place her white, short-sleeved chemise, shone the double badges of Engineers and Doctors Orders, their brass catching the sunlight. Her flying goggles were tightly clasped on top of her head over her black locks, of which a few tendrils had escaped over her temples to frame her face.

"Well then, Your Grace, shall we?" he said, offering his arm.

Soon, they were at the mews and in Annabella's steammotor.

"I am grateful, you know," she said, while waiting for the boiler to reach the right temperature. "Her Majesty's invitation for the four of us to join her aboard *The Cerulean Lady*, and for me to pilot her airship, equals a public recognition of us. Surely, she did this for your and Wyverstone's sake, but I am still grateful. This way, Society will receive us back in their midst, Rebecca and me." She turned to face him with a rather unladylike grin. "To be clear, I have no need for Society to receive me in their midst again. But I am ready to sacrifice myself for you and Mama."

He cupped her face and kissed her one more time before she steered the vehicle out onto the street. "Whatever my duchess wishes, I am happy to oblige. With the very small exception of traversing vast amounts of space in an airship."

Their laughter drowned in the engine noise of the steammotor driving towards Hyde Park.

Hyde Park was abuzz with activity.

Men, women, and children of upper and lower orders mingled in a colourful assortment of dresses, bonnets and reticules. Conveyances of all kinds, from modest hansom cabs, up to the most advanced steammotors, were lined up at the entrance. Above the park's fringes, gondotram wagons glided on their iron tracks towards the Hyde Park Corner skystation to disgorge yet another set of visitors.

As Edmund walked to England's pavilion where *The Cerulean Lady* was berthed, with Carmina at his arm, his peers greeted him with cold politeness. They could not downright give him the cut direct, as many most certainly wished. Not after the invitation Her Majesty had extended to him and his fiancée, Rebecca Beatrix Hammond. Her unspoken statement could not be clearer. She acknowledged and accepted the Earl of Wyverstone, his chosen lady, and his work as the country's spymaster.

Yet he was aware of the rumours that have been circulating around London's drawing rooms for the past two weeks. Of how Society regarded him as a pariah for consorting with someone they considered a liar, a cheat, and a fallen woman.

He could not care less. For the first time in years, he finally felt at peace.

A gust of wind caressed his face, accentuating the subtle fragrance of cinnamon and lavender coming from the woman beside him. She wore no disguise. Her dark green walking dress matched the bright green of her eyes. Her silken, black hair, which she had kept in its natural colour, gleamed in blueish hues in the mild early summer sun.

"I find it strange for me to walk like this, as myself," she said, a hint of a smile on her lips. "For us to walk like this. And yet so wonderful. Living with less burdensome secrets is rather exhilarating."

"We still have our share of them to keep." He returned her smile, locking his intense blue gaze with hers. "Whilst I closed the *Humautomaton* file, our work for the Crown will not get any easier. One never knows when some other madman will dream of overthrowing the current order, so we must be prepared. But I suppose it will be a great deal more interesting with you by my side on a permanent basis."

He could not help a grin, that kind of grin which carved dimples at the corners of his mouth and made him look five years younger. In just one week, they would be married. Until then, she would live in her mother's house, as part of her quest to get her old life back and build a bridge between Carmina Harcourt and Rebecca Beatrix Hammond.

"I would rather not think about lunatics," she said as they arrived at *The Cerulean Lady*'s berth. "Let us just enjoy this day. I have had enough of Ledburry, Sheridan, and their ilk."

The crowds had become denser around the entrances to the Crystal Palace, gawking at the magnificent glass and iron structure that stood tall and proud in the sunlight, housing the latest engineering wonders of the world.

Close to the main front doors, in England's pavilion, *The Cerulean Lady* was silently waiting, the anchorage grapples sunk firmly in the berth's walls. Royal guards lined each side of the stairs leading to the gondola, resplendent in their parade uniforms.

Edmund and Carmina climbed up to the gondola's lower level, where the crew was starting to gather in the navigation cabin, then took the small flight of stairs to the deck above. Half of the space was open. The other half was lavishly decorated with comfortable armchairs and settees, tea tables, bookshelves, a desk, and an escritoire – a magnificent drawing room or study to be used in the sky. Blue wallpaper adorned with golden leaves covered the walls, in the same colours as the spectacular envelope.

"She is breathtakingly beautiful," Carmina said, her mesmerised green gaze absorbing every small detail before finally settling on Edmund. "Thank you for making her possible."

Edmund led her to the open deck. Hyde Park unfolded before their eyes in acres upon acres of green.

"It was not I who made her possible," he said, just as

Herdforthbridge and Annabella alighted from their steammotor and went up the berth's stairs, as perfectly matched in everything else as they were mismatched in their attire. Hidden from their view, Jasper was climbing down a ladder leaning against the other end of the gondola, near an engine pod. Edmund nodded towards him. "It was he. He, Miss Blackwell, and their team. It was they who made the *Lady* possible."

Jasper jumped off the ladder, skipping the last rungs, and adjusted his cap on his dishevelled head. Dark smudges smeared his formerly white shirt, whose sleeves were rolled up to his elbows. A brass pocket watch was dangling from his waistcoat, escaped from his pocket. His trousers sported generous quantities of oil and grime, arranged upon an irregular pattern on the fabric. His coat lay forgotten on the grass.

He looked like a dockworker rather than an engineer in Her Majesty's service, assigned to fly Her Majesty's airship. Which he had decided not to do, to everyone's surprise and horror.

"Last engine cleared!" he shouted with a wide grin, shading his eyes with his hand to have a better view of the lively scenery around the Crystal Palace, his heart swelling with happiness with every new gawk from the curious visitors.

So many had come, and each one had stopped to admire the royal airship. He would rather not think of how close they'd been to not have her ready on time. To not have an Engineers World Gathering at all.

Among the onlookers, Gilbert Fontaine. He strode to him.

"An airship quite fit for the royals," the French engineer said. "You did well, Asher. Perhaps one of these days you'll visit *L'Étoile*. I'll take you on a tour myself."

Jasper wiped his hands on his trousers, his blue eyes

gleaming with interest. "That would be very kind of you. I'm glad things turned out well for your team."

"*L'Étoile* should have been our exhibit, to begin with," he said, a satisfied smile on his face. "Speaking of which, I should return to my lads. I don't trust that lot, not one bit." He took a few steps in the direction of the French pavilion and stopped, turning to Jasper again. "Thank you, Asher." Then he disappeared among the throngs of people.

A steammotor he recognised in an instant stopped close to the *Lady*'s berth, and Rowena alighted from the driver's seat. Her father, Ivy, and Avery Hamilton followed.

"Congratulations, my boy," Master Hollingsworth said, gently patting his arm. "You have accomplished your assignment beautifully." He stopped for a moment, his watery eyes locked on the *Lady*'s magnificent frame. "I reckon you'll want to return to your workbench. However, soon I shall have to name a successor to take my place as the royal mechanic."

Jasper understood. Yet, as dear as his master was to him, he had to disappoint him.

"You know me." A trace of sadness laced his voice. "I am the happiest when I'm in my workshop. Or at the airharbour. I am an airship engineer. This is what I want to be."

Rowena touched his elbow without looking at him. On impulse, he covered her gloved hand with his. "I think it's all right," she said. "Father surely understands. The Order has plenty of accomplished engineers he can choose from, isn't that so, Father?"

The royal mechanic nodded. "Indeed. Now, I believe we should go. Her Majesty will arrive at any moment, and it is not done to board the *Lady* after her."

Ivy stood still for a few more moments, and Jasper saw the sorrow in her eyes as she stared at the royal airship. "My parents would have loved her," she said, her voice shaking. "Look what we've done with their schematics."

He flicked her forehead, offering her his brightest smile. "They would. But I think you should go. Else Annabella will have the navigation cabin all for herself and she'll wreak havoc upon our piloting board, God forbid!"

He shuddered in mock horror, and she laughed, her eyes still shimmering with unshed tears.

She glared at him in the typical Ivy Blackwell manner he already knew so well. "You should have been there with us, you know," she said. "But you chose to leave me with those two aggravating, exasperating –" She stopped when he noticed Avery Hamilton's amused stare.

"I am exactly where I need to be," Jasper said, acknowledging once again the truth of his words. He was happy there, doing the last checks, shouting, and helping the ground crew. He was happy there, soiling his clothes and hands and face beyond recognition, carrying with him the pungent odour of oil and soot, of engines and pipes. Ivy and Annabella would do an excellent job as Her Majesty's pilots for that first flight. He was needed elsewhere.

Almost an hour later, when the *Lady*'s gondola door finally closed, he lifted his gaze towards the cabin, where Annabella and Ivy were waiting in front of the piloting board. His cap tumbled in the grass, but he didn't notice. With his lips curled in a wide smile, his heart thumping, he shouted in the berth's amplifier.

"Send her up!"

He watched as the *Lady*, *his* airship, slowly detached from her anchorage before the eyes of the mesmerised crowds, amongst the general cheer. On the gondola, Annabella's slender handwriting curled in shimmering gold.

Ea Caelium Superabit

He watched as the *Lady* soared higher and higher, her envelope glimmering in bright shades of gold and blue. He laughed as raw, fierce happiness coursed through him, filling his soul.

Against all odds, we are here, he thought, his blue eyes glued on the airship flying above the Crystal Palace. *If we came such a long way, she will too.*

He watched as *The Cerulean Lady* set her course towards Westminster, the letters on the gondola becoming smaller and smaller.

Ea Caelium Superabit.

"She will conquer the skies."

AUTHOR'S NOTE

Thank you for reading *Caelium*. I hope it was as enjoyable for you to read as it was for me to write. Now that the *Cerulean Airship* trilogy has come to an end, I must admit that I feel a bit nostalgic. This is why I am planning to write a few more novellas featuring some of the characters you met throughout the three books of the series.

In the meantime, I am working on a new book, *The Catcher of Souls*, which will be the first in my upcoming *Cursed Arts* series (this time, Victorian gaslamp). If you are curious about this Jack the Ripper retelling, you can read the first chapter at the end of this book.

As always, it would be lovely and much appreciated if you could spare a moment to leave a review on your favourite retailer's website.

You can also read a FREE short prequel featuring Jade Asher, set around the date of the *Golden Griffin* incident. The novella is available for download on my website as a bonus exclusively for my monthly newsletter subscribers. You will hear from me once a month or when I have news about my upcoming books, inspiration sources, behind the scenes, and many more.

I would also love to keep in touch. You can find me at www.delifictional.com and on social media, where we can talk about books and all things steampunk and Victorian.

ACKNOWLEDGMENTS

As always, a heartfelt thank you to all the wonderful people who are constantly supporting and encouraging my writing journey, especially to Monica, Alina and Rose. Without your help, this trilogy would not have been the same.

Turn the page to read the first chapter of *The Catcher of Souls*, the first book in my upcoming *Cursed Arts* series, a Jack the Ripper retelling with a gaslamp touch.

EXCERPT FROM THE CATCHER OF SOULS: CHAPTER 1

London, August 1888

D *eath comes in many forms. I am one of them.*
That little thought returned to the back of his mind like it did each time he concocted one of his strange potions, making the corner of his mouth twitch in a crooked, bitter smile behind the leather mask that kept the vile odour at a safe distance from his lungs.

An angel of death.

He almost laughed at the idea.

No, Sebastian Blackmore, Viscount Keswick, the only son and heir of the Duke of Allensmore, was no angel. Quite the opposite, in fact.

He watched as the liquid distilled, waiting for the vapours to turn into small droplets and fall to the bottom of the round glass container, his intense blue eyes almost dark in the sickly light of the lamp on his desk. His gloved hand brushed a few fair curls off his brow as he concentrated on the result in the sanctuary of his study-turned-makeshift laboratory.

At last, the transparent recipient of the distilling installation started to collect the bright pink substance Sebastian was expecting, a potent mixture of belladonna and laudanum, blended with three grains of strychnine, that would bring eternal sleep swiftly and with just the right amount of pain.

He poured his newest poison into the finger-sized, transparent phial, and secured it with a cork stopper before it vanished inside his waistcoat's pocket just as the mantel clock's hour hand moved to show nine in the evening.

Sebastian discarded his canvas apron, sleeve covers, and mask and plopped himself down into the leather armchair behind his desk, with little care for the evening attire his valet had so carefully helped him don a few hours before. Had he seen him, the poor man would have had heart failure.

Fortunately, such an incident was unlikely to occur, as Sebastian's laboratory was uncharted territory for the entire staff of his London house. The installation made of glass and brass where he prepared his deadly substances, the array of small bottles and phials filled with powders and liquids of various colours and degrees of toxicity, arranged in perfect order in the cabinets, the bunches of plants left hanging from a wooden beam to dry, and the strange old books on the shelves were not exactly part of the usual décor of a gentleman's study – of a future duke's study – so he would rather spare his household from a most curious sight. And from speculating about his activity for the Home Office's Department for the Handling of the Unnaturals, which only a few people knew about.

An assassin for the Crown. Of the most cowardly sort. That is what I am.

Not even one of the many unnaturals he had put to sleep in the past three years had actually seen his face. They had all died wondering who and what had killed them.

Just as those abominations deserved. People born with anatomical and physiological abilities that no living thing should possess. People who can control other people through the extraordinary power of their minds and bodies. Who are too dangerous to simply arrest and confine. Who are a liability to the unwitting men and women of London.

Just as his next victim deserved, the unnatural he would hunt that night, a man who had acquired a fortune through trade and believed he had the right to use his accursed power to terrify the poor and the weak.

Like all the bedevilled unnaturals believed.

Much as he loathed his damned assignments, he was a necessary evil for the stability of the city.

Of the Crown.

His face as blank as a stone slab, Sebastian rose and left the room, feeling the shape of the poison phial through the fabric of his evening waistcoat. After several days of tailing that man, it was about time to remove him.

He climbed down the stairs and crossed the narrow corridor, passing the ethereal landscape paintings that lined the wall up to the vestibule, where the butler was waiting to hand him his walking stick, cloak, and hat.

"Clerkenwell Green," he instructed his coachman and trusted aide, before disappearing inside the black, crestless carriage. The man was too used to his master's excursions in the most unlikely and sordid places in town to show any sign of astonishment.

He settled himself on the upholstered bench and rapped at the ceiling with his walking stick, prompting the conveyance to start its monotonous drive down the gaslit streets of London.

"Jonathan Maddings, tradesman," Sebastian said, his voice barely audible in the small enclosure of the carriage, repeating the information he had received from the Home Office. "An unnatural who can hypnotise his victims to bend them to his will. His wife and daughter have no knowledge of his criminal endeavours, which he exacts around the gin distillery in

Clerkenwell every Wednesday and Friday after half past nine in the evening, while his family believe he is at his club." He fiddled with the small phial of laudanum and belladonna extract tucked in his pocket, a corner of his mouth curled in a derisive grimace. "But not for long."

Outside, through the narrow slit of the window's curtains, London unfurled in a rapid succession of red brick buildings darkened with soot and smoke, their outline hard to distinguish under the yellow lights of the streetlamps. The day's heat had heightened the stench of the streets, which crawled inside the carriage, lifting the odour of rot and human waste into Sebastian's nostrils, making him cringe in disgust.

Bloody hell.

The timepiece attached to his waistcoat showed a quarter to ten when his carriage stopped in Clerkenwell Green.

A cauldron for London's radicals and agitators, Sebastian thought while alighting, pulling up the tall collar of his black cloak. *A most appropriate place for a such criminal to loiter.*

His hand on the phial, he strode towards Clerkenwell Close, which lay deserted and dark.

"I swear on me mum's grave I ain't a harlot!" A thin, desperate voice broke the eerie silence of the alley. "I was on me way home, guv'nor! Not taking the streets! Let me go! Please!"

A small, meagre bundle of a woman stood still against the dirty back wall of a lodging house, without moving an inch. In the almost non-existent light of the street, Sebastian could make out her dishevelled blond hair and half-torn dress, and the white bonnet lying in the alley's dirt.

A working-class woman, judging from her modest but clean clothes. One of the women working at the gin distillery for long hours and little pay.

Who was on her way home.

Sebastian held his breath and exhaled slowly, keeping his

rage under control. Another innocent would have died at the hands of an unnatural. Of a monster with a human face.

Jonathan Maddings' laugh cut the woman's words. "Oh, love, I'm afraid you'll miss dinner tonight." He took one step towards her, cupping her chin. "But keep begging, mind you. Seeing you so scared and defenceless makes our little encounter even more pleasant. I could enjoy some more of your begging before having my way with you."

With a swift move, Sebastian leaned his walking stick against the wall and extracted the poison out of his pocket, pouring the content over his gloves, soaking them in the pink liquid. He rubbed his hands and walked with steady steps towards them. For the first time since he handled unnaturals for the Home Office, he was going to show his face. But that abomination would carry it to his grave.

"You will let her go. Now."

His deep, baritone voice startled the man enough to turn his head to the unwanted guest, forgetting about his victim for a second.

"Run!" Sebastian shouted at the woman, who was gaping at him with terrified eyes in the dark. "His hypnosis only works as long as he focuses on you. Leave at once!"

She didn't wait for him to ask again. Grabbing her cotton skirts, she dashed towards the other end of the street without looking back.

"Where the bloody hell did you come from?" Maddings bellowed, trying to fix Sebastian with his stare.

But Sebastian was already behind him, avoiding eye contact. The other man turned quickly again, in a new failed attempt to immobilise him through hypnosis. While Sebastian was not as tall and sturdy as Maddings, his unrivalled agility made him anticipate his enemy's moves just in time to dodge them, always keeping himself behind him, away from his gaze.

"You could have lived a quiet life," Sebastian said, careful to remain hidden. "With your wife and daughter who love you because they have no idea what you really are." He jumped one step to the side, avoiding the man's eyes. "But instead of minding your comfortable life in Mayfair, you chose to use your mind power to hypnotise poor women and terrorise them in this wretched part of London where no decent human ventures." Another step, keeping himself behind his adversary. "But rest assured, Jonathan Maddings. Your wrongdoings will come to an end tonight."

The man stopped, too startled to continue his useless chase. "You know my name and my power. Who the devil are you?"

"Death." Sebastian's voice, no louder than a whisper, sounded like a doom bell's toll in the man's ear.

He covered Maddings' mouth and nose with his gloved hand and started counting. That new concoction should work in a matter of seconds.

One, two, three...

The man's body started convulsing uncontrollably, his arms flailing, struggling without success to escape Sebastian's iron grip.

Four, five, six, seven...

"I – I can't –" His muffled voice stuttered against Sebastian's wet glove. "I can't breathe –"

Eight, nine, ten.

All struggle suddenly ceased. One moment later, Sebastian cast a sarcastic glance at the man sprawled unconscious in the alley's dirt.

"It's dangerous to ramble about this place at night," he said, pushing the lifeless body with the tip of his perfectly polished black boot, anticipating what the general verdict would be the next morning when Maddings was found. *Footpads.* "Petty murder for robbery is too common a sight in this part of London."

Sebastian took off his gloves, peeling them off from the

inside out, ignoring the faint smell of poison and death that had mingled with the narrow street's foul air. He threw them and checked his hands. The impermeable lining had kept them dry.

He squatted and lit a match, watching his gloves turn into a pile of ashes near the dead man.

The alley returned to its silent darkness as he retrieved his walking stick and strode back to his carriage, without looking back.

"The Marquess of Hyden's house in Berkley Square," he said to his coachman, putting on a new, pristine pair of gloves.

I have a ball to attend.

For Abel Dunsmore, the fourth Earl of Wrenbury, balls were a most tedious affair, and that particular one reminded him why he preferred to avoid them, favouring instead London's most notorious gaming hells, his club or a mistress' bedchamber.

Or the most precious sanctity of his studio, among his lengths of canvas, pigments, and brushes.

But that night he was in neither of those places. And, while for most of Society's members, Lady Hyden's dinners, parties and events were among the most fashionable and sought-after social functions in London, he found the grand ballroom as confining as a cage, abuzz with gossip and impregnated with the lingering odour of body sweat that the lavish flower arrangements and perfume fragrances could not entirely hide.

Keeping a polite smile on his face and acting as the perfectly mannered gentleman while dancing with the host's youngest daughter was another challenge altogether. It was a matter of etiquette, he reminded himself, pretending not to notice the pairs of eyes glancing at them and the speculations sprouting behind the fans, whose tendrils were soon to envelop the entire female population congregated at the Marchioness of Hyden's house.

Will the Earl of Wrenbury marry Lady Madeline Walden, daughter of the Marquess of Hyden, one of the most powerful men in England?

Mischief glinted in his dark eyes. Oh, but let them wonder. Her infatuation with him was no secret.

Neither was his reputation, and his reputation was precisely what had brought him to Berkley Square that night. He hadn't attended Lady Hyden's ball out of social obligation, politeness, or for political conversation with his peers.

Abel was there for a woman. Who wasn't Madeline Walden, the Marquess of Hyden's youngest daughter, but Georgiana Lawrence, the widow of the late Earl of Carlton, a woman as elusive as the promise of clear sky in London in winter. A woman who loved art as much as he did, and who almost never attended any social functions.

The affair they had in Florence, which only lasted for a few days, would never be enough for him. So why not explain to her the advantages of taking him as her lover? At seven and twenty, he wasn't in a hurry to marry. He was managing his estate and his duties in the House of Lords just fine, and he could do without a wife for a few more years. They could enjoy each other as they wished, without any obligation.

"Well? Lord Wrenbury?"

Lady Madeline's voice brought him back to the reality of the ballroom – and of his dancing partner. He was considerably taller than her, his lean, muscular frame leading her with ease among the other dancers.

"Oh, I'm afraid I could not hear you." He offered her one of his most charming smiles. "The music and noise around us are the culprits, I swear."

"I was asking what I must do to convince you to paint my portrait."

His smile froze, turning into a grimace. Of all the things she – or anyone else – could ask of him, that was the most impossible one.

"Much as I loathe to disappoint, portraits are not my forte," he replied, regaining his composure in an instant. "It's been years since I last did one, but I could recommend several exceptionally talented artists who would be able to help you much better than I." Another dashing smile. "Surely, you do understand I would not want to make a fool of myself. Your beauty deserves better than my humble attempts."

"But I want no other exceptionally talented artist." Madeline Walden's haughty voice betrayed a woman who had never been denied anything. "I want you. Everyone says you are *the* exceptionally talented artist of London."

Abel lifted an eyebrow, equally startled and irked at her unexpected brazenness. Her blonde curls, spilling out of a carefully arranged chignon from the top of her head down to her bare shoulders, glittered under the chandelier's lights, complementing her blue eyes, fair skin and plump lips slightly opened in a delicate smile.

She was pretty, from an excellent family, and one of Society's most courted young ladies. And she let everyone know on every occasion and in no uncertain terms, defying her father's authority and the general rules of etiquette, that she had set her eyes on him. He should consider himself a fortunate man. Which he did not.

The music stopped before he could find the right answer, and he offered his arm to escort her back, silently grateful he was spared from continuing their conversation.

"Thank you for the honour, Lady Madeline." He bowed as he brought her to her sister and their friends. "It was a pleasure."

Finally free to pursue the real reason for his presence at Lady Hyden's ball, he searched for Georgiana Lawrence out of the corner of his eye, spotting her just as she was leaving the stuffy ballroom for the fresh air of the balcony.

He grinned, pleased at the perfect timing. *Excellent.*

It took him just a few strides to reach the French doors, his sharp ears picking up fragments of whispered conversation that lifted his eyebrow and curled the corner of his mouth.

I hear the marchioness asked Lady Lawrence to sing for us tonight. A private recital for her ball. I wonder what she did to convince her.

Oh, but Lady Lawrence will not sing. She will only play the piano. I am astonished she even accepted the invitation to attend Lady Hyden's ball.

My dear, she is an excellent pianist, but you must hear her angel voice. Unfortunately, though, she will never sing again.

Abel remembered the rumours that circulated two years before when Georgiana Lawrence had suddenly stopped singing – and attending her social circles. She had been terribly ill, bedridden for several weeks. A severe cold that had damaged her voice beyond repair, she had said, but Society's members had expressed various, usually different, opinions on the matter.

He breathed deeply, the night air a most welcome change to the heat inside, and watched her for a few moments.

Her light chestnut hair, gathered high at the back of her head, caught the moonlight, turning almost golden. The sapphire teardrop earrings, the same intense colour as her dark blue silk gown, led his gaze to the slender column of her neck and the silver and pearl necklace she wore around it.

By all gods and saints, she was as beautiful as he remembered – and he remembered more of her than his sanity could handle. Her long, thick tresses spread across the pillow, the gleam in her hazel eyes, the velvety sensation of her fingers on his skin, her soft voice murmuring his name.

No. His thoughts were taking a dangerous turn, and he needed his wits about him.

He closed the distance between them and leaned against the balcony's stone edge beside her, inhaling the flowery fragrances that a soft wind brought from the garden below.

"Have you not considered that standing here alone is a rather bold move?" Abel finally turned to face her, brushing a hand through his dark hair, which he wore slightly longer and more unruly than fashionable. "Society's gossip mill never sleeps."

"Lord Wrenbury." Georgiana Lawrence graced him with a curtsey, her voice polite and distant. "One of the advantages of married women and widows is the possibility of enjoying liberties such as relishing a breath of fresh air without the necessity of a chaperone."

She was keeping him at a distance. As he had expected.

"I missed you," he said, deciding that a direct approach would be a better option than wasting his words. "I even tried to call on you a few times after my return from Italy. But you kept your doors closed. And I wish for the key to open them."

She held his intense gaze, a hint of a smile dancing on her lips. "My lord, I'm afraid such an item does not exist."

Her eyes settled on the pleasant darkness of the garden. "Two years ago, I had just lost my husband, and you, your parents. Fate wanted us to meet on foreign soil, where no one knew us, out of our Society's eye. What pushed us into each other's arms in Florence was desperation. Sadness. The need for solace after the death of people close and dear to us." She turned to him again, with an expression he could not fathom. "But it was a mistake, one that we must forget and never repeat."

She bowed again and turned her back to him, disappearing inside the ballroom before he could fully understand what had just happened.

So that was it, he thought, almost laughing at her flat rejection, aware that he had grossly underestimated her. He should have known better. A woman like Georgiana Lawrence would never accept such a blunt proposal to be a mistress. Even if it came from the dashing Earl of Wrenbury, whom no other woman had ever rejected.

All right, then. An actress or an opera dancer would do. For now.

A dark shadow moving with feline agility and stealth through the garden caught his attention. His eyes had adjusted to the darkness, enough to recognise his closest friend.

Sebastian. If he used the back gate, he must have come to report to the marquess. No matter. If Keswick is here, this damned evening will be less boring.

A THICK, velvet curtain in dark brown colour at the end of a narrow flight of circular stairs marked the second, less conspicuous entrance to the Marquess of Hyden's study, opposite from the main door that led to the corridor on the first floor. Sebastian climbed the stone steps from the garden to the room and found the door slightly ajar. The marquess was waiting for him.

He stopped with his hand on the curtain at the sound of the feminine, musical voice coming from the study.

Lady Madeline Walden. He had to remain hidden until she left.

"But Papa, you must do something!" The muffled thud of her dainty evening slipper stomping on the carpet promptly followed her whining. "Wrenbury still refuses to paint my portrait. He dismissed me quite bluntly not half an hour ago, an offence I cannot simply overlook."

"My dear, I'm afraid your infatuation with Wrenbury has become intolerable." Annoyance laced her father's voice, who sounded like a man who had exhausted his last ounce of patience. Through the narrow space between the curtain and the wall, Sebastian saw Hyden rising from his chair and pacing about the room, his hands clasped at his back "You want your portrait done? Fine. Tomorrow I shall summon the best painters in London. But you must stop this nonsense with Wrenbury at once."

"You surely know there is no other painter in London as good as Lord Wrenbury." She seemed adamant about winning that battle. "I want him and no other and you are the only person who can help me, so I came to ask for your help. Please, Papa!"

Poor Wren.

"Be aware that I shall never entertain your illusions of a marriage with Wrenbury, and that is my final decision," the marquess said, his face almost as red as his thick hair and sideburns. "His actions, of which, alas, too few can be mentioned in polite company, have tainted the respectable title he inherited from his father. I have no intention to associate our family's name with that blackguard."

"Papa, I only want him to paint my portrait, not to ask for my hand. If you help me secure Lord Wrenbury's talent, I promise you will hear no more of that."

"All right, all right," her father said, raising his arms in an exasperated sign towards an invisible god. "But you must give me your word that, once you have your portrait, there will be no more talk of Wrenbury in this house."

Sebastian's mouth twitched in a grimace. She might have fooled her father, who never denied her anything, but she could not fool him. Her given word was a plain lie. She had no intention of leaving Wren alone, portrait or not, regardless of the polite, yet clear way his friend let her understand more than once that he had no interest in her – or her hand.

Hyden will try to use his influence to coerce him. But the marquess' power to coerce other people lies in information, and Wrenbury has no dark secrets to defend. He should be safe.

"Keswick, do come in," Hyden said after Lady Madeline left. "I was expecting you."

Sebastian entered the study, taking the same armchair the marquess' daughter had occupied moments before.

"I put Maddings to sleep," he said, taking the snifter of brandy his host offered him. "Quite a vile unnatural, that one."

"Did anyone see you? Clerkenwell Green is not exactly the most secluded area in London."

Sebastian sipped the drink, delaying his answer. If he told the truth, the marquess would chase Maddings' intended victim and make sure she never spoke a word about what happened that night – or about anything else. Never again. To anyone.

The woman would never recognise him, anyway. It was too dark, and she was too scared. He would not put her in danger after saving her.

"No, no one saw me," he finally said, moving his gaze from the empty glass to the marquess, his direct superior and the power behind the Home Office's Department for the Handling of the Unnaturals. "Do we have a new name?"

Hyden's frown brought his eyebrows together in a single thick line at the base of his brow. "I shall give you none for a while, as I have another kind of assignment for you." He refilled both glasses before pushing the newspaper on his desk in Sebastian's direction. "Have you read the journals today?"

He hadn't. A man who'd spent the entire day locked up in his laboratory had no time for such mundane activities.

"A woman was murdered in Whitechapel," Hyden explained while Sebastian read the article. "Polly Martin, possibly a prostitute. They found her mutilated body this early morning in a dark gate on Buck's Row."

Sebastian lifted his head from the newspaper for a moment, half intrigued, and half bemused. "I still fail to understand what this murder has to do with our department. And with me in particular. Last time I checked, I was not working for Scotland Yard."

"Her liver was missing," Hyden added.

"Christ!" The viscount put the newspaper back on the desk. "Do you believe she was an unnatural? And the murderer was after her for that reason?"

"I am almost certain that was the case, and I need you to investigate and confirm my theory. If I am right and she was an unnatural, we need to find out her ability and whether she was murdered because of it. I do not like this affair. And I'm afraid of what lies behind it."

Who the devil would like an affair that involves hacked unnaturals and missing organs?

Sebastian rose. It was past the time he went to the ballroom. "Give me a day or two and you will have your answers."

Hyden remained seated, his short, plump fingers drumming on the mahogany desk's polished top.

"Wait," he said, just as Sebastian was opening the study's door. "Send Wrenbury here. I would like a word with him."

ABEL DIDN'T HAVE to turn his head to know that the one who had opened the French doors to the balcony where he was still lingering, relishing the pleasant night breeze, was Sebastian. His strange aloofness and unmistakable air always preceded him.

He brings the smell of London and death.

"You have been out after someone again," Abel said almost matter-of-factly. "Another kill for Queen and Country."

Sebastian leaned against the balcony, his back to the garden, pretending not to notice Abel's sarcasm. "At least London has one criminal less."

"How do you know he truly was a criminal? How do you know he wasn't just an unnatural?"

"I always know," Sebastian replied sharply. A gust of wind tousled his blond hair, covering his unreadable blue eyes for a moment. "In my experience, being an unnatural and being a criminal are essentially the same thing."

Abel frowned, holding back a derisive snort. "What makes you so certain?"

There he was, arguing with his closest friend all over again about the same old thing. The one thing that meant so much to him.

Sebastian's answer came swiftly, in the same assured tone he always used in their arguments since they were children. "The people I put to sleep. Society's dregs, whose abnormal abilities were a danger to the rest of us. You are a dreamer, Wren. You believe in their redemption, but no such thing is possible for them. They are too wretched to atone, and you are too much of an artist to understand."

Oh, but he did understand. He understood too well.

"Why won't you paint Madeline Walden's portrait?" Sebastian eyed him with an inquisitive, yet amused, look. "She is chasing you to a ridiculous extent for that whim of hers."

Abel clenched his fists until his knuckles turned white under his gloves. How he wished he could tell his oldest friend everything and shed the burden he had been carrying for far too long. But he could not. As long as Sebastian's theories remained unchanged, he could not answer his question truthfully.

"I never do portraits."

"Hyden has requested your presence in his study." Sebastian straightened his back, ready to return to the ballroom. "Most certainly to ask for that portrait. I am not sure what is worse, dealing with his daughter or facing him."

Abel laughed, halting for a moment before the French doors. "I can handle the marquess."

～

"IF YOU SUMMONED me here to ask for your daughter's portrait, I'm afraid you are wasting your time. And mine. My answer will not change."

Abel almost stormed into the marquess' study. He had no time, nor was he in the mood for chatter or formalities. Greetings and polite introductory conversations be damned. That portrait story had already strained his nerves to an unbearable extent, and he intended to put an end to it.

Hyden lifted an eyebrow, as emotionless as ever, the very image of a man too certain of his power to let anything or anyone affect him. He waited for his guest to finish, without rising to welcome him, his elbows and clasped hands forming a triangle with the base on his desk.

"Is that so?" His voice sounded as placid as the expression on his round, plump face. "Perhaps you would like to enlighten me with an appropriate explanation."

The man's arrogance knew no end.

Abel cleared his throat, aware that his chances of convincing the old snake were small. "Because I lack the skill. I am not good enough to paint portraits."

The marquess rubbed his chin, eyeing him with the dark glint of a predator ready to corner its prey. "And you expect me to believe that the man who could paint a most astonishing portrait of the late Earl of Wrenbury's brother at such an early age lacked the skill? On the contrary, Wrenbury. That boy not only had the skill. He also was a prodigy."

Abel froze in the middle of the room, his gaze locked on the cast iron lamp mounted on the wall behind the marquess' armchair. Not many people knew about the portrait he had painted when he was eleven years of age, as a present for his uncle's birthday.

He clenched his teeth, unable to utter a single coherent word. How much did Hyden know? A little? More than a little? The entire story?

"Too bad he died too soon to enjoy it," he said when Abel didn't reply. "I wonder what became of that painting."

"That was my last portrait," Abel finally said, regaining a small portion of his composure. "I choose to draw what I know, and I only know landscape and architecture."

"Landscape and architecture, he says!" Hyden snorted, leaning into his upholstered armchair, his clasped hands over his round, prominent abdomen. "Instead of wasting your talent on such dull subjects, perhaps you should consider painting my daughter. It would be a good start for you to shift your preferences to living things."

"No."

The marquess finally rose and took a few steps, frowning deep in thought, before stopping in front of Abel.

"All right then," he said, looking up at the taller man. "I tried to use logic and good sense, but you never seem inclined to listen to either." A short pause. "Which leaves me no choice but to appeal to more coercive methods."

An icy sense of foreboding gripped Abel's throat. "I fail to understand what you mean."

"If you still refuse to do what my daughter asks of you, all scandal sheets in London will find out about your secret incursions in Whitechapel and the black-haired beauty you visit so often at her shop. London Society is always hungry for fresh gossip, especially for the scandals that are always associated with your person, so they will be delighted to hear about the Earl of Wrenbury's latest private endeavours. Now you choose whether you want that to become public information."

All colour drained from Abel's face. He clenched his fists, fighting the urge to hit the unscrupulous bastard. His uncle's portrait be damned. Hyden knew more than that. Through his extensive network of spies, he had discovered Abel's most precious secret. One he had vowed to protect with his life.

One the marquess would throw to the scandal sheets

without a second thought, without remorse, just as he promised. His words never were idle threats.

"I agree," Abel said, his voice broken, his shoulders slumped in defeat. He would find a way to extricate himself from the bloody mess, but that night he had more urgent things to protect. "I shall be expecting Lady Madeline in my studio tomorrow. For her portrait."

www.ingramcontent.com/pod-product-compliance
Lightning Source LLC
Chambersburg PA
CBHW020314160726
47992CB00004B/1529